TWILIGHT
in Danzig

A Novel by
Siegfried Kra

SECOND EDITION

Pleasure Boat Studio: A Literary Press
Seattle, Washington

First Edition by Canal House, 2015

Copyright © 2018, Siegfried Kra, M.D.
All Rights Reserved

ISBN 978-0-912887-58-6

Library of Congress Control Number: 2017956627

Edited by Jack Estes, Nancy Seewald, Jeff Welker
Cover and Interior Design by Lauren Grosskopf

Pleasure Boat Studio books are available through your favorite bookstore
and through the following:
SPD (Small Press Distribution) Tel. 800-869-7553
Baker & Taylor 800-775-1100
Ingram Tel 615-793-5000
Amazon.com and bn.com

and through
PLEASURE BOAT STUDIO: A LITERARY PRESS
www.pleasureboatstudio.com
Seattle, Washington

Contact Lauren Grosskopf, Publisher
Email: Pleasboatpublishing@gmail.com

For my daughters,
Lisette & Annice

Siegfried Kra as a boy, with his beloved dog, Astor.

TWILIGHT
in Danzig

Chapter One

"JONAS, TIME TO GO HOME," Fräulein Marlow called after the small boy. Jonas was bent over a circular pond, prodding a small sailboat to reach the other shore. He rose from his crouched position, looked up at the woman in the starched blue uniform, a white collar around her neck, and ran to her obediently.

She knew all about nobility, being herself a descendant of Prince Lefevre, once the Duke of Danzig. The end of World War 1 had also brought an end to the nobility of Danzig, except for a few. She was young, beautiful, and well-bred, with long silk-blonde hair, and she was poor. The position as governess in the rich Kruger household was ideal.

The late autumn afternoon air was chilly as the sun began to set over Danzig, leaving a blood-red glow on the Baltic Sea. The governess pulled her blue frock securely around her young narrow body. The little boy, shivering, held onto her hand as they briskly strolled on the white-pebbled path through the park.

All in all, life with the Kruger family was decent enough. Her living quarters on the top floor of the house gave her a marvelous view of the harbor, of Stefan's Park, with its trimmed hedges, wide lawns, and musical pavilion, and of the tall medieval Marin church in the old city.

Below her window were the manicured gardens of the estate. After three years, she felt part of the family, not just a servant. Little Jonas, with his soft pompadour and dark eyes fringed with long curving lashes, was very special to her. She admired his fine, flat ears that sat close to his head, unlike those of his little playmates that stuck out as though standing at attention. She was going to make him a Prussian prince, a gentleman by all standards of nobility she knew, in spite of his birth as a Jew.

An asphalt staircase, flanked by two marble lions, led to a large terrace that was the main entrance to the house. Jonas raced ahead and kicked on the heavy carved door because the bell was too high for him to reach. His cheeks were like two red apples plucked from the cold air.

"Who is banging on my door?" A sweet voice came from the other side.

Slowly, his mother opened the door.

"Why, it is my little Jonas!" Lucia Kruger wrapped her slender arms around her son. "And what sea battles did we win today?" she asked as the governess followed behind the boy, carrying the still-wet sailboat. Lucia surveyed her son, dusty and breathless from his afternoon romp. "We will give you a warm bath and a nice supper," she continued, "and Fräulein can be free for the night."

As they stood in the spacious entrance hall, Prince Eric Brandenberg came trailing in, wearing a magnificent green riding outfit and smoking a pipe. He was an attractive looking man with a delicate face and high cheekbones.

"Fräulein." He nodded to Fräulein Marlow in his aristocratic way and then approached Jonas, taking the boy's small hand in his and shaking it.

"I am pleased to see you again, young man." With his long tapered finger he gently pushed on the boy's belly, making Jonas giggle.

"Ah, I almost forgot; I read in the newspaper someone has a birthday soon, and you know who that is. So I brought you a little present, an early birthday gift." From behind his back the Prince brought forward a little Hessian soldier riding a horse.

"For your collection, which is getting bigger and bigger, as large as the Prussian Army once was." Jonas clicked his heels, bowed and took the soldier with delight.

"Thank you, sir."

"Do I at least get a little kiss?" Brandenberg bent down as Jonas planted a light kiss on the Prince's smooth cheek.

"I really must be going, Frau Kruger. It has been a charming afternoon."

The Prince bowed again and kissed Lucia Kruger's hand. He gave her a small, careful glance as he departed.

"About eight o'clock tonight, Eric," she said. "I do want so much for you to be here."

"Eight, indeed, and not one moment later. I don't want to miss one minute of the gracious Kruger dinner."

"He is such a dear friend to all of us," she sighed and took Jonas by the hand, singing as they ascended the spiral staircase to the nursery.

The nursery was as large as the downstairs hall, lined with long windows reaching to the floor. Adjacent to the space was a marbled bathroom decorated with painted figures of Rumpelstiltskin, Hansel and Gretel, the Katzenjammer Kids, and the Seven Dwarfs. A small bathtub supported by gold legs stood in the center of the bathroom, and against the north-facing walls were tall white-painted radiators with rounded pipes that heated three white bath towels. Lucia undressed the little boy, then swung him in the air.

"And now the Zeppelin is slowly coming down for a landing, and Jonas is the captain, into the pine water." The child liked his mother undressing him and then giving him a bath. It was a special treat because his birthday was coming, he thought. The tepid green pine water and the odor of pine forest soothed him from the cold air outside.

Brand Kruger arrived home earlier than usual, carrying a German Shepherd puppy under his arm.

"Where is my son, the soon-to-be birthday boy?" he shouted.

"Your son," Fräulein Marlow said, standing by the circular staircase, "is having a bath." Brand raced up the stairs into the bathroom, tiptoed inside, carrying the animal in his arms, and then allowed the puppy to roam freely.

"Muttie, there is a dog here," Jonas squealed. Brand picked up the dog and placed it next to Jonas, watching as it licked the water off his son's face.

"For you."

Jonas climbed out of the bathtub and hugged his new playmate.

"Every boy should have a dog," Brand exulted. "And how is my darling wife today?"

"You are in a cheery mood." She reached for a thick, warmed towel from the pipes and tried to encircle Jonas' small body as he ran naked after the dog out of the playroom and into the hall. Hearing all the noise, the governess came upstairs shaking her head in disapproval.

"Fräulein, you have a new charge."

"So I see. Of course, he isn't housebroken."

"A German Shepherd has excellent manners, Fräulein. In a few days, with your superb perseverance, he will know his place."

"As you say, sir," she answered politely as she turned away to arrange for the boy's supper. With dinner guests expected, he would eat at a small table set up in the nursery.

Lucia was at first angry, but when the small dog ran to her and licked her face as she bent down to pet him, her face broke out in a radiant smile.

"What a nice dog. We will love him forever," she said.

"A wonderful present for our Jonas."

"What do you want to call him?" Lucia asked Jonas, now standing beside her wrapped up like a little mummy in his great towel.

The boy had a perplexed look on his face.

"We'll call him Astor," Brand broke in. "That was once the name of my dog."

"Then you should call him Astor the Second." Fräulein Marlow's sarcastic tone was barely detectable.

"Astor the Second it shall be!"

"I like Astor only," Jonas said, although the attention of the grown-ups had moved on.

"Well now, dear wife, and who is coming to dinner tonight?"

"I invited Uncle Herman and his girlfriend. I haven't seen my brother in weeks. And the Prince is coming."

"Does the Prince have to be at all our dinner parties?" Brand asked with a bit of irritation.

"He is a good friend, and he is our neighbor. And he adds so much class to our table."

"He reminds me of one of our Lalique vases that you place on the table to impress people. Besides, I think he has a crush on you."

"Well, what of it? Don't you like your wife to be appreciated by other men? I thought men get a certain, how should I say, frisson of pleasure from their women being admired?"

"Yes, but not from a mignon." Lucia chose to ignore that remark.

"I also invited Grecia."

"That madman! A Russian anarchist, a Hessian Prince, Max the industrialist, and your nutty brother. What a group."

"And Grecia's beautiful wife. You like her, with her gorgeous boobs that hang out like ripe apples."

"Lotte is a beautiful woman."

"The most beautiful woman in all of Danzig, right, Lover?" She cast a sidelong glance at him.

Jonas was sitting on the floor playing with Astor.

"What are boobs, Mummy?"

"Go ahead and tell him," Brand dared.

Brand had to look away so his son or Lucia couldn't see him smiling.

"That is just a funny term for a woman's breasts, sweetheart."

"Fräulein Marlow has nice boobs, too," Jonas said.

"I invited Grecia because it is his birthday," Lucia smoothly continued. It was unclear whether she had chosen to let the remark pass or hadn't heard it.

Brand looked at the boy, suddenly quite pleased with him. "How do you know that, Jonas?"

"Because I saw them."

"Jonas, it is time for your dinner." Lucia lightly clapped her hands together. "Hurry now and when you have finished I will tell you a story before bed."

"No, please. I like to hear you and Papa talk."

"I bet you do."

With a teasing tone, Lucia turned to her husband, "There is also someone else coming whom you don't know."

"Oh?"

"A young man I met a few days ago at the Beaux Arts. He is American. He came to Danzig to study the architecture. He is here by himself, and I thought we could learn English from him. We all must learn English. It is the language of the future."

"I don't need to know the language of the barbarians, and I will never have to. They eat filet mignon with jam, I am told. Why should I spend an evening with a cowboy?"

"What is a cowboy, Papa?" Jonas asked.

"A cowboy is a man who rides horses and drinks beer."

"Papa, you ride horses and drink vodka."

"Jonas, that is enough! Go and get your supper," his father said. "Fräulein Marlow!" Brand yelled. "Jonas is waiting for you."

Dressed in baggy pants, a striped yellow sports jacket, and a blue vest which covered his protruding belly, Uncle Herman was the first to arrive for the dinner party. He was short, fat, and round as a gourd. He always wore a broad grin partially hidden by a big cigar. His smile and twinkling eyes always made it seem he had just pulled off another clever scheme. At his side was his new girlfriend, Frieda, who recently sang the role of Brunhilda at the Danzig Wagnerian Opera Festival. She towered over Uncle Herman like an Amazon. He liked big buxom women with long blonde hair.

Gerta, the chambermaid, greeted Uncle Herman as he let himself in through the mammoth oak front doors of the house.

"Good evening, sir."

"Gerta, you are looking slick tonight. Do you have a little date later?"

"No, sir," she giggled.

"Where is my nephew, that little momzer?"

"Upstairs asleep, sir. They just got him off. You better not wake him. Fräulein will be furious."

"The hell with Fräulein. Frieda, you stay here and look at the paintings or something. See how my rich sister lives."

He handed the gray fedora to Gerta and whispered, "Don't tell anyone."

He then dashed up the stairs bouncing like a pleased hippopotamus. Jonas was soundly asleep and Astor was at his side, propped up on a woolen blanket and pillow.

He picked Jonas off the bed, and hugged him, and Jonas awoke smiling.

"Hello, Uncle Herman. This is Astor."

"Welcome to the home, Astor," he said appraising the puppy. "Now Jonas, my boy, I have a present for you, right from Budapest." He handed the sleepy boy a brown teddy bear. Jonas took the stuffed animal, placed it carefully on the other side of his pillow, put his small arms around his uncle in a hug and lay back down. Fräulein Marlow, hearing the commotion as she was getting ready, entered the bedroom partially dressed. She left her robe slightly open, revealing her long beautiful legs. "Please, Uncle Herman, the boy needs his sleep." She had the night off along with the following day. Tonight she would be joining her employers at the dinner.

"At 8:00 p.m.? It is much too early to go to bed."

The governess did not like Uncle Herman. To her he was a wise-cracking Jew, a flashy, perpetually sunburned merchant who kept company only with Gentile women, or *shiksas*, as he liked to say. She felt especially resentful that he barely noticed her, as though she was a piece of the household furniture. His eyes did not even acknowledge her naked legs.

"I know you don't like me, Fräulein. Well, I don't like you either, so there. But my nephew comes first, and if I were head of this household you would have been long gone back to your milk farm or wherever you came from, no less be invited to my sister's table."

"As you wish, sir," she curtsied and gave him a disdainful look. There was more she wanted to say, much more. The time will come, she thought to herself. Milk farm, did he call it? The landed estate that had been sliced up and laid to waste following Versailles? Yes, his time will come, that arrogant pig.

Jonas, watching from the corner of his eye, wondered why Uncle Herman didn't like his governess.

Returning downstairs Uncle Herman regained his jovial sense and saw that the Prince had arrived. He was dressed in a perfectly tailored tuxedo, his chest festooned with medals and decorated ribbons.

"Prince Brandenberg, I feel I should bow to you. You are, as usual, the paragon of elegance."

"Dear man, I never tire of your compliments."

"You know, Prince, if those are pure gold, you better not wear them so obviously. The price of gold is going up as our guldens are disappearing."

"Who would dare to steal a medal from a Prussian officer?"

"If the Prussian officer is drunk enough, he won't know they're gone," Herman said with a short laugh. "Let me introduce you to Frieda. She's never met a real Prince before."

The Prince bowed and kissed the singer's hand.

"Charming, charming."

"She is, incidentally, Hungarian, your highness, not German."

"She is still charming, a handsome woman."

Lucia entered shortly, looking stunning. She wore a black rayon jersey evening dress by Madeleine Vionnet with a long exposed back and a beautiful chain of diamonds around her neck. Her auburn hair was gathered in an upward sweep.

"All my favorite men are already here, promptly. How wonderfully nice."

She embraced her brother and Uncle Herman said, "You are some gorgeous woman," as he stared at her cleavage. "If you weren't my sister . . ."

"And you are a lewd brother, dear, and I wish you would get rid of that disgusting cigar. Please don't smoke until we go to the drawing room after dinner."

She moved on to her other guests. "Prince, how marvelous you look." He took her hand and kissed it, and she in turn gave him an affectionate kiss on his clean-shaven cheek. Then she turned back to her brother and waited for him to make the introductions.

"Lucia, I want you to meet Frieda, the opera singer. She is Hungarian, and understands little if any German or Polish. So you can say what you wish. She will smile politely."

Lucia took both of the opera singer's hands and warmly greeted her.

"Why does my brother always go out with women who can't speak the language or understand?" She sighed, smiling, knowing that the handsome woman hadn't a clue of what she'd said.

"You guess. I give you two, my baby sister."

"Why don't you settle down with a nice Jewish girl? Next you will be telling me you are going out with Americans. Last month it was a Moroccan, but I know very well she was Africano, a *Schwartze*."

"I like exotic women. Now, tell me, what is the occasion of a dinner party midweek, although that is a silly question to ask around here." Still, it seemed wise to change the subject as it tired him to continue this sparring.

"Tonight is Grecia's birthday, and your little angel nephew will soon have his."

"How is that little devil doing these days?"

"Not to be trusted for one second. That little devil ran off the other day and for one hour Fräulein and I searched frantically for him. He was hiding behind a rock with the little girl from next door."

"Good for him. Why waste all those days waiting for the sperm to flow?"

"I knew brother Herman would approve."

"As soon as he is old enough I am taking him to a brothel."

The doorbell chimed and Lotte and Grecia made their grand entrance. Grecia, the anarchist, six feet tall, had a sharp Roman nose and dark, intelligent, penetrating eyes. His wife, Lotte, a magnificent-looking woman with the striking features of

Marlene Dietrich, wore a simple dress of olive green velvet with rhinestone shoulder clips. She held her head proudly, elegantly, like a Russian princess. She was, in fact, a Romanoff, and had escaped to Danzig with Grecia. Grecia had fought in the White Army under Dochek's command, and when Trotsky's Red Army prevailed, they had fled in 1917. Now, in Danzig, he was employed by Burkhardt, the provincial governor appointed by the League of Nations under the Versailles Treaty.

"Grecia, you scoundrel, I am glad you're here to provoke us, not of course like your beautiful Lotte." Uncle Herman's eyes nearly popped out of his head as he appraised her.

"Where is our elegant host?" Lotte asked.

"As usual, he is up to something. He is in conference with Max Schiller in the library. However, once he knows you're here, Lotte, he will appear like Haley's comet," Lucia trilled.

Brand appeared just at that moment, tall, powerful and graceful, dressed in a blue pin-striped suit, white shirt, and blue tie. His full head of black hair was pasted down and shimmering against his lean face. Max Schiller accompanied him. A medium-sized man with gray hair and carbon-black eyes, Max was the board chairman of the Luirgi firm. They had discovered an efficient method for converting coal into ammonia and oil, two ingredients of ammunition needed by the Germans.

"Two industrial giants in one room can be dangerous," Grecia said.

"Not as dangerous as three beautiful women," Max quickly returned.

"Max, my good Prussian friend, it's the men, it's the men who make the women dangerous," Brand slyly added. By now all the guests were holding champagne flutes in their hands, and the Prince raised his. "Our first toast, then, to the men and their dangerous women."

Next to Lucia was an empty chair, as the American had not

arrived. Prince Brandenberg was seated on her left. The evening flowed as easily as the champagne. The main course, a traditional goose, braised with port and roasted vegetables, was sumptuous, and the dessert, a chocolate soufflé drowned in Drambuie, was a marvelous delight. Throughout the evening Lucia felt unusually gay and flirtatious. The Prince at every opportunity grasped her hand and kissed it.

"Madam, you are as delicious as the soufflé."

Even if he might be mignon, Lucia thought, he is charming and sexy. She thought just then of John Barrymore and his aristocratic profile. Anyway, there are some mignons who do like women equally, she continued to herself.

"You are such a dear friend," she told the Prince as she touched his ringed hand, the Brandenberg crest.

Brand sat next to Lotte, who had no objections as he playfully touched her thighs at least five times during the course of the evening. Uncle Herman, with his voracious appetite, asked for a second helping of soufflé. "Nu," he looked at Lucia, "Where is the rest?"

"Don't be a pig, Herman," Frieda whispered in broken German.

"You love me being a pig," he whispered into her ear.

Lucia gently shook the Lalique bell to the right of her water goblet, which made a sweet tingling sound. Another soufflé was brought into the dining room and placed in front of Uncle Herman along with a bottle of Grand Marnier. Using a large silver spoon with the letter "L" engraved on the handle, Herman gouged out the center of the soufflé and poured the Grand Marnier into its depths. A round of applause followed as the dessert was passed from seat to seat.

Fräulein Marlow remained quiet, languid, beautiful. She was dressed in a simple blue dress that accentuated her flawless skin, and her ashen eyes wandered towards Brand. She wanted him right at that moment. He looked so handsome tonight, his dark eyes seductive and impenetrable. She relished sitting with the family at dinner, their secret lending a provocative spice to any meal she shared with him. When she had first joined the household, she had been served separately. Then Lucia had decided that "the Fräulein needs some relaxation after being alone with that little comet all day."

Brand raised his glass and struck another glass with a spoon, making the crystal ring.

"Ladies and gentlemen, and others, a toast. A toast to my son, who will be nine years old at the end of next week, and also to Grecia on her birthday, whose age is more secret than Max's method of converting coal to oil."

"Bravo! Bravo!"

"And to peace, to peace," Grecia said, "because it is not here for long."

Lotte shot a sharp look towards her husband. "Please, Grecia, not tonight. It is your birthday. Just have some champagne."

"I must say what I have to say. Perhaps this time will not come again."

"Come on, Grecia, stop it," Uncle Herman implored.

"Wait," Max Schiller said, "it is his birthday. He should have the right to make a speech, unless, of course, our gracious hostess objects."

"I quietly object, but please go on, Grecia."

"Germany wants Danzig back. Right now, in Berlin, the National Socialist Party may have lost seats in the last election, but still, they remain the Reichstag's largest party. And the party, even if you choose to pretend otherwise, is headed by a very convincing man who is a real threat. Most intelligent people think Hitler is a maniac, but his following has increased. Hitler and his Brownshirt hoodlums are screaming to have Danzig returned to Germany."

"Why shouldn't Danzig again become a part of Germany?" Max asked. "For five hundred years it was part of Germany."

"The League of Nations would never allow Germany to annex Danzig," the Prince joined in.

Max Schiller knew better. His industrial colleagues Farben, Bentz, and Krupp, and even some Americans were supportive of the new party with Adolf Hitler at the helm.

Uncle Herman also believed economic chaos was about to begin. He was in the money business and was selling guldens as fast as he could get them, buying gold and American dollars instead. He had already convinced his brother-in-law to get rid of some of his guldens.

"I, for one, care little for politics," the Prince said, temporarily setting down his spoon. "Politics belongs to the proletariat. My politics are contained in this beautiful, luscious, soft soufflé. To be devoured, beginning with its crowning peak, until I am satiated."

"That sounds so sensual, dear Prince, that it makes me tingle," Lucia said. "Or maybe it's the champagne now reaching my head."

"And in fine music and beautiful women," he continued. "Brand, where is the little music in the night? A little Mozart or Chopin to mellow Grecia, or should we prepare our ears for the ride of Valkyrie?"

"Wagner is so coarse," Lotte said softly.

"Well, then," commanded Brand, bringing the fine linen napkin to his lips for a final swipe, "if the guests desire music, then you shall have it. I have a little surprise for you all in the library. So, come, children, the entertainment is about to begin."

The library was magnificent. Flemish tapestries closed off the windows to protect the rare books enclosed in the glass cases from the light. Biedermeier furniture crowded the room. A large Tabriz Persian rug covered the parquet floor. A Dürer painting was hanging on the far side of the great room, and a newly acquired Kokoschka hung beside it.

Standing in the corner of the library were four musicians. "Les Quatre Ensemble de Genz," Max introduced. "The four musicians of Genz," and everyone applauded.

A roaring fire warmed the space as the quartet struck their instruments, playing Mozart and Hindemith. Fräulein, accustomed to these evenings, sat peaceably on the armrest of a Directoire blue velvet couch with her long lovely legs crossed in front of Brand. By his brief glance, she knew he would visit her this night.

She knew those eyes; they belonged to little Jonas as well as to Brand. She flushed with excitement, and hoped Lucia Kruger was too preoccupied to see the hunger in her husband's eyes.

During the concert, a tall handsome young man stole into the room and quietly sat down next to Lucia. He wore a blue tie, shabby gray pants, and a heavy tweed jacket. After the applause had died down, Lucia, her beautiful face animated against the firelight, said, "Ladies and gentlemen, this is William Harrington, from Columbus, Ohio. He is an architecture student at the university."

"I am pleased to meet you all," he said in halting German. Uncle Herman staggered over to him. "I speak a little English. Nobody else can."

The American smiled.

"Not so. I speak English, too," Grecia announced. Everyone applauded and howled.

"Where did you learn English, sir?" Bill asked.

"Grecia Greenspun is my name, and I learned English from Americans in Russia. The expeditionary American force came to help the White Army, and I was their guide."

Uncle Herman added in Polish, "Another one of Woodrow Wilson's idiocies. Hundreds of American soldiers died there in the brutal cold, and then Trotsky won Russia."

Lucia whispered to Herman, nodding at her young new friend, "You know, we are the first Jews he ever met."

"I don't believe it. There are so many Jews in America."

"Not many in Columbus, Ohio. He told me so. They are all in New York. He is much older than he looks. Isn't he beautiful?"

Lucia went through the formality of introducing each one in the room. "This is Prince Brandenberg, Bill." Fräulein Marlow was the only one who noticed the look in the Prince's eyes. It was arousal; there was no mistake. The Prince straightened his body, clicked his heels, and bowed slightly.

Lucia said, "Bill speaks French, so we can all talk to him."

"Maybe Bill wants to learn German," the Prince said. "Would you like to learn German?"

"I would like that very much, and I will teach you English," Bill smiled politely.

Fräulein Marlow wondered how an American would behave in bed. He was tall and strong-looking; it would be an adventure to have an American push into her, just once. She would have to see if she could manage a tryst.

As the little group settled around Bill, who became the center of their conversation, Brand moved close to Max Schiller.

"Let's finish our talk in the billiard room, Max. They won't miss us. Leave your glass here. I have a special brandy for us."

On the other side of the library, two rolling doors opened to a carved inlaid paneled room with cushioned velvet sidings. The billiard table was handcrafted by British carpenters who copied the style of Mariot, dating back to 1450, from the Chateau de Blois in France. On the fireplace mantel were trophies Brand had won in tennis, pool, and bowling.

"Take off your jacket, Max. A little billiards while we talk?"

He served the industrialist brandy in a Baccarat snifter. "Napoleon, 1893. I found two bottles."

"This brandy is superb," Max said, sipping on the enticing aromatic drink.

"Farben is extending its dye plant," he said, coming to the point now. "It is no secret. Our past conversion process will only work if we have coal. We need oil to put German industry on its feet. You can supply us with the shipping and divert the coal you have been sending to England to us. We will pay you more, of course."

Max Schiller, an elegant Prussian aristocrat, was a second cousin of Bleichroder. The entire business world knew of Gerson von Bleichroder, with whom Bismarck had consulted on all his financial dealings. Few knew that Bleichroder or that his cousin, Max Schiller, were Jews.

Brand pressed his case.

"With Gdynia, the new port being built by the Poles, we will be able to float our barges during the wintertime. The new port is situated in a peninsula and never freezes. Ships can enter in the heart of the North Sea winter."

Schiller leaned toward Brand. "We must cast our lot with the Germans, my friend. They are the future. The League of Nations is tired. Its members are old men. It was a noble idea of Wilson's, but it will soon be totally ineffective. Danzig will be in the hands of the Fatherland, where it belongs. You are a businessman, Brand. Business is always above politics. Governments change; ideals are a luxury for the philosophers. Guns and butter make a country run. No matter who runs the show, there will always be the rich and the less fortunate. Europe has thousands of years of history. The governments change like the weather, but the businessmen endure."

This man learned well from his cousin, Brand thought.

"You will have your coal," he said in a strong, confident

voice. A handshake was all that was necessary to bind the deal.

When they returned to the library, Uncle Herman was sitting at the piano surrounded by the guests. They were singing old Russian and German folk songs. Lucia was singing happily, surrounded by the Prince on one side and the young American towering over her on the other, her light soprano no match of course for Frieda's who sat politely by and listened. "Are all Americans so tall?" Lucia whispered coquettishly to her new friend.

"Only those from Columbus, Ohio," he laughed, making himself appear more endearing to her.

"How do you like Danzig?"

"It is one of the most ancient, elegant, charming cities I have ever seen, and after tonight I never want to leave."

Uncle Herman overheard the tail end of the conversation, gave his sister a knowing look and squeezed Frieda's hand. He had picked Frieda up on Motz Street in Berlin, at a nightclub called El Dorado. The club was known throughout Berlin for its famous clientele. Prostitutes, transvestites, and cocaine dealers mingled with Europe's cafe society. Each table had its own telephone for making rendezvous. Cocaine was sniffed as freely as champagne was poured.

Max Schiller was dozing in a chair, the real work of the evening concluded, while Uncle Herman sang his last song of the night. "Berliners are singing this inflation song," he said, and with a high-pitched, slurred voice, he began:

"Broke, broke, the whole world is broke. And how about selling Granny's house to buy booze? And if America had their way, 'Yes we have no bananas.' Everyone sing together," Herman yelled.

"Yes, we have no bananas, and my parrot won't eat no hard-boiled eggs."

Jonas, awakened by the loud singing, crawled out of bed with Astor at his side. He lay on the floor like one of his toy soldiers at the top of the staircase. He liked seeing everyone so happy and pretty looking. He saw the Prince place a small gold engraved card in Bill's hand. "English learning. Yes?"

Jonas watched wide-eyed. A secret message, a code to the American! He imagined the entire scenario: The Crane Gate, where the wheat was stored for shipment, was to be destroyed at ten in the morning by an invading fleet from Norway. The American agreed to carry out the plans of the Prince. Jonas thought he must inform his friend Gerhardt to try to stop the battle.

"Oh, yes," Bill said. The Prince bowed and clicked his heels. Jonas raised himself up from his prone position and imitated the Prince, clicking his heels and bowing his head. Lucia saw the movement at the top of the stairs.

"Jonas! Get into bed immediately," Lucia called.

"Only after he bids his uncle good night." In seconds Jonas was at the bottom of the stairs as he slid down the banister into Uncle Herman's arms.

"Now, where did you learn that from, Fräulein?"

"From an American movie."

Uncle Herman hugged his sister. "Time for us to go, my dear. The blonde is getting impatient to go to bed."

Lucia burst out laughing, finding her brother both deplorable and adorable.

"Herman, you are a disgrace to our family. If mother and father knew about your behavior, they would disown you. I love you, anyway."

Chapter Two

PRINCE BRANDENBERG WALKED across the sprawling lawn towards the stony mansion built by his ancestors two hundred years earlier. Most of his family had died; others were living in Paris and Switzerland. He was the last to remain in the family home. His elderly, aristocratic-looking butler greeted him at the door.

"Did the Prince enjoy the evening with the Krugers?"

"Yes, Otto. I expect a young American to be calling in a few days, a Bill Harrington."

"That is good, sir. You need some new friends."

"Is Emile home yet?"

"No, sir. He's gone out for a nightcap, he said. If I might say so, sir, Emile has been carousing around a little too much. He is seen on the boulevard each night, and we don't know what he will bring back. Perhaps it is time for Emile to return to France."

"Perhaps."

"Did anyone call?"

"Just Rudolf Hess from Berlin. He said he must talk to you, and I quote, 'before a big change occurs.'"

"Shit on Hess. I have no use for his political crap."

"None of us do, sir, but it would be best if you could remain on friendly terms with them for now."

"Good night, Otto. Are you still planning to go to America?"

"If things change the way I think they will, yes." The loyal manservant paused, scanning the Prince's face. "Perhaps, sir, you ought to give that some thought, too."

"What will I do in America?"

Otto shrugged, but continued to gaze at the Prince.

"Good night, Otto."

Upstairs in the Prince's bedroom, the mirrored wall reflected a thirty-five-year-old man who suddenly looked ten years older. The flowered design of the wallpaper complemented the brilliant design of the silk sheets of the massive four-poster bed. A tufted chaise lounge was on the other side of the room, next to a statue of Adonis standing on a small French inlaid round table. A portrait of a young man painted by Edvard Munch hung over one wall. Brandenberg didn't see the letter from his old friend Hess, inviting him to meet the future chancellor of Germany, Adolf Hitler, on the inlaid table beside the bed.

The Prince undressed and stood naked in front of the long mirror, viewing his slender body. His thoughts turned to the young American at dinner tonight, as he ran his hands over his smooth chest, delicately massaging his nipples. From the large armoire, he pulled out a pair of pink bloomers and a black silk nightgown. He slipped into the bloomers, dropped the nightgown over his head, and sat down in front of the dressing table. After covering his lips in pink lipstick, he sprayed cologne on his body, tweezed his eyebrows and climbed into bed. On his night table was a small ceramic bottle. He took a silver spoon, tapped a bit of white powder onto it, brought the cocaine to his nose, and closed his eyes.

His arms had held many young men before – sailors and salesmen, and others passing through town, their eyes meeting ahead of their bodies in rushed and urgent grunts. There had been bell hops, Emile most recently, a take-home souvenir from a recent trip to the City of Light, but never an American. When the rush from the powder started in his body, the Prince twisted in ecstasy, rubbing himself and thinking about Bill, strong, fresh, and virginal, just as he imagined America itself to be. "Bill, Bill," he moaned. "What a splendid evening," was his final thought as the cocaine took over. And then he remembered nothing.

Most governesses' bedrooms in Danzig were bleak looking, deliberately furnished sparsely to encourage these ladies to spend most of their time caring for their charges and not lounging around their room. Fräulein Marlow's chamber was an exception. She had a large bedroom and sitting area with her own private bath; a small apartment, really, and a luxury by anyone's standards in the early thirties. Lucia furnished the space for her with a velvet couch, two soft easy chairs, a Biedermeier armoire, and two Caucasian rugs, while Brand, unbeknownst to his wife, brought her exotic undergarments when he traveled to Belgium and France, along with perfumes and oils for her bath. Her rooms were not located in the servant's quarters on the other side of the house, but instead were a short distance from where Jonas slept, yet far enough away to afford her the privacy for which she longed.

She undressed and filled the upright ceramic bathtub with pine oil and closed her eyes as her entire body softened. Lately, she had been vowing that the time had come to leave, settle down, get married and begin her own life. She was, after all, a beautiful well-bred country girl, though she'd been in town for ten years now. She'd come to seek a husband of means, and if not that, then a position that would allow her to forget where she had come from, and what she had lost. Her memories of a sun-kissed childhood, before the War and Allies took that all away, had dimmed. Her officer father killed on the Marne, and her mother exhausted by debt and disappointment, the champagne country of her youth was now an embittered empty land. She had considered herself lucky to get away. All she knew was that poverty, genteel or inherited, was a disease that was hard to shake off. But now, even as her dead dreams dropped from her heart like tree leaves in a cold wind, there was reason to hope again.

First, there was her employer, who was also her lover, and a lover like none she had ever experienced. The other men she met were far less exciting, certainly less wealthy. Even though he usually stayed with her for only a half-hour, it was enough. Sometimes, when Lucia went to Warsaw to see her parents, he would stay long enough for them to briefly sleep locked in each other's arms. It was a marvelous time of freedom. And then, there was this dynamic new movement that promised to change it all. There would be food and jobs again, security and hope. She heard about it at the cafes where she'd sometimes go with the other governesses on their evenings off. This movement of, and for, pure Germans. Let the Communists and capitalists, the trade-unionists, and the gypsies and the Jews trade places with them. Yes, let them endure a life without money, a life of loss and new rules. She imagined putting the heel of her shoe to the head of that despicable Uncle Herman. As she lay in the bathtub, she took the nozzle of the douche and placed it between her legs, her breaths shortening. Brand was going to visit her soon. She had another lover, Bruno, the meat cutter who worked in town. She met him at one of the cafes where he was espousing the new political party that was going to restore Germany to its former glory. Bruno was young, strong, and a German; rough, but she liked that, too. Brand was gentle, sensual. She liked the imaginative ways of the rich Jew. It gave her pleasure knowing that her mistress' husband was her lover. It reversed her envy of the Jewess's soft life. Fräulein Marlow's body was fuller, younger, and Brand liked her full breasts.

Tomorrow was her day off. She would meet Bruno at the beer hall and then return to his room for the night. She climbed out of the bathtub, dried her ready body, and climbed into bed, waiting. It was well past midnight. All those Kruger dinner parties bored her. She would have rather stayed upstairs. Lucia had the mistaken notion that she wanted to join the family's friends, whom she resented. "You are part of the family, Fräulein. We want you to share in our good fortune."

Downstairs, meanwhile, sitting in his favorite room – the billiard room – Brand was exhilarated with happiness. The evening was a monumental success. He had forgotten entirely about Fräulein Marlow. The excitement of a big business deal that would double his fortune was stronger even than his sexual hunger. He filled his glass with more Napoleon brandy and saluted his company. In his mind he made a quick calculation of the increase to his fortune as his coal-filled barges steamed up the North Sea to Bremerhaven. The rolling doors of the room softly opened as Lucia appeared in a diaphanous white silk dressing gown. The lamplight illuminated her lovely curves.

"Still up, Darling? Wasn't that a beautiful evening? Your idea of the quartet was so clever. Don't you just love Bill? He is such a doll."

"It was a great evening during which I, my dear, concluded the largest deal of my career."

"You mean we are going to be richer than now?"

"Much richer."

She fell into his lap and her robe opened. She was naked underneath. "But more coal means more barges, doesn't it?"

"Right, my smart wife. We will have to double the staff, and the swampland I bought years ago is going to be part of the new port called Gdynia that the Poles are building. The entire harbor will be opened all winter."

The silk gown slid off her shoulder and Brand kissed her still youthful breasts.

"Not bad for an old lady."

"Not bad at all," he said as his mouth closed over hers.

He still couldn't sleep after they made love. He returned to his study and looked out the window. The night sky was dull and heavy, and he wondered whether this augured for an early snow. In this medieval town on the Baltic Sea, snow sometimes fell in late fall. He suddenly remembered Fräulein Marlow, and imagined she had waited for him. He sighed and then poured himself another brandy. Usually, with Lucia upstairs reading in her boudoir, thinking Brand was at his desk reviewing contracts, it had been easier than he could have anticipated to steal thirty minutes with the alluring young Fräulein. The risks he took frankly thrilled him. After all the drama it had taken to get here, so much else in his life seemed settled now.

It was only twelve years ago or so, he reflected, that he was in Zakopane. The only Jew in the Puszauaski elite cavalry division out in that barren field. World War 1 had ended, but not for Poland. He joined the Polish cavalry because he was starving and he was alone. Raised on a farm, he was an expert horseman. His mother had abandoned him to go to America, and his father had long been dead. At the age of fourteen, he was on his own, and hungry. Each day he hoped there would be a letter with a ticket to America, but the letter never came. It was not long after he joined the army that he was promoted to lieutenant in the cavalry. He had been careful to conceal his Jewishness, for no Jew could ever achieve officer rank. He knew how to read and write, and he had the instincts of a fox. He let his mind float back to that dark, distant time.

The Red Army under Trotsky was at the gates of Warsaw, ready to march into the Polish capital. Out on the field with the ruffian cavalry, Brand was a pariah. The men did not trust him because he did not drink. For weeks they waited for battle to come, soaking in vodka and gambling. Then one morning, in the late fall, it began to snow, and his drunken men were about to run away, to flee from the barren land and from their fears and boredom concerning the fight that fortunately hadn't come, to return to Warsaw. They were camped in the middle of a field, surrounded by their horses. As the first morning light fell on the sleeping men, barrages of gunfire opened upon them on all sides. The Red Army had surrounded them, and in less than half an hour the field was covered in blood. Brand was thrown off his horse when a cannon shot struck his arm. The Bolsheviks swept down on them with their swords, slashing the throats of his fallen men. Brand rolled over towards some high grass and hid himself from the ongoing slaughter. Later, much later, he was found by a gentleman farmer who took him to his estate and nursed him back to life. The slaughter had taken place on his land.

The aristocratic Polish gentleman who saved Brand's life was named Stefan Metchnik. It was Metchnik who owned the coal mines in Zakopane, and that was how Brand, the pauper, eventually became the industrialist. Metchnik gave him a job, sending him to Danzig to represent his interests. Brand devised a plan to ship coal up the Vistula River from Krakow to the port of Danzig. He was twenty-two years old, and soon formed his own company with Metchnik's blessings, and his coal. Since then, Brand had been both son and protégée to the old gentleman.

It was good that his arm ached once in a while to remind him of how it was to starve, to be poor, and how much nicer it was for him to be rich and powerful. Brand's son, Jonas, was never going to have to beg for bread or sleep in only his clothing on the ground. The gods had been good to Brand and he wouldn't allow that to change. He had survived being killed.

Bill Harrington had come to Danzig to learn architecture and to have an adventure. Life in Columbus was all about going to football games and drinking beer before inevitably marrying and entering your dad's business. With the Depression in America deepening, it was a fate one had to feel grateful about. Still, Bill knew the satirist James Thurber, a friend of the family whom Bill thought of as a wise uncle, who had heard about his dreams and encouraged him to study architecture in Europe. As his main interest was medieval Nordic architecture, Danzig was an ideal choice. Most of the buildings were still intact, dating back to the fourteenth century when the city had belonged to the Hanseatic League, an association of northern German towns and merchant communities.

The adventure that he was seeking had seemed possible when he met Lucia Kruger at Beaux Arts School, and now he knew a Prince. The morning after the dinner party, an engraved invitation was lying under the door of his modest rented flat, adorned with the Brandenberg seal: "Please come to my home for cocktails and dinner at seven o'clock."

Dressed in the only suit he owned, with a white shirt and red tie, Bill arrived promptly at the Prince's home. Otto met him at the door, followed by the Prince, in a blue smoking jacket with a red scarf around his neck. Emile had been given a one-way train ticket back to Paris that morning and the Prince was feeling chipper indeed. "Welcome to the Brandenberg home," he said. "I see you like red, too. How nice."

Bill didn't know where to move his eyes first. Everywhere he looked was stunning: ancestral portraits hung in the hall; a large crystal chandelier was suspended from the tall ceiling. "It is like living in a museum," Bill stammered slightly.

"It is a museum. I let the public in every spring for a tour. Come, dear friend," the Prince spoke in French. "You do understand French?"

"A little."

"Good, then we will speak in French and English."

Cocktails were served in a small sitting room around a delicate table stacked with liqueurs, canapés, and decanters of Scotch and rum.

"Scotch? Americans like Scotch, isn't that so?"

"Yes."

The Prince sat in a Pope chair with his legs crossed. When he smiled, he displayed a fine row of white teeth. Bill smelled the cologne his host was wearing and began to feel uncomfortable.

After a third tumbler of Scotch, however, he felt more relaxed and continued to listen to the Prince discuss the poet Verlaine, and how he had killed his lover.

"It was a terrible scandal, terrible." Brandenberg put down his Scotch glass and looked at the young American. "But come, let me show you the house."

They started in the wine cellar, which was as large as the living room.

"You pick any wine you like for dinner."

"I don't know anything about wines."

"Perhaps someday soon you will."

"What is your oldest bottle?" Bill asked.

"Here in this corner." They moved to the far side of the cellar and Bill stumbled on a rack. The Prince quickly caught him before he fell, holding fast onto his arm.

"These old places sometimes are dangerous," the Prince warned, and Bill felt a strange sensation as the Prince put his arm around his waist.

"Come, we don't want any more falls."

Dinner was served in the small dining room, at a narrow dinner table, surrounded by more family portraits hanging on a velvet wall. Bill drank more wine and champagne than he ever had in his life. He barely remembered eating the delicate pheasant or the dessert, a coeur a la crème with caramelized strawberries.

After dinner, the tour resumed. When they arrived at the Prince's bedroom, the Prince placed his arms around Bill and opened the large armoire.

"Have you ever had cocaine?" he asked.

"No," Bill admitted, "they even took it out of Coca Cola." The Prince laughed.

"Take some. It will give you courage to do what you dare not."

He placed the spoon against Bill's nose, and removed a gold jewelry box from the armoire. He reached for a small ring with the Brandenberg crest.

"For you."

Bill blushed and felt his body shift almost inexorably; the cocaine suffused into his head, mixing with the alcohol. It made him feel like a different person.

"I can't take that," he protested as the Prince handed him the ring.

"For our friendship, today and tomorrow. English lessons we will start tomorrow and I will pay you. Students are so poor."

"But I have no present to give you." Bill's voice came from another part of his brain. He knew what the Prince would say next.

"You have a present for me. It is late. Stay for the night and my driver will take you back in the morning."

Adjacent to the Prince's bedroom was a guest room with a large four-poster bed. A pair of silk pajamas was already set out across the bed, and a robe.

"Make yourself comfortable. It is getting late and you are so tired," the Prince said. "Or, are you drunk?"

"A little of both, I guess."

The Prince's face was flushed. He left Bill alone in the room and when he returned in his robe, Bill was fast asleep. The lines of the Prince's face seem to advance him five more years from his utter disappointment. He quietly closed the bedroom door and filled his nose with the white powder.

It was the morning of Jonas' birthday. Brand, in his gray and white Duesenberg, sped up to a gabled building, the home of his company, Baltic Kohlen. He wore a fedora hat with a silk brim, dark striped pants, and a double-breasted blue jacket. He entered the marbled hall where his secretary, Fräulein Giesela, greeted him. It was precisely ten o'clock. "Good morning, Herr Kruger. Mr. Metchnik has been waiting for you for two hours."

"God in heaven! This is a surprise," he bellowed as he entered his office. "I wasn't expecting to see you until later."

A tall, simply dressed young man with the face of a bulldog followed Brand. He had been a bouncer in a Berlin café; now he was a doorman, a bodyguard, an errand man – and he carried a Mauser in his pants.

"Karl-Heinz, ice up the 1920 champagne! Metchnik, you are a devil. We missed you last week at the party."

Metchnik, an elderly, elegant, aristocratic looking man, was seated in a deep armchair sipping a demitasse. "Yes, we were sorry to miss it. Sonja has a new protégée, you see. So we had to go to Venice. She has fallen in love with a bunch of nuts. Expressionists they call themselves. She made a party for a young man called Weber, and invited the Guggenheims from New York. It is the craziest art I ever saw, but what does a coal dealer know about art?"

"Where is she now?"

"Shopping for a present for your son's birthday tonight, what else? We arrived on the overnight train. You see, we always honor our promises, which, when it comes to young Jonas, also happen to be our priority."

Metchnik and his wife would be dining tonight with them, of course, when the family celebrated. Jonas was like a grandchild to them, one whom Sonja, without children of her own, loved to indulge.

"Stefan, you didn't come to my office so early in the morning to discuss art."

"You are right. I am here about a serious matter, Brand."

"Such a beautiful morning and you want to be serious?"

"Very serious."

His face looked gray and old. Worry makes even the most elegant face look old.

"You have made a deal with Max Schiller. The rumor is out. I heard it in Venice," he said in a solemn tone.

"A big deal, Stefan, a very big deal." Brand's face became flushed. He was surprised by the speed with which this news spread. Impressive. His eyes sparkled like crystals.

"Thousands and thousands of tons of coal," he continued. "The mines will be working again. All those men, hundreds of them, that you were so worried and concerned about, will be working. You won't have to ride on your stallion to their homes, giving them food parcels so they don't starve. I wanted to save the good news to tell you tonight at Jonas' birthday party. Just think: work and money. Now, it is my chance to help you." Brand paused. There was an awkward silence.

"Of course, that is good news."

"Why are you down in the mouth? Is Sonja ill, or you?"

"No, thank the Lord. We are well. Frankly, Brand, you are dealing with the devil."

"What?"

"No wait, let me finish. Max Schiller, who is, if you didn't know, part Jew, represents a group of men whom I am not happy with. They are supporting the National Socialist Party headed by that crazed maniac."

"You mean Adolf Hitler. He is a big joke as far as I am concerned. He is as ridiculous as your new Expressionist painters."

"Do you know what they are going to do with that coal?"

"Of course," Brand said. "They will turn it into fuel. Let them build up their economy. Europe is in a deep depression and so is the world economy. Heaven knows if the new American president-elect will be able to do a thing about that. Things are just as bad there, too."

"Brand, for heaven's sake, the coal is not for industry. They want to make ammunition, guns, tanks."

"The Versailles Treaty will never allow it."

"That Treaty is as dead as ancient Rome, Brand. You have plenty of money. Don't send them the coal. There are plenty of other markets. Take your excess cash and buy things in America. That is where the future lies. Europe is dying. Don't send them the coal."

"All right, we will send the coal to England, and then it will end up in Germany by a different route. I know very well that fellow, Farben, can and will, overnight, convert his aniline factory to powder. Don't you think I realized when those ridiculous Americans at Versailles said, 'We will never let Germany make arms again,' that they were lying? Who in industry did not know the truth? If they really cared, they would have forced Farben to make pancakes. No, instead they let him be a dye maker. You have to agree, that is a funny joke. A first-year chemistry student knows that with a few changes in aniline production, you have gunpowder, so to speak. I'll tell you something else I know. There is a guy in the U.S. by the name of Goddard experimenting on a new form of air travel called rockets. Did you ever hear of a place called Peenemünde?"

"Now, where is that?" the elderly gentleman asked.

"Not more than fifty miles from here by our favorite summer retreat, near Koningerberg, on the isle of Usedom, there are some German scientists who are hoping to do the same thing. There are two guys called Von Braun and Dorenberg. Do you want more names? Not much is happening – yet. And it's very hush-hush. But it's only a matter of time, maybe three, four years before this place breaks out and becomes a viable proving ground. So don't tell me I don't know what is going on. They want to go to the moon."

"My dear Brand, you are reading too much science fiction. Anyway, my good friend who sees no limits, it's 1932 and another year is soon ending. I can tell you the world is going to be a different place in ten years. Hitler is not to be taken lightly. He is appealing to frustrated, angry, hungry Germans who are ripe for a leader who promises them the good life again. The Jews are to blame for the German's starvation and loss of dignity, so he preaches, but the master race will prevail. And Max Schiller is playing with fire, if you want my opinion."

"That is just political crap; let's not overestimate a former house painter. In the meantime, Jonas is having a birthday party in a few hours and if you and Sonja are not there, in good spirits, there will be a war like you have never seen."

When Sonja and Metchnik arrived, the birthday party was in full swing. The birthday boy presided over the long tea table where fifteen of his cronies sat while their governess weaved to and fro trying to keep some order. Jonas wore brown lederhosen, a white shirt, and a red tie. His brown hair was neatly pressed down on his scalp with his father's English pomade. Fräulein Marlow, hours before the party got under way, had prepared

Jonas for the occasion.

The boy had been sitting on the floor of his large playroom, which stretched on like a bowling alley, when Fräulein came into the room. His tin soldiers were lined up facing each other for another battle as Astor quietly sat on the floor beside him. On one side of the room was a desk with a small graphite blackboard still showing the morning's writing lessons.

"Did you practice your letters yet, Jonas?"

"Yes, Fräulein."

"We better get ready, then." She bent down and raised Jonas up from the floor.

"Come, let's put away your army because once your friends get here you won't find them again." Her soft white blouse opened and Jonas caught a glimpse of her large breasts. It wasn't the first time.

"Now, you remember how I taught you to be a good host. You know what host means. You don't fight with your friends, and you let them play with all your things."

She helped him bathe and dressed him in his birthday outfit. "A good German boy has to be neat, courteous, strong, and wear a red tie." She gave him a kiss on his cheek and he felt her breasts against him.

"Your parents will be waiting for you." She pressed his brown hair down with the pomade and placed a pin to hold it.

"Now, don't run your hand through your hair, Jonas." She took a step back to assess the results and smiled. "You look like a little Hessian prince."

At the head of the table, covered with platters piled high with assorted tea sandwiches, meats and smoked fish, and small cakes, Jonas laughed and chattered with his friends. Fräulein Marlow looked on proudly as she watched Jonas acting like a gentleman, the host, the master of the party. Astor was underneath the table scrounging food from the guests while Lucia, Brand, Metchnik,

Sonja, the Prince, and Bill Harrington were crowded around a small table, sipping champagne as they listened to Uncle Herman tell off-color jokes.

After the lemon ices were eaten, the light dimmed. Hilda, the cook, carried in a towering birthday cake with a small statue of a little boy made of marzipan standing on its apex. Nine candles plus one for good luck surrounded the small marzipan boy.

Lucia came over to the table with Brand and placed her arms around her son. "Now, Jonas, make a wish and blow out all the candles."

Jonas stood on the chair and closed his eyes, and with one quick blow, all the candles were extinguished, followed by a round of applause as Lucia kissed him.

"Are you going to tell us your wish?" Brand asked.

"Don't you dare," the Prince broke in. "It is good to have a little secret that you keep for yourself."

Fräulein Marlow quietly smiled. "Well, everyone in this household has secrets," she said, and in the darkness she eyed Brand who was staring at her. She had missed him these last several nights and so disliked wondering whether or not he would show. Still, she thrilled whenever he did, rousing her from a delicious half-awake sleep, and climbing in next to her, crushing her voluptuous breasts with his muscular body. He knew how to touch every part of her body that was the most exquisitely sensitive. She trembled like a caught bird in his arms. And she knew things about Brand that his wife never would dream existed behind his outwardly stoic demeanor. She doubted sincerely that the frivolous Lucia, who had gone from her father's house to her husband's, understood what a man like Brand needed from a woman. His eyes told her he missed her, too.

"And now," Brand proclaimed, "I have a surprise for the birthday boy and his friends. Everyone can come to our little theater for something special."

Jonas led his friends to the small theater in the basement of the house. The grownups followed with their champagne glasses, and Uncle Herman carried the champagne bucket. The lights dimmed and a live bear appeared on the stage with its trainer and began to dance to a background of Viennese waltzes. The children applauded and screeched with happiness.

"The birthday boy may now dance with the bear," announced the skinny trainer who reached for Jonas to come forward. Reluctantly, Jonas left the table and amidst all the cheers, took the trainer's hand and the bear's paw as the threesome made a circle going round and round to the music. Lucia watched nervously and was relieved when Jonas was freed from the circle and ran back to the table with his arms raised high like a true warrior.

Fräulein Marlow was anxious for the party to end because tonight was her night off. She was thinking of Bruno now. Her need for him was very different than what she experienced with Brand. It was raw, and political, and also just a little bit dangerous, although differently so.

Tonight she had promised to go to a meeting with Bruno at the Kammastrasse Hall where the new Socialist Party was having a rally. "You owe it to your Prussian ancestors to be there," he had told her when they were together one night in bed, his massive hands cupping her ample breasts and making them feel girlishly small.

"Danzig can not be a free state run by the Jews. We must bring Danzig back to the Fatherland."

Thursday night was a big night for all the maids and governesses of the town, and, for that matter, for all of Germany, Switzerland, and France. It was the one night that household help vanished, except for Karl-Heinz, Brand's chauffeur bodyguard. The cafés in the old city were crowded with domestic help who came to drink beer, eat wurst and seasoned potatoes, and dance to accordion music.

For Prince Brandenberg, Thursday was also the night to make new conquests. As he pretended to enjoy the spectacle of young Jonas dancing with the bear, the Prince imagined himself hunting for bear later that night.

The Café Geiger was located in the waterfront district of the city where some of the low-lifes congregated. No one knew who the Prince was because he came dressed just like one of the ruffians, wearing worn-out baggy pants and a sailor shirt. He was a regular client of the Café Geiger, where the back rooms catered to the bizarre sexual needs of the clientele. It reeked with the smell of opium and wine, and the only politics were sex and drugs.

This double life of his suited the Prince and he had come to appreciate his darker nature. It worked for him, so long as he was careful – and he was – so that the darkness within him did not swell, like the walls of a bubble, and the toxins within him did not burst into the sedate and civilized world from which he came. On other nights, when the people of Danzig gathered in fancy drawing rooms where the conversations were gossip, theater, and politics, he knew all too well that were it not for his noble background, Danzig society wouldn't tolerate him. So he had learned to be cautious.

Now sitting beside Bill and Sonja, he glanced at the small group of adults in the downstairs basement theater who were sitting apart from the laughing children – Brand, Lucia, Uncle Herman, and yes, even the honorable Metchnik – and wondered what their secrets were. One thing life had already taught the Prince was that no one could live with too much truth.

The party finally ended and all the children and grownups left, including Brand and Lucia. The little girl, Alexandra, was invited to spend the night. She and Jonas had the house all to themselves, except for the chambermaid, Frau Gross, who was left to care for them. Jonas was looking forward to opening his presents and going to his secret hiding place.

Alexandria, whom he called Ala, was one year older than he, with adorable dark round eyes and long black hair. Her parents, Prussians, were in the shipping business and lived next door on the famous street called Langfuhr, which was lined with magnificent mansions. Each residence had a majestic stone staircase at its entrance, and stone balconies, the famous carved balconies of Danzig.

The children were sitting on the floor of the kitchen as Jonas opened his first present, from Ala. It was a round paperweight with a tin soldier and a young girl inside. "Shake it," Ala directed.

With his small hands Jonas shook the paperweight and snowflakes appeared. "Oh, that is beautiful," he exclaimed.

"Tell me a story," Ala said, "about the soldier and princess in the bowl."

"I am the soldier and I was wounded from a battle with the French and the princess came to help me get better."

"What about me? I want to be in the glass, too."

"All right, you are the princess and you came to me and then we lived together forever in the glass."

"I like that story better," she said.

"Come on." Jonas stood up. "Let's go exploring, but don't be afraid; it will be dark."

"I won't be afraid if I am with a soldier."

They ran up the long winding stairs to the master bedroom. The late afternoon light was quickly fading.

"This is where my mother and father sleep," he said. Three large French armoires stood on the side of the bedroom.

"Follow me. I have my own secret place." They squeezed behind the armoires, climbing into what appeared to be a very tiny alcove where Jonas kept a small blanket on the floor and some toy soldiers and two books. Astor also wriggled through the narrow separation between the tall chests.

"Here is my hiding place," Jonas explained. "No one knows it except you."

"It is dark here," Ala said, "but I am not afraid. Can you keep a secret?" Ala asked. "You can't tell anyone, not even Fräulein Marlow. I heard my parents whisper that we are going to leave for America soon."

"Why America?" asked Jonas. "It is very far away."

"I know. But Father said the streets are lined with gold."

"I want to go to America, too," Jonas replied, "and I will bring Astor and walk on the gold streets."

"Not so loud, Jonas. Someone may hear you."

"Let's play doctor," Jonas said. "You lie down and I will examine you."

Ala reluctantly lay down on the blanket.

"You have to pull down your pants."

"I don't want too. It is too cold."

"Then we can't play doctor, and I won't let you come here again. It is dark and no one can see you. Come on, Ala."

She pulled up her dress and partially pulled down her panties a couple of inches. "That is all I am going to show," she said. "You can touch me just here and not lower."

He ran his fingers around her belly button, tickling her. Ala then sat up and rearranged her panties. "No more today. I want to leave your secret place. Let's play with your new toys."

Frau Gross was waiting on top of the stairs when they emerged flustered from the bedroom.

"Where have you two been?" She scowled at the blushing children. "I have been searching for you. It is time for your supper, and then to bed. What have you been doing?"

"Nothing, Frau Gross, we were playing hide and go seek, and I could not find Ala," Jonas answered in a weak voice.

The Prince and Bill Harrington marched through the dark streets near the waterfront, heading for the Café Geiger. They heard their shoes echoing on the brick pavement as they passed old houses dating back centuries. In the alleyways stood sinister-looking men smoking cigarettes.

"These are the cocaine sellers. Mostly sailors. You don't have to be afraid," the Prince told Bill. In the week since their dinner together the two men had met daily, for coffee, for tea, for walks and English lessons. The Prince was careful to avoid by word or gesture anything the young American could construe as a seduction. Still, the Prince was enchanted, smitten by just about every pivot, and even how Bill said good morning when they would meet, without shaking hands, after the American fashion. What was more, the Prince sensed something about Bill that the young American didn't know himself – yet. It was his mouth that gave him away. It was pink and soft, despite the all-American frame. Still, Bill, oblivious perhaps, seemed to genuinely enjoy the Prince's company, quickly ascribing the nobleman's after-party invitation tonight to just another "adventure." That, after all, was what had brought him to Europe, to Danzig, and to what the Prince had described as a most "unusual" club.

To that point, the Prince continued, "In this port, ships from all nations arrive from all other ports. The Turks like this port because it is an easy market. You will enjoy the Café Geiger. The philosopher, Schopenhauer, used to hang around here, and there are some interesting characters. They are like owls; you can only see them at night. Night people whom you never see during the daylight."

The Café Geiger had a flickering light, illuminating a small violin hanging over the side of the entrance. They climbed down the dark, narrow, sinister-looking stairs, which led to the café. The late afternoon sun that had bathed the Krugers' birthday celebration in golden hues had given way to a clear, brisk late autumn night. The men had been walking for nearly an hour now. Bill welcomed the opportunity to warm himself.

Inside the smoke-riddled room was a man with a large mustache playing the accordion. A waitress brought them to the dark far side of the dreary room where two men were already sitting sipping beer.

"For a moment I didn't recognize you," one of the men said. "Your outfit is like a Sicilian sailor's."

"This is my American friend, Bill Harrington, from Ohio."

The smaller man with jet black hair and wild-looking eyes stood up and greeted Bill.

"This is Rudolf Hess, a crazed intellectual from Berlin who wants to change the world," the Prince said in French. "We are all friends from Berlin along with his architect friend, Albert Speer. I spent several years with him in Heidelberg."

The Prince placed a small bottle on the table.

"Anyone? Here, Bill, have you ever tried this stuff? Everyone in Germany who is anybody uses it, or you can have a pipe of opium."

"I think I will stick to the beer," Bill said, embarrassed.

The Prince turned to his old friend. "Don't worry, Rudi, you can talk freely in front of my friend. He already knows why we are here."

Hess' face reddened with anger and he told the Prince in German, "You are a fool! Why did you bring that boy here?"

"He hardly understands any German," the Prince said.

"I told you before I am not interested in your madness. You are German, and you love your country, or so you told me hundreds of times. If we lose the next elections coming up, Germany will go communist and, my dear Prince, you will have the Bolsheviks living in your home. I just want to get your support because Hitler is a genius, and he hates fags, but he will leave you and me alone if we support him. I have some plans laid out for you for some demonstrations in the town square next week, before the election. I want you on the viewing stand with me cheering or just to say a few words."

"My friend here from Berlin," the Prince said again in French to Bill, "is pleased you have come to visit us, and he thinks if all Americans are so handsome, he wishes to visit your country soon."

"He isn't a Jew, is he?" asked Hess crossly. "Is he, Prince? You cross all lines when it comes to love."

"It's not like that," the Prince answered as Hess dumb-foundedly looked on. Turning back to Bill he urged, "Now you will try the great German sauerbraten, or a frankfurter like you have in New York, and the best beer in the world."

By the end of the evening Bill Harrington was drowned in beer and a cute German maid was sitting on his lap, running her hand between his legs while Hess and the Prince disappeared to an upstairs room.

Then the maid took Bill by the hand and led him to a room upstairs, too. The young girl giggled and pulled her dress down. Bill collapsed on the narrow bed, closed his eyes and felt her warm naked body on top of him. She fumbled with his pants then he felt the wonderful sensation of her mouth on his penis, which, however, would not harden. Frightened, he thought about his first girlfriend back home, a local pharmacist's daughter, who left him, frustrated each time they lay together on a blanket he would spread out on the hill overlooking the Allegheny River. And there had been Jean, whom he'd taken out a few times when he was at the University and had liked very much. The girls back home had looked at him questioningly, much the way this young woman was now. Would she mock and ridicule him for his failures, too, and still demand his money?

He wanted to cry. But then the maid gripped his hips and flipped him over. She climbed on top of his naked backside, slid her hands beneath him to massage his testicles and then gently flicked her tongue into his anus as she simulated a pumping motion with him beneath her.

Seconds later he burst his semen into her hands, and fell asleep.

Chapter Three

*O*F ALL THE PRESENTS THAT Jonas cherished most dearly, Astor excepted, was a wonderful crystal radio. Now, sitting on the floor of his playroom, he placed the silver prongs in his small ears and, listening to the martial music, he marched his Prussian tin soldiers to the stirring sounds. The French soldiers, sitting on feathered horses, were lined up in an attack formation. Today, Jonas decided the battle would be won by the Prussian cavalry. One by one the boy pushed the French soldiers to the ground while advancing his Prussian army to victory. Suddenly there was silence. The music stopped and Jonas adjusted the prongs in his ears and shook the crystal radio. He then heard screeching, the frantic sound of a man making a speech, constantly interrupted by cheers and wild shouting – "Heil Hitler" – swelling into a crescendo of what seemed like thousands of voices joined together.

Jonas laughed, thrilled by the excitement of it all. He repeated the salute he had heard, his lips mimicking the shouts. Fräulein Marlow was standing by the rolling doors of the playroom, observing the boy giggling with delight. She walked towards him.

"Jonas, what are you laughing at so much? Is there something funny coming over the crystal?" She ran her hand across the curve of his face as she crouched down. Jonas pushed her long blond hair aside and gave his governess the plugs of the crystal fingers to listen for herself. He waited for her to giggle; instead, he saw the lines around her eyes tighten, her mouth purse.

She had heard Hitler speak before, but never with such force, never with such inspiration. Now he was speaking directly to her, the underdog, a subaltern to that filthy rich and impure race, the *Juden*, those Jews. True, her boss was also her lover, a Jew no less, but sexual desire goes beyond politics. But this will all soon change! She nodded her head in agreement, which Jonas took as a sign that she found the speaker funny, but she did not laugh. The face looked harder than ever. Perhaps grownups don't laugh at the same things children find funny, he reasoned. Five minutes later, when the speech was over, she removed the plugs from her ear, returning them to the child.

"Yes, that was very nice, Jonas. If you hear that funny man again, promise you will call me."

"Yes, Fräulein." He was happy he was able to please her. She was so strict, and he was always in at least a little trouble.

At the far end of his playroom were two large French doors that opened onto a stone balcony. Although the parapet was too high for Jonas to reach, there were two circular openings on each side of the concrete wall that made it possible for him to see beautiful Stefan Park and the wide roadway below. Now he played captain of a great sailing ship, stood at rigid attention, saluted, and looked out at the distant horizon, his open sea. Uncle Herman had bought him a white sailor suit from Copenhagen that he wore on occasion. The best time to play captain on his magical balcony was when he was wearing his suit.

He opened the French doors and went outside with Astor, who sniffed the cold January air. "Yo ho! Yo ho!" Jonas shouted. "Here comes the captain."

He was startled by what he thought was an echo, but he realized it was the beating of drums and the sounds of marching.

It was against the Fräulein's rules to climb into the turret, but how could he resist seeing where the sound of the drums was coming from? His head hung through the opening, a small cherub straining his eyes. In the far distance he could make out a column of men that looked like an army of slowly moving ants.

"They are coming, Astor, to attack the ship. Prepare the ship for battle. Raise the flags!" he yelled. Just as he had seen in the pirate cartoon with the Katzenjammer Kids, which he watched on Saturday with Uncle Herman at the movie palace.

The ants grew larger. They were much closer now. Suddenly they wore uniforms, short pants and arm bands, and carried small drums tied around their necks, beating them in time to their marching. In the center of the parade there were tall boys proudly holding aloft a huge photograph of a man with slick black hair and a small mustache.

"Links, links (left, left), recht, recht (right, right)!" they chanted, and then they sang the song he had heard over the crystal set, the "Horst Wessel," the Nazi anthem. Minutes later, the procession was gone, except for the receding sound of the drama.

Jonas climbed quickly out of the turret and rushed to the special closet in his playroom, the spacious one where his larger toys were kept, and found his drum. He ran to his bedroom and slipped on his lederhosen, and spread a large white handkerchief on the floor, drawing on it a crisscross sign in red crayon so that it looked like what the marching boys wore. Folding it, he tied it around his arm, the crisscross showing. Now he was ready, dressed just like the boys he had seen.

With the drum suspended from his neck, he marched down the long, winding stairs. "Links, links, recht, recht!" His right arm was raised in the erect salute. "Dumm, derumm, dumm, dumm," he whispered to himself. The only thing missing was the knife the boys carried on the side of their leather pants, encased in a leather pouch. Uncle Herman will bring me one if I ask,

Jonas thought. Uncle Herman gives me anything I want, not like the mean Fräulein.

In the spacious library, surrounded by stacks of rare books, Brand Kruger and Metchnik sat at a large Louis XVI desk, discussing their plans for future coal shipments. Both men were dressed in dark suits and had serious expressions on their faces.

"I went to Gdynia last week," Brand said. "You know, where all the swampland is. The Poles have already filled it in and the docks will be finished by the fall."

"That means we can send our barges up the Vistula to the port all year around," Metchnik said, "because they will be enclosed in the peninsula and the waters won't freeze. This is the best deal in your life, and the most dangerous. I don't know how long they will let the Jews work."

"They won't bother me. They need me too much," Brand replied.

"Dron, dum, dum."

"What the devil is that?" Metchnik asked.

"That is your little angel, Jonas," Brand said. "He wants to come in."

"Let him in, Brand. We need a break!" Metchnik pulled the heavy rolling door open as both men began to politely applaud, and in came Jonas, head straight, eyes front, right arm upraised, marching across the length of the library, chanting unintelligibly.

At first they saw only the boy with his brown hair combed to one side and the drum suspended from his neck, Astor yelping behind. He was a welcome relief from their complicated business matters. Jonas often brought a smile to the grown-ups because he used their language without quite knowing what the words meant, and he had an innate ability to imitate people who struck his fancy.

They stopped applauding and Brand rose to his feet when they saw the child stretch out his left arm, displaying his Nazi armband.

Fräulein, hearing all the commotion, hurried down to the library and stopped short. Her eyes widened in amazement, as if she were witnessing a birth, a miracle.

"Jonas, stop that at once! What are you doing?" Brand yelled, ripping off the armband. Jonas' face twisted with astonishment and tears immediately rolled down his cheeks as Astor jumped on Brand, barking at him. "Where did you learn this from? God in heaven!" Brand continued. "Don't you ever wear that again or march like that."

"I saw the boys in the street marching like that, Boy Scouts on parade. I'd like to be one, Father."

"They are not Boy Scouts!"

Metchnik looked upon the ugly scene with great sadness.

"Not so hard on the boy," he whispered.

"You belong to the Boy Scouts already," Brand said, more softly now, "The Maccabee Club," he said, referring to a gymnastic program at the synagogue for Jewish children. "Don't you march with them every Sunday at the gym?"

"It is not the same thing. We have to exercise and wear white shorts, and I don't like climbing on the wooden horses and the ropes. Besides, Gerhardt always pushes me down on the mat. I hate him. I wish he was dead."

Fräulein, without first knocking on the heavy library doors, quickly entered, placed her arms around Jonas' small shoulders, and escorted him out. Unseen by the others, her lips were curled in a sly smile.

The next week, on Sunday, Jonas refused to go to his weekly Maccabee Club.

"If not the gym, would you like to play Schlagball, or perhaps go to the park?" Fräulein asked him. "I did promise your parents to take you to the gym today," Fräulein said to Jonas, who remained preoccupied with his soldiers.

The boy said nothing and just shook his head.

"Well, then, we can't waste a whole day with you moping around. I guess I will have to surprise you with something wonderful."

"What? Tell me, Fräulein, please!" a suddenly very alert Jonas pleaded.

"I am going to dress you in your nice Sunday outfit, and then we will take the trolley car to the old city. Not today, but one day soon. We'll take a little walk down Long Street, past the tall mysterious Marin Church where the dungeons are, and go to the Crane Gate, where all the wheat is stored as it comes off the boats by the water. We'll watch the swans and the boats."

"But what is the surprise, Fräulein?"

"You will see. You have to learn to be patient. It is much better to wait around for something good, my little man, than to get it all at once."

It was much colder than usual, even for the middle of January. A cutting wind blew from the North Sea; the clouds were gray as dirty cotton balls. They had to walk for ten minutes to the end of a wide street to meet the trolley car. Passing by the elegant estates, Fräulein pointed to the largest one, the one owned by the Prince. It was enclosed by a very old, tall iron gate, the family crest mounted above its entrance. The Prince enjoyed displaying the colorful banner with the family crest from the upper stone balcony when he was in residence. The banner was up, whipping in the wind, smoke was rising from the chimney, and Fräulein caught a glimpse of Bill Harrington through the large, wide library window standing by the stone fireplace. She surmised he was there for the Prince's daily English lesson.

She held Jonas' hand tightly. He was shivering, the wind cutting right through his long pants. They were both relieved when they finally mounted the red-colored trolley car and sat down on the wooden seat by the window. It snaked through the narrow streets into the old town, twisting and screeching. Fräulein had an arm around Jonas' narrow shoulders, and this made him feel warm and secure, like rising from the bathtub and having a towel encircle his naked body. Fräulein Marlow pointed out the historical houses where once-famous Danzig citizens resided, like King Ziygmunt, the ruler of Prussia and Danzig. When the trolley arrived at Hellagasse, they got off and briskly walked down the narrow brick streets flanked by old Flemish buildings. In front of the entrance of each house were posts crowned with the heads of lions guarding charming stone balconies. Jonas liked touching posts as he trotted along, imitating a horse. Fräulein held fast to his hand, and her arm stretched taut as Jonas pulled her. She knew that if Jonas was let loose he would disappear within seconds, galloping down the curved streets and alleys. He was far into his imaginary world. He was the knight on his horse returning from another glorious battle.

They arrived at Halengasse, or Jew Street, named by the Hanseatic League when the Jews of the thirteenth century were given the right to form their own trade guilds. This was the street where Jewish shoemakers, carpenters, hatters, tanners, and tailors were allowed to run their businesses relatively un-harassed. It made Jonas laugh to pass a street with such a funny name. He pictured dozens of bearded rabbis living on this street like the Rabbi who presided over his synagogue. But he saw none. They walked on to Geisengasse Street, with its medieval buildings and a magnificent Gothic structure called the Marian Church. Just behind the street was a small square with a statue of a noble warrior in the center, which marked the spot where the Danzigers once defended themselves against the invasion of the Teutonic Knights. Fräulein pointed to one of the older Hanseatic buildings in the center of the square. It was a narrow, five-story rectangular structure with small windows lined by white frames, contiguous with other buildings of the same size.

"Do you know what that place is, Jonas?"

"Father's office," he answered proudly pointing to a small sign engraved in stone. The Gothic letters read *Baltic Kohlen.*

Another block to the right and they were at the old brown wooden grain elevator on the waterfront. The sun broke through the Baltic skies as they sat down on the brick edge of the Mottlau River to watch the fishing boats and barges. Some of the barges, carrying mounds of coal that looked like small volcanic hills, had large blue letters on their sides: *Baltic Kohlen Company.*

"Your father's boats," Fräulein remarked.

"Father said he will take me on one of the barges soon and I can be the captain."

Swarthy-looking men were leaving the schooner, their wet trousers tucked into shiny black rubber boots, carrying large, slimy, straw baskets overflowing with bass and flounder. Behind them, the concrete wall known as Long Street was bustling with people, mostly elegantly dressed ladies and their maids shopping in the quaint shops that lined the dock. The air was filled with the peaceful sounds of Danzig. Occasionally, a small gunboat passed, flying the German eagle, reminding those who cared to be reminded that peace was but a passing thing.

Jonas sat on the concrete parapet, dangling his feet, staring at the busy scene before him. He kept his eyes fixed on the gunboat, imagining that he was the captain and that he was directing the cannon fire toward the shore.

"Fire on the grain gate," he shouted, "when I give the orders, but don't hit any of the fishermen."

"That is not nice, Jonas," Fräulein Marlow corrected in a stern voice.

A tall coarse-looking man suddenly appeared from the crowd, wearing a fisherman's cap, black leather jacket, and black pants.

"Jonas, this is my friend, Bruno," Fräulein said.

The boy jumped up, clicked his heels, and offered his small hand to the large man. "It is a pleasure to meet you."

"What a splendid gentleman," Bruno responded. But Jonas felt repulsed by Bruno's hard, unrefined face, and resented him deeply as he saw him touch his governess' hand. Fräulein Marlow instinctively placed her arm around Jonas' shoulders and drew him close to her.

"And now, my little Jonas, comes the surprise." He felt reassured once more as he smelled her closeness to him.

"Do you remember the Boy Scouts you liked so much? Well, I am going to take you to meet them. Bruno is one of their leaders, and he is nice enough to take us with him. This will be our little secret, Jonas."

They arrived at a small street called the Toppengasse, and came upon a large building of whitewashed brick which had been the headquarters of the British Army during the Allied occupation after World War 1. Now it was the headquarters of the National Socialist Party – the Nazis. A large flag was flying over the entrance; it had the same insignia on it that Jonas had drawn on his armband. Almost directly across the street was the medieval Central Synagogue, the pride of Danzig's Jews, built by Lithuanian immigrants in the fourteenth century. It was the very proud depository of the most ancient Torahs and holy books in Europe. For a moment, Jonas thought they were going to the synagogue. During the High Holidays, Fräulein often brought him there to visit with his parents during the long service. Every year, the shrewd governess would place a red rose in his hands which he then gave to his delighted mother, who showered him with kisses as the worshipers looked on at the charming, elegant little boy who showed so much love for his parents. But this was certainly not the High Holidays, and judging from Jonas's excited little face, his parents were the furthest thing from his mind right now.

Any confusion felt by Jonas was soon eased as they turned away from the synagogue and mounted the stairs to the white building. He felt uneasy and embarrassed as they entered a large hall brimming with young boys and girls, many his own age, sitting on small wooden folding chairs. Up front was a long wooden table surrounded by men wearing brown uniforms. Hanging from the wall in back of them was a huge poster of a man with a small mustache, in uniform. Each side of the hall was flanked by flags flying the colors of Danzig, and there were red and black and white swastika flags, too. The boys wore brown uniforms; the girls were in blue skirts and white blouses.

"We will sit here in the back, Jonas, so we can watch," Fräulein whispered to him.

Bruno left their side and was soon sitting at the long table with the other men. A tall, young, blond man was standing in front of the stark room. He had a warm pleasant smile, and was speaking much more softly than the others.

Jonas surveyed the audience of children. The governess removed his warm fur-lined leather coat and then took off his woolen cap, holding it in her hand as she placed her other arm around his shoulders.

"Boys and girls, I want to tell you today about our great city, Danzig. All of you born in Danzig are Germans, proud Germans. Even your birth certificates are written in German. Danzig has been part of Germany for hundreds of years. It is like living in a big house. Germany, the fatherland, is the big house, and Danzig is one of the rooms of the house. For now, Danzig is called a Free State and everyone, all kinds, are living in this house when it really should be reserved only for our German family. But soon, I promise you all, our leader, Adolf Hitler, will unite us and we will be one big happy family again. You are Aryan. That is a big word for you to remember. Aryans. Aryans. You know there is not enough food in our homes, that our people are living like rats. The food is taken away by those ugly people, these foreigners who are not part of our family."

Jonas felt his stomach grumble. He remembered it was getting near dinner time. He began to worry that there would not be any food when he returned home.

"We are forming clubs all over for you to join. We will teach you German songs. You will learn how to march. The boys will learn to wrestle and box, even how to use a knife, and later, how to shoot a gun. We want you to be little soldiers for the new country, for the new Germany. We want you to be strong. You do want to be strong, don't you?"

Jonas nodded his head affirmatively and felt for the muscles in his arms. "I am strong enough to jump the pommel horse at the Maccabee Club," he said to himself.

The tall man in front continued to talk, his voice growing louder. "You, too, all of you, will someday become leaders. When you march on the streets all the people will shout and be proud of you, the strong German youth, as they see you in your uniforms, strong and tall, and they will talk of you as the real Germans of the future, their hope. We have enemies out there who want to take the food away from your tables and leave you without your homes," he said, and then repeated the sentence three times.

"Let us all now give the salute to our leader, to the man who saved us all."

All the children in the hall shouted, "Heil Hitler!"

"Say it louder! Louder!" And they did, over and over.

The hall became warm and stuffy as the children started to

sing German songs.

Today Germany, tomorrow the world!

Jonas liked stamping his feet and he enjoyed the shouting. When it was over he was wet with perspiration. Fräulein Marlow proudly slipped a small band around his arm.

"This is for you, my little Jonas, you are now a member of these scouts. Next time, I will get you a uniform to wear, just like the other boys."

As they forged their way back outside through the sweaty crowd, she said, "You were such a wonderful boy that I am going to reward you with some hot chocolate with a marshmallow."

They went to Springers, the popular ice cream store on Long Street, and sat inside at one of the small wrought iron tables. Jonas sipped on the hot chocolate drink, while he fingered his armband.

"Now, you remember, this is our little secret. You must not tell your father or mother, not yet. Later, we will surprise them."

In the long months that followed, every Thursday Fräulein and Jonas could be seen boarding the red-and-black trolley car to go to the Toppengasse to attend the Nazi Youth meetings. Lucia thought it was sweet of Fräulein to sacrifice her day off to take Jonas to the museums. Some days, his governess would put Astor on his leash and together the three of them would go to Stefan's Park.

There – the Brownshirts – the Hitler Youth, would gather to practice marching and running.

"Go Jonas, you can join them, run with them," she urged.

"I don't want to Fräulein. I'd rather stay with you and Astor." Going to the meetings was fine, but to be out in the open cavorting with those boys made him feel uncomfortable. Besides, then it would no longer be a secret, a clandestine meeting, and his parents would learn of it. They might even see him and become angry with his Fräulein and make her leave and he would be left all alone.

Chapter Four

$\mathscr{T}$HE CAFÉ DES ARTISTES was so named became it was Danzig's favorite hangout for writers and artists. They would meet in the evenings, smoke hashish, sip a Pernod, and sniff cocaine. It was not as glamorous as the fast Rue Flaubert crowd in Paris, but it was still their café, and Lucia liked going there very much. During the day, throughout the afternoon, it served as an elegant tea house and a nice place for a rendezvous with a lover, with fresh flowers on every small round table, carts with delicate patisserie circulating around the room, and a Hungarian violinist playing Liebestraum or some Strauss love songs, and more recently the songs of Kurt Weill.

Bill Harrington was sitting at one of these tables on this February afternoon waiting for Lucia to arrive. Surprisingly, for a destination so popular, this was his first visit. In the three months since his arrival in Danzig, he had discovered it was not uncommon for her to be late an hour or more. This tardiness was not deliberate. It was just that by the time Lucia finished her toiletries, spoke to Cook about dinner that night and to Fräulein Marlow about Jonas (already long gone at school by the time she rose), she had simply lost all sense of time. Lucia had her own clock, Lucia Time. She was so charming a woman, so lovely and adorable, that it was not possible to become angry with her ways. She also had her own peculiar style. Her clock was the reverse of most people's. Her best hours of alertness, productivity, and sexuality were after 11:00 p.m. It was at this hour she read her newspaper, wrote her letters, and munched on marzipans and plums while reading poetry. At three in the morning she might then go and awaken Brand, who could always be counted upon to have a nocturnal erection. Satisfied, she then slept until noon. The only time she was up in the morning was to attend funerals, to catch a train, or to meet Bill Harrington near the Beaux Arts for their weekly lunch. Today, Lucia wanted something a little more *soigné*. A late lunch *a deux*.

Bill had become a fixture in the lives of her little set. He was so fresh and unspoiled, and as an American and a university graduate yet, he was interesting, well-read, and just delicious to look at. Certainly the other ladies at the café today had noticed. As he sat at one of the corner tables while finishing a second cup of tea, they saw a tall handsome man with a certain understated sexuality about him that made him dangerously attractive. His thick, uncombed brown hair, his marvelous blue eyes, like corn-flowers, and his comfortable and casual brown corduroy jacket gave him the appeal of a young poet. And of course it would only be when Lucia arrived that they would be able to admire the row of healthy white teeth that only an American diet of fresh food and whole milk, lots of milk, could produce as he greeted her with a wide smile. For now, they saw that his complexion was soft, unblemished; and his shoulders were well-developed, round, sturdy, and certainly roomy enough for a delicate, forlorn, young woman to nestle her head on.

Today, they may have also have been enchanted by the look he wore of a bemused school boy as he struggled to read the local Danzig newspaper, moving his pale lips while trying to interpret the German. The Prince had advised him to read the local newspaper rather than the English one because that way he would learn the language. Bill had grown surprisingly close to the Prince, perhaps closer even than to Lucia. The young American had quickly come to admire the Prince for his exquisite manners, and for his charm and generosity. A highly cultivated man and true Continental who really knew literature and music, the Prince had even recently finished re-reading *Crime and Punishment,* in French. Most important, Bill discovered how disarmingly easy it was to make conversation with him, real conversation, beyond the superfluities of polite society. Each had spoken frankly of their very different upbringings, about the books they best loved, and about ideas – from art and architecture to philosophy and politics. And the man was, after all, a Prince! He had listened intently to all Bill had to say, and his responses, always crafted with insight and rendered with such respect, made Bill feel important. So of course, the Prince's suggestion that Bill improve his German by reading the daily paper made excellent sense to him.

Bill was reading now about last week's news, the elevation of Adolf Hitler to German Chancellor. It felt that there would be no stopping the National Socialists now. If he had read on he would have learned that certain elements in Danzig seemed energized by this event, coupled with the conscious hatred for Jews, homosexuals, gypsies, and non-Aryans felt by all classes of society. But Bill had stopped reading to wonder instead what strange, sick society would struggle with this difficult, impossible language. Why did the verb have to be at the end of a sentence? It was really as ridiculous as Hebrew, which had to be read from right to left.

Oscar, the notorious maître d' of this café, who normally knew everyone there, was circling the tables like a dragonfly. He kept eyeing the American, the only person new to him. He was unable to answer the ladies' inquiries about the mysterious young man who was sitting alone struggling with the newspaper.

"You are English?" he asked Bill.

"No, American."

"Ah, I speak a little English. This place is very nice also. We have some Negro players, a combo, who come some nights to play American jazz. It is very dark and much smoke here, but much people come. You could speak to them. Are you a student?"

"Yes, I am here to study architecture. I am waiting for a friend."

"Some Pernod for you?"

"Yes, please," Bill said, suddenly quite pleased with himself for accepting – just another little piece of the adventure, drinking before lunch as opposed to with lunch! He crossed his long legs and put down his paper, and he decided that if he had only a glass before Lucia arrived, it should not be difficult to concentrate on what she was saying. He began thinking about everything that had happened since he'd decided to leave America.

Just half a year ago, he was a senior with no clear post-graduate prospects, shooting baskets in the gym at the state university of Ohio, cheering at football games, captaining the wrestling team, and cleaning tables in the school cafeteria to help pay for his tuition. His father, a successful merchant with a small chain of hardware stores, had wanted his son to take upon himself some of the responsibilities for his education. Bill had no desire to spend the rest of his life selling nuts and bolts and lighting fixtures in Columbus. He was a good architectural student, but hardly a brilliant one. His teacher, a Prussian, suggested he take a year in Europe to learn the real stuff.

"We copy everything from the old world," the Prussian had said. "Go to Germany. The Walter Gropius School is where you will learn. Study Gothic medieval buildings and places like Danzig. Everyone is going to Florence and Venice. You go to Germany, Berlin."

His father consented and gave him enough money to get started. He paid the fare for the trip on the *SS Bremen*. If Bill was still determined to apply to architecture school when he got back, his father would let him try for Carnegie Mellon in not-too-far-away Pittsburgh, though Bill himself dreamed of Columbia and Yale. But in exchange, Bill had to promise to first work a year in one of the hardware stores like his two older brothers, and to give the family business a serious try. Now, however, he knew he could never return to Main Street in Columbus. He had met Lucia the second day after he arrived in Danzig, at the Beaux Arts, when he was looking for student housing. He was standing in front of the bulletin board in the dimly lit medieval hall, trying to read the announcements.

"Do you speak English?" he asked the petite, pretty woman who was looking at the board, reading announcements of courses and special lectures. Bill would later learn that Lucia loved to drop in to the Beaux Arts. Marriage and early motherhood had arrested any hope she entertained of an art school education. But she believed that as the wife of one of Danzig's most powerful men, it was useful for her to display not only a quick wit and a lively way with conversation, but to have ideas of her own on the important interests of the day: furniture, painting, decoration. These requisites the Beaux Arts handsomely satisfied.

"A little," Lucia had said.

"I am looking for a room in which to live. I am a student."

She took him to a charming rooming house minutes away from the university. Although many students from all over the world came to the famed University of Danzig to study philosophy and art, this was the very first American Lucia had met and, rather like taking up a new hobby, she had befriended him ever since.

It was beginning to get dark when she finally arrived. Her cheeks were red as rouge, completely the effect of the cold air.

She was wearing a Persian lamb jacket.

"Of course, I am sorry to be late." She stretched her small body as Bill bent down to kiss her on the cheek. "God, I am frozen. I must have some coffee at once, and perhaps a little Pernod."

Oscar was quickly at her side, clicking his heels and kissing her hand, helping her off with her coat. She wore a simple wool dress of navy blue and her cherry-stained mouth popped against her white skin and dark lashes.

"Everything is mixed up," she said as she made several circles with her small soft hands and then brought them to her lips. She looked up into Bill's eyes as she gently blew warm air on her fingers. "Now that's better. They are alive again. Brand left for Berlin this morning, as usual, leaving me with this house and all that. Thank God for Fräulein." She spoke in English, sprinkling her words with French and German phrases, which made her even more charming.

"How is young Jonas?" Bill inquired. He liked to hear Lucia speak and to watch her animated hands, which spoke their own language. Occasionally, her right hand brushed against her brown hair and her eyes would focus on him as if there was no one else in the room.

"That little monster." She laughed as menus were brought to them. "I never get to see him these days, except when he is sleeping at night, like an angel. The other day I saw him with the forbidden books on the upper shelf of the library."

"The forbidden books?" Bill asked blankly.

Lucia laughed. "Brand has a collection on exotic women of Africa, some kind of anthropological survey of women's breasts. Jonas managed to find one of the volumes. I caught sight of his little body stretching on the tall ladder, and he was gaping at the book in complete fascination. I was afraid to startle him because he might tumble off. I watched him for a while. He didn't look at all like my innocent nine-year-old. The Fräulein was in the library with him pretending to be reading. I silently closed the door. I was really too embarrassed to do or say anything."

"Boys are always curious. Who isn't fascinated by the naked body?" Bill remarked nonchalantly.

"I see my little boy changing, but I really can't put my finger on it. He is as loving as always, but something is different." The waiter came to the table and took their order. Bowls of steaming potato soup and more Pernod.

"Perhaps he is having an early change. Some boys do, you know," Bill opined with an air of authority.

"Enough of Kinder talk. How is the American architect?"

"*Ganz gut*, very well, thank you. I am seeing buildings, studying and having the best time of my life."

Her eyes now focused on his hands, which were resting on the checkered red tablecloth, and her fingers gently brushed them, as if she were painting.

"Your hands are so smooth. The hands of an artist, a great pianist. I always wanted to touch the hands of an artist. You know, once I saw Schnabel up close, performing in the Opernplatz in Berlin, and I kept wondering how his hands must feel, thinking those wonderful fingers must lead an independent life, have an intelligence of their own."

She continued to chat, her head now bending down slightly, while continuing to stroke each of his fingers. If she had looked up she would have seen Bill's face flushing crimson.

"You can tell so much about a person by his hands, his work, his rung in society. No wonder gypsies can tell your fortune from your hands. Here now, let me see the lines of your palms and I will tell your fortune."

Harrington maintained a respectful silence as Lucia turned his hands over and traced the lines of the palms with her well-manicured fingernails.

"Now, let's see. You will have a very long life." She slipped into German. "There is soon to be a great and beautiful and fantastic love affair, one you will never, ever forget." He understood "love affair," but the rest of what she said was lost. "And you will become a famous architect," she said in English, smiling charmingly.

He felt something soft touch his leg, which he thought was Lucia's thigh. It was almost imperceptible. Unsure of himself, but somehow excited about just where all of this was going, he responded by placing his hand on top of hers, squeezing. Then came the soft movement under the table once more. He instinctively moved his hand beneath the checkered tablecloth, only to burst out into roaring laughter.

"My God, it's a dog!" he yelled. "Lucia, I have to apologize," he said. "What is a dog doing here?"

"Everyone brings their dog to this café," she said, not without a smile. "Not so in America?"

"Not in America. It is against the law." The small schnauzer returned to a nearby table, to his mistress, a tall, elegant, elderly woman.

"Fritz, come here! You naughty boy!" she began to scold him, affectionately.

"And you don't have to apologize, Bill. I like when you squeeze my hand."

The owner of the café, Jan Goldberg, dressed in a dark suit, approached their table, bending his body slightly to speak.

"It is always an honor to have a beautiful woman here." He took Lucia's pretty hand and kissed it, then gave Bill a friendly but incisive look.

"Jan, this is Bill Harrington, an American."

"Sir, welcome. A friend of one of the best families in Danzig is more than welcome here. And where is the famous industrialist?"

"In Berlin, where else?"

"Not getting into much trouble, I hope. These are rapidly changing times, *n'est-ce pas?*"

Jan Goldberg was obviously more than just keeper of an inn. He had arrived in Danzig before 1917, along with many other Jewish intellectuals. A pogrom against the Jews – another one, but especially violent – had wracked Russia, while many Jews fled from Poland to escape being drafted to fight against the Bolsheviks. Jan was a writer; now he was a Zionist, too. He bought a small café, making it a place where the intelligentsia could comfortably meet, drinking tea and reciting their works through the day. Soon the bare tables were replaced by elegant settings, the walls bedecked by fine works of art, and violinists played romantic scores. At night it was quite a different matter. A black combo from New York played hot jazz, and the patrons, still mostly intellectuals, also included some anarchists and revolutionaries, unemployed artists and cocaine sellers. Danzig was also a stopover for poor immigrants such as Jews from Russia and Polish shtetls on their way to America and Palestine with the help of Jewish-American money.

Jan was also a money-changer and the head of the young Jewish organization called the *Judenbund*, or freedom fighters. They met once a week in the high school gymnasium, which was still allowed in the Free State of Danzig. They were few in number, but they knew exactly what Adolf Hitler was up to. In three years they would plan the assassination of Hess, Himmler, Goering, and Hitler himself.

"He likes you a lot," Bill said somewhat disconcertedly, after Goldberg had left the table.

"A little jealous over an older woman?" Lucia teased him.

"You are not so much older than I, I think," Bill said a bit defensively.

Lucia's eyes were sparkling now, dazzling jewels. Everything that needed to be said was written on her face.

There was a certain magic that engulfed them now. They were on fire. The waiter came by with more Pernod.

Just as they were about to drink again five tall young men, perhaps no older than sixteen, entered the café. They were dressed in brown dilapidated uniforms and carried small round frayed straw baskets. They wore bright Nazi armbands, and approached each table requesting money. Oscar and Jan Goldberg sternly looked on and dropped some groschens into one of the baskets. When they came to Lucia's and Bill's table, the Brownshirts gave them a long hard look. Bill reached into his pocket and threw coins into one of the baskets. They then moved to the center of the café, and the youngest of the group, who looked to be not all that much older than Jonas, said, "We thank you for the disabled, homeless war veterans of Germany," and he began to sing in a sweet voice: "We are the youth of Germany, and tomorrow, tomorrow, is our future for the world."

The patrons sat silently.

"Who are they?" Bill whispered.

"They call themselves Brownshirts. They are fascists, and some people say they are very dangerous."

"Why does the owner let them in?

"This is the Free State of Danzig. The National Socialist Party, the Nazi party, is allowed to exist, along with a host of others. The Brownshirts represent the Nazi party."

As soon as the youths left, the violins played "Mack the Knife" and the café once again became filled with the sound of afternoon chatter, but for Lucia and Bill, the mood was ruined.

"Let's get out of here," Lucia said. "Come home with me and I will make you my favorite dish, Russian eggs and champagne. Thursday the help is off, and the house belongs to us," she whispered seductively. Bill's heart was alive in anticipation and he could almost feel its beat. He fingered the Prince's friendship ring which he had stopped wearing some time ago though kept wrapped in a handkerchief in his pants pocket, not sure why he had done so but perhaps too tipsy now to give it more thought.

When they arrived at Langfuhr, at the Kruger's home, all the lights were out except for some upstairs, including those in Fräulein's quarters. Astor met them at the hall, jumping on Lucia and growling at Bill.

"Shame on you, Astor. Bill is our good friend. He's not used to you yet, Bill. It means you must come to be with us more often," Lucia told him, the American's face glowing from the Pernod.

She took the dog to the kitchen and returned with two Romanoff flutes and a bottle of Veuve Clicquot, 1920.

"Let's sit in my private study. No one is allowed in except scholars and lovers," she teased.

"I am both of those," he said, emboldened both by the drink and willful desire. He could feel that this rendezvous would end, yes, in the loss of his virginity, finally.

"You must sit on my swooning couch. Take your shoes off while I take a peek at Jonas to see if all is well."

It was a small colorful room lined with books. A large gilt desk stood by the window and a carved ivory mantel over the fireplace was crowded with miniature works of art and colored gems. Dozens of large amber gems collected from the beaches of Danzig caught his eyes. Bill held an amber stone in his hand and sat down on the Victorian fainting couch. In front of the couch was a small table with a glorious collection of Romanov eggs. If he knew the value of each of those beautiful pieces of art he would hardly have been so casual in handling them.

Jonas was not in his bed. Lucia softly made her way to the very end of the long hall, past guest bedrooms and Jonas' playroom to the Fräulein's apartment where she found him napping, his small body languidly stretched over his governess, who was also, apparently, in a deep sleep.

Bill removed his shoes, stretched out on the sofa, and sipped his champagne, his eyes studying the room, especially because it was Lucia's: small Lalique and Meissen figurines; first editions of Verlaine, Baudelaire, and Pushkin; and paintings by Klimt all lining the walls along with photographs of Jonas in his gym suit and sailor's outfit. There were also pictures of Brand on his horse and another with a tennis racket. He spotted a small plate with the inscription "Casino, Sopot 1928." To be asked into this lovely space, so feminine and private, stirred Bill mightily.

Lucia returned now wearing an Oriental kimono and sat next to him. "I am so much more comfortable," she sighed. "Don't look so surprised at my outfit. We went to Shanghai last year on one of those wild trips that Brand likes to take. It was the longest, hardest trip of my life and the most exciting one. We were at sea for almost a month."

"You look beautiful, Lucia," Bill said. At that moment he was not interested in hearing about her travels, but moved closer to her staring into her eyes, those beautiful sparkling eyes. But just then he wondered about the Prince, who also had brown sparkling eyes, and whose look excited him, too.

No, it was not the same thing, dammit. Still, he worried that Lucia must feel his mixed confused feelings. What would she think? Focus, man, focus! Bill told himself as he looked back at the paintings on the wall. His eyes fell on a small George Stubbs, of a horse about to be mounted by a tall man dressed in equestrian clothing and polished riding boots. He blinked. Fortunately, Bill got a reprieve as Lucia started to ramble on.

"This is my special room," she said. "Here is where I can sit quietly, read, write letters. I love to write letters to my friends. I am going to write a letter to you. And one day, when you go back to America and have forgotten all about me, then you will get a letter from Danzig."

"I don't think I will ever forget you or Danzig," Bill said, meaning it. And suddenly, it was clear to him, the whole messy incoherence of it. "Perhaps I will never return to Ohio."

"That will be good, but then I will write you anyway. I know you want to spend some time with Walter Gropius in Weimar, at the Bauhaus. I heard he is moving the Bauhaus to Dessau to establish the International Style. You see, the Beaux Arts has taught me a little something about architecture."

She moved closer to him and very suddenly kissed him gently on his lips. Her kimono opened and her full breasts were exposed to him.

Clumsily he touched them and her sighs rang in his ears, deep womanly sounds of arousal. Lucia reached for him, gently rubbing him through his wool trousers. But she was surprised to find that he did not respond, and when his pursed lips failed to open to her mouth either, she gracefully retreated, closed her kimono and tried to hide her disappointment and said no more.

"I guess I am just nervous that your husband will come marching in, or Jonas," Bill said with a pained voice.

Lucia understood.

Fräulein Marlow was a sneak and voyeur. She had feigned sleep, and when Lucia left her room she silently crept down the stairs and stood breathlessly behind the closed doors, listening while peeking through the keyhole. The hallway was bathed in darkness – the scene inside Lucia's study reminded her of a snow globe, small and glittery and utterly ridiculous. She smiled to herself and thought of Brand. How stupid men are. If only he could see his wife now. Oscar Wilde had something to say, she once read, about marriage killing a woman's passion. He was wrong. It simmers slowly. These Krugers were volcanic.

She quietly tiptoed away, exhilarated by her knowledge. Another secret to be stored away for the future.

Bill, the good-looking American stud, just didn't like women.

Chapter Five

JONAS LIKED THE CHANGE. His governess was not always scolding him now. He no longer had to drink a lukewarm glass of milk with slimy skin floating on top. She had Cook prepare things he liked most – soft-boiled eggs and chocolate pudding at dinner, when they ate alone. When they went to Oliver Forest with Astor, and Jonas ran ahead disappearing in the brush, she strolled patiently, not yelling at him to return. They collected baskets of walnuts from the ground, and then in the evening she threaded them on long pieces of string and made necklaces. When the first snow arrived, they put a harness around Astor's neck and attached him to the sled that pulled the giggling boy through the beautiful forest near their home.

After supper, Fräulein Marlow removed her stiff white blouse and black skirt and placed a housecoat over her naked body. No longer did Jonas resist going to bed. She warmed the feather bed covers by the radiator in his bedroom, and after his mother and father came to say good night, he knew that Fräulein would come in to tell him a story. He could hardly wait. Astor was allowed to stay in his room, and as soon as his parents left, the dog jumped on the bed, snuggling against Jonas' feet. Jonas had once been afraid of the dark, but no longer. A sliver of light crept under the rolling doors as he waited. Soon the governess would enter his room. He liked the subtle spiced scent of her perfume. It reminded him of warm cinnamon muffins. He waited, humming to himself the two stanzas of "Horst Wessel," the Nazi anthem. Fräulein told him the song was written by a young student killed by the Communists in Berlin in 1930. So saddened were the Germans that the original poem became the Nazi anthem.

The child closed his eyes blissfully and smiled as he heard the Fräulein tiptoe into the room.

"Jonas is fast asleep, but now I am going to wake him to tell a story." She bent down, encouraging her robe to open, her full breasts touching his face as she hugged him and kissed his forehead. Acting surprised, he opened his eyes and broke out into a big grin. He sat up and placed his legs up against his body.

"Before I begin the story, I want to ask you, are you my little boy?"

"Yes," Jonas answered.

"And do you love Fräulein?"

"Yes."

"Just as much as Muttie and Daddy?"

He nodded. Yes, he did. His governess never left him at night, preferring the company of grown-ups to his. His parents rarely took him to Stefan's Park, or out for lemon ices.

"And will you always keep our little secrets forever, all the things we do together like grownup people?"

"Oh, yes."

"Good, then come and give me a big hug, and you can lay your head right here if you want to." She placed his head on her naked breast, his lips near her nipple. She closed her eyes and sighed.

"Tonight I am going to tell you the story of a boy called Jonas, who lived in a very big house."

"Like me," Jonas said in a small voice. The Fräulein's breast against his cheek was so smooth and warm. "And does the boy live with a dog called Astor?" he continued. Hearing his name, the dog raised his head from the edge of the bed and licked Jonas' feet.

"And the dog called you-know-what. One day he wore his brown uniform, and he received a present, a little knife in a leather sheath. He walked down the aisle at the meeting house and there he met the great man, the leader, who shook his hand, and said, 'Soon I am going to make you a leader, a captain of the boys, and you will lead them in a march, and your mother and father will be proud of you.' And then everyone clapped, and we decided to change your name from Jonas Kruger to Jonas the Great Captain, because Kruger was not a good name to have for such a great leader."

"Great Captain Jonas," he repeated to himself. "And then what happened?"

"Tomorrow I will tell you what happened, but now you have to go to sleep. You have to grow strong and healthy to do all those things."

She pulled the down quilt over his body and kissed him on the cheek. After the governess left the room he could still smell her perfume on the sheets. He fell asleep dreaming of being a famous soldier, his Fräulein at his side.

When Brand returned from Berlin he was reluctant to tell Lucia what he had witnessed. Although the newspapers were filled with descriptions of the rioting in the streets of Berlin against the Communist Party, the brutal beatings were omitted. The bread lines were growing longer, and people were so poor that they were living on the streets, in shacks, begging for food. The American Hoover Commission and other relief agencies had failed miserably. Suffering and want was everywhere.

"I am happy to return," Brand told Lucia. "Things are very horrible in Germany."

"They must get their factories going, and with Kruger coal, of course," Lucia answered. But she was not interested in hearing Brand's story of Berlin. She had been waiting a long time to discuss Jonas with him.

"You have been away so much you probably haven't had a chance to notice, but your son seems different now. I don't know exactly what it is, but he seems far off, preoccupied. He is no longer loving. He doesn't want to go to the Maccabee Club, and he absolutely detests the Hebrew lessons with the Rabbi," Lucia said, referring to religious instruction that would culminate a few years hence in the child's Bar Mitzvah. "He mimics the Rabbi and makes terrible fun of him. His disrespect is alarming. Also, he won't let go of his governess."

"You are imaging it, Lucia. He looked and acted fine with me. The Rabbi is always complaining. What young boy enjoys Hebrew lessons, an archaic language that is only used at the Holidays?"

"I think we should get rid of her, Brand. I have a woman's intuition that something is very wrong."

"She is a terrific governess. Look, Jonas is like a little prince. He is so well mannered. . . ."

"Exactly, and he acts like a grown-up instead of a young boy."

"He will start gymnasium before long," Brand said, referring to the boy's academy Jonas would be attending the following fall. "It will be good for him to be with other boys beside those isolated here in Langfuhr. You'll see. It will be fine."

That night Brand was sitting on his son's bed, reflecting on Lucia's observations. True, the Fräulein was somewhat mysterious, and he and Lucia had very little idea of how the pair spent their days together. Then again, Jonas was a happy child and wasn't it mystery that made her so exciting in the first place? He slowly shook his head. My son has good taste at least, thinking it had been a while since he had last shared the lovely Fräulein's bed. And surely she would not harm the child – my child, he thought. Jonas stirred and opened his eyes.

"I hope you will like these trains. I bought them in Berlin and they come from America. They are called Lionel trains. On Saturday we will set them up together."

"I love them, Papa. We can build a fort together."

"Jonas, are you feeling all right?" Brand decided to test the water. "Is there anything wrong? If you don't like your governess, we can have her leave."

"Oh, no, Father. I love Fräulein Marlow," he protested, almost in panic. "She is wonderful to me. Just because I don't want to go to the Maccabee Club, Muttie thinks something is wrong." Of course, thought Brand. Of course that's all it is.

Nonetheless, Brand and Lucia insisted he continue with the group which met on Sunday mornings at the gymnasium of the Sankt Johann High School. Several weeks later twenty young boys were lined up in a straight line, all wearing white shorts and white shirts. The little Maccabees had just finished body-bending and jumping jacks ten times. Jonas' school friend Gerhardt stood next to him.

"Now, boys, everyone run to the ropes," ordered the gym master. "Take your rope and start swinging back and forth."

"Did you ever see a woman's tits?" Jonas casually asked Gerhardt as he swung back and forth like a pendulum of a clock.

"No, have you?" Gerhardt whispered.

"Yes. At first, I saw them in some secret books in our library. Black tits of all shapes and sizes."

"I don't believe you. You show them to me next time I come to your house, yes?"

"I also saw them – real, live, and touched them with my hands and kissed one, right on the nipple, and I almost . . ."

"Jonas, you are such a shit liar. You make everything up."

"No, I don't. My Fräulein always lets me see them and touch and kiss them. She even promised to show me her hole and touch it." Gerhardt snorted. Goaded, Jonas continued: "And you know what else, Gerhardt? I belong to the German Youth."

"You are crazy, Jonas. I am going to tell Herr Ott."

"I have a uniform, and carry a knife, march, sing songs, and have an armband like the Nazis. If you want to become a member I can ask Fräulein to let you come with us."

"You make me sick, Jonas, with your lies. I hate you and all your stupid lies!"

"I hate you too, Gerhardt, and if I had my knife with me I would stab you."

Gerhardt waited for Jonas to swing back into his path and then punched Jonas in his face. Jonas let go of the rope and fell to the ground crying. His nose was bleeding. Gerhardt stood above him waiting to strike him again. One of the gym teachers came running and picked Jonas up from the ground. "He hit me!" Jonas cried.

"Well, he lies too much! He lies about terrible things!"

After the gym hour was over, both boys took the short walk to the trolley car that would take them back to their homes. As they walked in silence, Gerhardt suddenly kicked Jonas, who pulled off his leather knapsack and began to swing at Gerhardt's head. Gerhardt ran off laughing and yelling, "Asshole! Liar!" with Jonas in hot pursuit. As Jonas neared him, Gerhardt turned, stuck out his tongue, and dashed off the sidewalk into the gutter. A fast-moving car came from around the corner. There was a scream, and Gerhardt was on the ground, his head covered with blood.

Jonas and other boys ran out to him, surrounding the unconscious boy. Jonas bent down, shouting, "Gerhardt, I didn't mean it! I didn't mean it! Please don't be dead!" He was stricken with fear and panic, slapping his thighs, pulling at his hair.

Grown-ups arrived and then the ambulance. When the trolley car came, Jonas, frightened and trembling, quickly boarded it. A very long ten minutes later he was on Ranestiffe Street. Astor was waiting at the window of the Kruger's house as usual and ran downstairs as Jonas opened the door, jumping on him and kissing his face.

"Mother, Mother," Jonas yelled. "Something terrible happened!" But Fräulein Marlow was not at the house and Lucia was lunching in town. "Astor, something terrible happened. We have to go to Gerhardt's house and tell his mother." With Astor following in pursuit, both ran as fast as Jonas' young legs could manage to Gerhardt's home, just a few houses down, past the Prince's mansion. Still out of breath, he rang the doorbell, and when the boy's mother answered, he quickly said, "Frau Baum, come quickly! Gerhardt was hit by a car and he is bleeding from his head."

"What? Jonas, is this another one of your stories?"

"No, Frau Baum," he cried. "I saw it with my own eyes."

Frau Baum began to scream hysterically, and Jonas became frightened and ran away, down the street back to his house, with Astor barking beside him.

Lucia was waiting at the door as Jonas came stumbling in, tears streaming down his face.

"My poor Jonas, what happened? Your face is all bruised." She pulled him toward her.

"Who hit you? Astor, why did you let Jonas get hit?"

"Astor was not there. Gerhardt was hit by a car because I chased him into the street."

"What are you talking about?"

Several days later, in school, Jonas learned that Gerhardt was in the hospital. The boy had sustained a severe concussion and multiple cracked ribs, but he would live. Jonas was ashamed to cry in class, but was unable to hold back the tears. His teacher, Frau Zahn, was a tough Prussian who wore a long black dress and black shoes, and who deeply resented the few Jewish children in her class. She had a picture of Adolf Hitler hanging by the blackboard and forced the children to recite the oath to the Fatherland each morning. In spite of the protests of the Jewish families, she was allowed to conduct her class as she wished.

"There is no crying in my classroom," she chided Jonas. "If you continue this way you will stand outside."

That night Jonas was unable to sleep; his guilt mixed with relief, the tears would not stop coming. He lay under the bedcovers, shaking. Brand and Lucia had called on Gerhardt's parents. Evidently, the child remembered only exchanging angry words with Jonas but none of the pushing and shoving that resulted in the accident. So Jonas escaped punishment, but on his own he remained inconsolable. Not even Fräulein Marlow was able that night to soothe the shattered boy. He laid awake crying and remembering.

Gerhardt had been his best friend. What had he done?

Just the previous weekend they had spent a wonderful day together. At 8:00 in the morning, Gerhardt's mother had come in the chauffer-driven Rolls Royce to take Lucia and Jonas to the transit camp at Troyl. The mothers were bringing bags of provisions donated by their friends to the unfortunates and had decided that an outing among the refugees would develop the boys' characters. A small island near Danzig, Troyl housed Jews from revolutionary Russia and Poland who were on their way to Palestine and America, and even to Shanghai and Brazil.

As soon as the car halted, the two boys jumped out like mad dogs and ran toward the large gray barracks in front of them. It was useless for the two mothers, for all their cajoling and threats, to try to slow them down. The boys saw old men with beards who looked like their Rabbi and young boys with long sideburns and skullcaps on their small heads, dressed in shabby clothing, sitting around a long wooden beat-up table eating their breakfasts out of wooden bowls. Jonas was dressed in a splendid dark green leather suit complemented by a leather cap and blue scarf. He gamely walked into the large hall which was lined with a row of beds. Gerhardt stood by the door, afraid to move. One small boy sitting on a bed beckoned Jonas by waving a small toy car. The boy was dressed in light clothing and was shivering. They just stared at each other, neither of them able to say anything. The shivering boy pushed the small car over the bed.

"That is a nice car," Jonas said in German, and then the Russian boy, still shivering, said something that Jonas could not understand. He touched the leather on Jonas' coat and stared at the leather button-down shoes. The little boy gave Jonas the car to push on the blanket. Jonas saw how pale and thin the boy looked. From his coat pocket he gave him some chocolate marzipan that he had taken before they left from the living room candy dish when no one was watching. Jonas watched the boy eat the candy with blissful pleasure, then gave him all the rest he had in his pocket. The little boy offered the car to Jonas, who refused it, but the child placed the toy in Jonas' pocket anyway. Jonas removed his leather hat and blue scarf, placed the hat on the boy's head, left the scarf on the bed, and ran outside. He found Gerhardt standing by the long dock where a steamer was anchored. It was leaving for Palestine in the afternoon.

Both boys climbed the steep gangplank. Once on deck the first mate, a tall blond Swede, assumed that these two were some of the refugee boys he was going to be transporting.

"You boys are early, but get along with you. I don't blame you."

Jonas led the way down the stairs to the engine room, climbing over the wheels and pipes and brass railings. They were touching and pressing everything, while a Portuguese sailor with black grease smeared on his face looked on, astounded.

"Let's go up on deck, Gerhardt," Jonas called excitedly. They raced up the many long steel stairs until they got to the very top deck, to the pilot's room. "Get down from there, you two devils, at once, before I get the police."

"We are not leaving," Jonas called. "I am the captain now, and we are going to America. Everyone aboard."

One of the sailors grabbed both boys roughly by their collars, pulling them back to the dock. "I should keep you on board and put you both in shackles in the boiler room to teach you rascals a lesson," as he handed them over to their apologetic mothers.

They were driving back from the island when Lucia noticed that Jonas' hat and scarf were missing.

"You are impossible, Jonas. Where is your beautiful leather cap and scarf?"

"I must have dropped them somewhere."

Gerhardt gave Jonas a secret look, and said nothing, saving him from a certain scolding.

"He was a real friend," Jonas said under his bed covers, now remembering that look.

He began to cry some more. "I am sorry, Gerhardt. I don't hate you, and I didn't mean to chase you into the street. Gerhardt, please, please, please forgive me."

Chapter Six

THEY HAD BEEN LOVERS for almost two months. Since the day after Lucia's attempted seduction, in fact. Worn out, Bill was tired of fighting his attraction to men. This was what it is, wasn't it? This nameless intruder that had stalked any attempted encounter he'd ever had with women. If he couldn't do it with Lucia, then who? He had arrived at the Prince's for their usual afternoon English lesson over tea and drinks. This time, the Prince sensed a change. He saw Bill's mouth had the expression of trustfulness, like a child's, and the gentleness of surrender. The Prince saw that Bill was back to wearing the Brandenburg signet ring. He put down his cards of vowels and English conjugations, and took Bill into his arms. Inseparable since, the Prince had experienced a tenderness he had never known and Bill, who cried that first time after they held each other in the Prince's large bed, experienced a release, like a fist unclenched.

"Now you look like a Berliner in your green jacket and pants, instead of those boring chinos and sweaters," the Prince said approvingly to Bill. They were walking on the Wilhelmstrasse, toward the old Gedachtniskirche. It was Bill's first visit to the German capital. The Prince was proud of the figure Bill now cut in his fine clothes. He was handsomer than ever, if that were possible.

"With this nice outfit you bought me, are you taking me to see another church?"

"We are going to the center of intellectual life in Berlin, the famous Romanisches Café. It is even better than Le Dôme in Paris, or the Café Central in Vienna."

"You have been everywhere," Bill admired.

"Not everywhere. Not yet to America."

"Then it will be my turn to show you something. You can't imagine how different America is."

On all the streets, crowded with beggars, shabbily dressed, Bill saw hungry and desperate-looking people, and long banners with the Nazi insignia hanging from the buildings. Children and old people were scavenging garbage pails for food.

A decorated horse-drawn wagon suddenly passed by them, carrying barrels of ale. The horse was festooned with white feathers around its thick neck, blue leggings and a colorful blanket over its back and down its sides. The driver, an old man wearing a Tyrolean outfit, had a warm smile on his weathered face and was speaking to the horse gently, lovingly:

"Hilda, you old mare, just a little longer, hang on. Soon we will dump the barrels and take a nice slow ride home to eat. You'd like that, yes?"

"Each beer-maker has his distinct wagon," the Prince explained. "The Lowenberg Brewery in Munich has an entire stable of beautiful Arabian horses to pull their wagons. They decorate their horses as if they were nobility."

As the men were about to enter the café, the horse suddenly slipped and lost its footing, rolling over on the ground, tossing the wagon on its side. The barrels rolled off the wagon into the streets like ungainly bowling balls, spilling beer. The old man, unharmed but distraught, ran to the horse, screaming, "Hilda, my poor Hilda, what in God's name have you done to yourself, my dearest sweetheart, so old and noble. How can you fall like this in the streets?"

He placed the head of the stiff horse against his face, crying. Consumed in absolute grief and trying to soothe the stricken mare, he took little notice of the dozens of young and old men and women who ran to grab the barrels of beer. They rolled the barrels with their hands and knees down the inclined street. Others placed their mouths against the barrels as beer spurted into their desperate faces.

"They are so pathetic, these Berliners; they have lost all their dignity," the Prince said as he surveyed the chaos. "I heard things like this also go on in America now with your Depression."

"I didn't see this in Columbus. There were bread lines and lots of beggars, but nothing like this."

"We better go into the café," the Prince said quietly.

"No, I have to see."

"It is going to become ugly."

"I have to see," Bill repeated, shaking his head.

"Very well, then. I will wait for you inside."

By the time the police arrived, the driver of the wagon was screaming from frustration, and all the beer barrels were gone. The policeman walked toward the horse on the ground.

"His leg is broken. Do you want to shoot him?" the police sergeant asked the frantic driver, not unkindly.

"No, I can't kill Hilda. Let me leave, please," the old man begged.

The policeman waited for the old man to disappear down the street, and then he pulled a revolver from his holster. He pointed at the mare's head and shot the quivering horse. The decorative feathers were now covered with blood. The horse lay motionless on the street.

Minutes later, after the police were gone, the street smelled of death. Everything was still, frozen in time, a lantern slide.

Like silhouettes on a movie screen, people began to appear from nowhere – small children, old men, young, gaunt, shabby people, looking like corpses. Some carried large knives, and others cleavers or hatchets. They all carried something as they circled, like stalking animals, the dead horse. Suddenly, as if someone had given a signal, they all broke out in a run, making directly for the mare. Bill could only see stooped bodies and the frantic sounds of cutting and scraping, and sucking. Then one young boy broke free from the crowd. He ran with a slice of raw meat, still warm, in his hands, his mouth and face covered with blood. Others like the boy also ran away – mad wolves with their bloody bounty. When the crowd finally dispersed, there was only a pile of feathers and the butchered, pitiful remnants of a once-strong steed.

Bill felt sick to his stomach. He was about to fall when the Prince returned to his side and placed his arms around the American.

"Hunger is a terrible thing," he whispered, his fingers softly grazing Bill's cheek. "I am sorry you saw this. These were once proud people."

"How did you know it would happen?" Bill asked weakly.

"I saw it once before. Come, let's go into the café. Just a few feet away a great culture still prevails, an oasis where some sort of sanity still lives."

The café was poorly lit, filled with stale smoke and the smell of sausage, wine, and cheese. Hordes of interesting-looking people were sitting at decrepit tables. The café looked old, worn out, seedy, devoid of charm.

"Its decay," the Prince said, "gives it a certain *gemütlichkeit*. Unfortunately, that is a word not possible to translate into English. How should I say it to you? It means warmth, friendliness. It is like a big warm cushion to sit on while you sip on good brandy and smoke a Havana. So don't be fooled by its appearance. All the greatest minds in the world have come through this café at one time or another.

"I don't think I am up to this," Bill said haltingly. "I can't get that horrible picture out of my head. That poor horse, devoured by people who have also become animals."

"Very well, then, try hard my good fellow," the Prince said gently, his arms still around Bill's waist.

Bill's eyes focused toward the bar where three beautiful women were standing in long black gowns, smoking and laughing with each other. Occasionally, they hopped to the different tables, exchanging greetings. They looked at Bill, giving him a seductive look as they blew small smoke rings in his direction.

"Now, then, I knew it would not take long for you to erase that heinous scene of the outside world. It's different here."

Bill could not restrain a smile as his eyes and brain and sense adjusted to the Café Romanisches. His friend was right. He did feel better.

"Here in this marvelous place sit lawyers, doctors, actors, artists, politicians, writers, conductors, musicians, dancers, and publishers – bohemians of every sort, size, color and sexual persuasion. Here, on the right, is the smaller room, called the 'swimming pool,' where the artists of the day gather. Look over, my friend, there you see Bertolt Brecht and George Grosz, the caricaturist, sitting in the corner. The large room which looks like a beer hall, called the 'non-swimming pool,' is for the American literary people. You can see Thomas Wolfe, Sinclair Lewis and his wife, Dorothy Thompson."

"I read Wolfe's *Look Homeward Angel* on the crossing over here!" Bill exclaimed, clearly awestruck to be in the man's company.

"Ah, the Prince comes to Berlin with his American protégée," greeted a neat-looking man in a dark suit with a red tie, a white handkerchief in his hand.

"This is Berlin's most notorious gossip columnist," the Prince nodded. "Meet 'Rumpelstilzchen,' as he is called. But we know his real name is Adolph Stein. He is part of the regular crowd, and they don't like the casual drop-ins, *nicht wahr?*"

"Quite, but you are an exception."

"My young friend is seeking interesting conversation," the Prince gestured around the room. "Whom shall we have him meet?"

There were girls standing at the bar, gesturing to Bill, others placing their hand on their breasts, and licking their lips.

"Any interest?" the Prince asked and then threw his head back and laughed.

Bill felt uneasy and was annoyed by the Prince's tone. "No, it's all right," He said hesitatingly, not sure what his friend meant.

"A wise decision, Sir," nodded Rumpelstilzchen, "because 'things are seldom what they seem; 'skimmed milk masquerades as cream,' as wrote your English geniuses, Gilbert and Sullivan. These women are our impersonators."

"Men," the Prince nodded, laughing again and enjoying Bill's naiveté. "They are in the theater."

They sat at one of the empty tables, and the Prince ordered something Bill could not understand. The waiter brought two large glasses and cups of coffee. Inside each of the glasses were soft-boiled eggs.

"The specialty of the house," the Prince explained. "Do you see the man with the mysterious eyes and mustache? That is the writer Stefan Zweig, and in the corner is Erich Remarque. His book came out a few years ago, and it is still raising many eyebrows. Bitterly anti-war, you know? I believe it's English title is *All Quiet on the Western Front.*"

"What do I do with the soft-boiled eggs?" Bill asked.

"You gently divide each with your spoon, and mash the yolk and the white." His companion demonstrated.

On the periphery of the large room were dozens of telephone booths occupied by reporters, their ID tags around their necks and many of them speaking English. The room had a busy, almost carnival atmosphere. They were gathering information about the turbulent, tempestuously changing, political picture of Berlin, and then contacting their home offices.

"I am going to leave you here for a while," the Prince said. "I have to take care of some business matters, much to my disgust. Stay for a while, if you wish, and then take a walk. We will meet at the Zoo Station and take the midnight train back to Danzig. Don't let one of the sexy 'girls' get hold of you. We will meet, then, at 6:00 p.m., yes?"

The Prince had planned this in advance, and Bill was prepared for his swift departure.

"I regret to leave you like this, but I am late for that goddamn meeting as it is."

Not long after the Prince departed, an accordion player stood in the center of the large room and started to play a sad lieder with lyrics by Heine. A tall woman appeared in a black top hat and tuxedo. Bill had seen pictures of Marlene Dietrich and felt certain it was she. She sang a song in accented English that made Bill melancholy. Everyone had become lugubrious.

"Do you want to buy an illusion? I have some to make you laugh and some to make you cry. One penny."

Bill had many illusions in his young life, and plenty of confusions, too. The Prince had enriched his life beyond his wildest dreams. He had moved into the Prince's mansion, where he had his own room and dressing room. And although for appearances sake Bill had kept his flat, they were together every night.

And then there was Lucia, a lonely and lovely coquette, so marvelously happy and bright, whom he had disappointed. When he was a teenager he used to fantasize about seeing naked women and making love to them. He had the chance that night when she tried to seduce him in her private salon, but he just couldn't. Now she was another bead in his short pathetic string of failed conquests. But it had woken him up.

"Do you like our Marlene?" a young voice interrupted. He was startled by her voice. She was an American woman, not much older than he, plain-looking and preppy, the type Bill used to see at college football games on Saturday afternoons.

"My name is Saunders. They call me Dee. I work as a 'gopher' for the *Tribune*. Hang around here and you'll find more action than outside. Those fucking Krauts are serious business. Are you an artist or a lover?"

"Both." Bill laughed. "Where are you from?"

"Boston," she said. "Beacon Hill, and the rest is bull."

"And you?"

"Ohio, Columbus."

"Is that in the United States?" she smirked. When she smiled she did not look so plain, he thought. Her face took on a warmth that made her look almost attractive.

"You seemed to be beguiled by our Marlene. But, she is a he, and don't you know, I swear he could double for the real thing. May I sit down? Don't look shocked. This is Berlin. An open city. Did you try cocaine yet?"

"No," he lied. Yes, the Prince had introduced him to the pleasures of that powerful powder too. "Can I buy you a drink?"

"Just order a hamburger for me, with lots of French fries."

"Do they have that here?"

"Are you kidding? I would give all my passion to anyone for a hamburger. That is some ring you are wearing," she said with admiration, and Bill was glad he had slipped it back on his finger after that night at Lucia's. He had done it with a calculated fatefulness. It was a signal. If the Prince noticed, what would be would be. He was willing to see where it led.

"Are you in love? Were you in love? Do you want to be in love?"

"All of the above," Bill responded with a sickly laugh.

"This is the sexy spot in town, for sensitive souls, and you have such sensitive eyes. You are a writer, of course?"

"No, I am sort of an architectural student."

"Well, mystery boy, I have to run. I heard a hot scoop: The Nazis have forbidden the playing of Jewish composers at the Berlin State Opera, but they will allow Bruno Walter and Otto Klemperer to conduct. Both are Jews. You aren't Jewish by any chance, are you? Because if you are, keep it to yourself." She lowered her voice. "I am Jewish. No one knows that. See you again," she said, returning to her animated self. "I am here every day. Let's have coffee."

"That would be nice." She left like a windstorm before Bill had a chance to tell her he was going back to Danzig.

He smoked one more cigarette and looked at his watch. He still had more hours ahead of him before he was to meet the Prince. "Marlene" kept singing, and he became sadder when he/she sang "Falling in Love Again," huskily.

It was in Danzig, in Europe, far from Columbus, Ohio, that he found his real self, unashamed, free. Meeting Lucia was important, and fortuitous, because his real sexuality was tested. It was not guilty feelings or fear that had prevented him from "cutting the mustard," as one of his high school friends called it; he was just not meant to be with women.

And fortunately Lucia, if disturbed, failed to show it. She adored the Prince and was genuinely happy he had found someone to love him. The incident in her private study, designed to spark a harmless affair that never happened, an afternoon delight, like those of which many of her women friends boasted, was in her mind forgotten.

The two remained good friends, however, sharing their secrets together. Bill realized that she was using him to make Brand jealous. She confided in Bill that she suspected Brand, like so many of the men in his society, had a mistress. "The best way for a woman to keep a man is to make him realize there are other men out there who long for her."

And what about himself? Sitting in the Café Romanisches, somehow enjoying the bittersweet languor of it all, he tried to rationalize his perversion, this beautiful unexpected love that had found him at a ripe moment. He was young and in Europe, after all. He knew the stories of Rimbaud and Mann, and Verlaine and Wilde. But he wasn't like them. This wonderful freedom, this uncorked self, this "new" Bill, this "real" Bill...would the genie ever return to the bottle? Yes, of course it would. This mad intoxication would end eventually, and he would return home. He was an American, after all, a midwest boy, and in his head, if not his heart, a heterosexual. Wasn't he?

It was late afternoon when Harrington walked down the prowling boulevards towards the Zoo Station, its name derived from its proximity to the famous Berlin Zoo. In some ways Main Street in Columbus was not that different from many of the streets he passed. Bakeries, pharmacies, shoe shops, small lingerie shops – he stopped at each one, studying the styles used in displays. The confectionery stores were wonderful. Varieties of chocolates and marzipans, formed into shapes of people, animals, houses and small mountains, were more beautifully displayed than he had ever seen. The architecture of the city was beautiful too. The museums and monuments, the wide boulevards and the lovely Tiergarten, had captivated him. He had been right to come here.

But now the young American came across a line of shops with white paint splashed on the windows, and he recognized the word *Juden* with the Star of David painted underneath. Posters crying out that "German children are starving!" were pasted on the doors. Other signs read, "Germans – defend yourself against Jewish atrocities." The only other anti-Semitic signs he

had ever seen were those displayed on the classy inns in Columbus: "Christians only. No Jews are welcomed."

Somehow, here, the white paint made it all look so much more
perfidious and dangerous. Germany, after all, was not Ohio. The
air here was charged with explosives. The fuse seemed to grow
shorter and shorter.

He noticed an elderly man walking ahead of him, a small
man with a full beard and skullcap, carrying several heavy and
worn books. He had never met any Jews in Ohio. Now, for the
first time, Bill had the Krugers and their friends. They bore no
resemblance whatsoever to the pictures he had seen all his life.
The man in front of him must be a Jew. He quickened his pace
to get a good look. Perhaps that is how Jews look in Germany:
bearded, wearing skullcaps and long black coats.

Coming from across the street at that same moment were
four teenage boys dressed in Brownshirts and green pants. He
remembered the scurrilous boys who had come into the Café
des Artistes. They blocked the bearded man's path. Bill stopped,
listened, and watched the scene unfold.

The bearded man tried to continue on. One of the boys
pulled off the old man's glasses and smashed them with his foot.
Another one pulled the skullcap from his head and tossed it in
the air while the others laughed like hyenas.

"Please let me go. I am late. You can have the cap and anything else I have."

"He sounds afraid," they guffawed.

"You can have the cap, you filthy Jew. Beg for it. Get on your
knees."

One of the boys grabbed the man by the neck and pushed
him to the ground. "Get on your knees and cross yourself, pig."

Bill watched the pathetic scene with pity for the old man.
Surely, they were only going to molest him and intimidate him,
nothing more.

"He won't cross himself," one of the other boys yelled and took a leather baton he was carrying in his belt and struck the helpless man across the face.

The American was no longer able to restrain his anger, as he saw blood running down the elderly man's face. He ran up to the boys, insisting, "Leave him alone, you bastards!"

Bill was much taller than any of the boys, and with one swift jab he punched one of them in the face. They backed off as they saw blood appear on the stunned face of their comrade. As Bill helped the man up on his feet, he felt his body pummeled with fists. He was not able to intercept a swinging leather club that struck his head. The excruciating pain he felt unleashed all his rage. Only one other time had he felt such anger, and that was while on the wrestling team in college. It was just after Jean, that college girl he liked, had broken up with him and his nerves and self-esteem were already frayed. The break-up smarted for, although she had hadn't said as much, they both knew why she had dumped him. He heard she was already seeing a player on the football team while, if things weren't bad enough, his parents could not understand why he wasn't dating. Then one of his teammates had kiddingly called him a "fairy" during practice. Suddenly something Bill had never felt took hold of him, a raw seizing feeling erupting from a deep channel inside him. The coach had become alarmed when he saw that Bill would not release the body hold of his accuser.

"Take back what you said! I mean it!" Bill yelled. The boy kept silent and Bill had tightened his grip.

Finally, the boy sputtered, "I give up. Let go, Bill." But Bill kept squeezing the boy's chest until there was barely any breath left and his ribs were about to snap. Bill's mind had traveled to another zone of reality.

He was deaf to the pleas and cries of the boy and the coach. Two other wrestlers and the coach struggled to pull him off. After that episode he quit the wrestling team, fearful of his own strength and the madness that overtook him.

Now Bill felt the same uncontrollable anger. He grabbed one of the Brownshirts by the neck and squeezed it in a wrestler's hold. "Run!" he yelled to the wounded man. But the old man just stood there. The other boys, like Lilliputians, pulled at Bill's legs and arms as he brutally smashed his strong fist with the Prince's large ring into any face that was before him. But it was to no avail. The boys piled on him, kicking and beating him with their clubs, which only angered him more. Bill flung his wrists at them like a wild man. Across the street the police watched, making not even a weak gesture to interrupt the struggle, until the police saw that the boys were being brutally mauled. They finally stepped in and broke up the fight. Before the beat-up hooligans ran off, they pulled the old Jew to the ground, stomped on his head and kicked him in the ribs as Bill lay panting on the ground. An ambulance finally arrived, picking up the old man, who was already dead from the beating.

"Do you want to go to the hospital? You are bleeding," the paramedic asked.

"Are you kidding? Just let me out of this fucking country. Take me to Zoo Station, and give me a towel to clean myself."

Across town, while his paramour seethed, Prince Brandenberg checked his watch and waited for this interminable meeting to finish. The Prince's wealth came from ancestral property holdings, and the family owned a grain and lumber company. After the world war, the Hanseatic company was decontrolled, but Brandenberg still sat on the board and received a generous yearly stipend of fifty thousand guldens, some forty thousand dollars a year.

It was a sum ample enough to allow him to live lavishly.

He had also befriended his neighbors, the Kruger family, and through Uncle Herman he profited greatly, following their good advice to buy dollars when the gulden was becoming worthless. In Berlin, meanwhile, people were hoarding barrels of worthless currency to buy a loaf of bread. The government simply kept printing more and more paper money, while all this time the Prince was flush with gold and dollars.

The parent company had re-established itself in Berlin, and what had brought the Prince to Berlin this day was to attend their monthly board meeting. The board members, mostly Danzigers, some from the new and increasingly powerful Nazi Party, were meeting privately before the Prince had arrived. They wanted Danzig reunited with the Fatherland since, they argued, it was only a matter of time now that Hitler would become chancellor of Germany. Besides, they had the blessing of their American business associates.

"Prince Brandenburg is the most undesirable member of our board," Wilhelm Brenner, the chairman said. "He is one of the major stockholders, however, and there is no way we can legally wrest away his interest. At least his association with the Jew coal dealer can help us for the time being. But he has to be convinced that his future lies with the new Germany."

"Or we could arrange to discredit him, get him arrested, if we can catch him in one of his flirtations. I gather he now has a young American boy living with him," said another of the members, his lips curling in distaste.

"You are insane," interrupted a third. "It won't happen. Hess is an old school friend and whatever else. He will protect him."

"True; so we have to tread very lightly. Luckily, he has no interest in fiduciary matters. The only reason he comes to these meetings is to pick up his check."

And so, when the Prince arrived, all the board members rose and greeted him warmly. A few matters were discussed, in particular the Baltic Kohlen deal with the Luirgi company, which was under the direction of Brand's friend, Schiller.

"Prince, you are good friends with Brand Kruger. Propose to him to use his barges to ship our lumber. Tell him this will be the Hanseatic League of 1934, a Baltic merger. Tell him he will be the chairman of the largest consortium since the original league was formed in 1430, and it will be headed by a Jewish merchant, no less."

The meeting was interrupted by one of the clerks who handed a telephone to the chairman. "A matter of great urgency, sir."

The room became silent as the chairman listened, a frown on his face. Then he slowly spoke in an ominous voice, looking at the Prince.

"That was the chief of police," he said. "There was a bloody incident on the Kammerstrasse. Four teenagers were badly beaten and an old Jew was stomped to death. Your American friend was involved in the incident. One youth has a broken nose, another is almost blinded, and the third nearly had his neck broken. All the boys are no older than fourteen or fifteen. The parents are demanding the American's immediate arrest."

"That young man is a gentle soul," the Prince responded vehemently. "He would not hurt anyone. They must have made a mistake." The Prince was troubled, agitated.

"Not from what was reported by the police. They saw him brutally attack the teenagers, and they were going to arrest him when he told them he was your guest in Berlin and displayed a ring you gave him. He did not carry a passport to prove he was an American. They want to verify if he is your friend."

When the Prince rushed out of the meeting, the chairman said, "Gentlemen, we now have an answer to the problem of our Prince."

Bill was sitting on a bench near Zoo Station facing the Tier-garten. His new outfit was torn, covered with blood. With his swollen right hand he inspected his face and felt his chest for any broken ribs. A passerby could have taken him for just another drunken street person on the bench, hungry, dirty, dissolute, a quotidian scene these days in Berlin. He was in pain and embar-rassed that the Prince would see him like this. Bill took his beat-ing as just punishment from Providence. He felt disloyal to his parents, to the Prince, to himself. Never had Bill Harrington ever witnessed such vicious violence. But he was like those ruffians, no better, ready to destroy them any way he could. This city, he thought to himself, is where the devil lives. It makes monsters out of ordinary people. Although it was chilly, his body was still hot, sweating. The violence was still in his soul. Could this happen in America? He thought. Never. Not like this.

For a few minutes the Prince stood at a distance, shaking his head in sorrow as he saw his beautiful young American friend, to whom he was now so deeply attached, once so splendidly naïve, looking ten years older than himself.

"We'd better stay the night at the Europa Hotel, Bill. I am so sorry," the Prince said, his arm clasping Harrington's shoulders. "We'll get you cleaned up and find a change of clothes. But good for you. You tried to help an old innocent man. We have a lot to learn from you. If you had merely stood and watched you would then be as guilty as they. For me, the biggest crime is to be indif-ferent. The silent onlooker is as guilty as the predator."

Chapter Seven

*L*UCIA HAD MADE SOME of the arrangements for their spring pilgrimage to Marienbad. The beautiful and unsullied spot, far removed from the feverish events of Berlin, sits in the soft foothills of Czechoslovakia. Long the restful retreat of European aristocracy, surrounded by sloping hills and long paths through ancient pine forests that wind between the gently running brooks, it was Arcadia, a pristine retreat where one came to be rejuvenated after a hard winter of frolicking. Here they came to have the sulfur waters flow soothingly over exhausted joints, and to drink the elixirs of lime water to flush out kidneys, relieve melancholy, and relax nerves stretched taut.

Regarding the party's accommodations, the Prince arranged for three suites at the Park Hotel, which was off limits to Jews and "common people." In spite of the world Depression, all the area hotels were booked years in advance. Everything was normal in Marienbad this May of 1934.

Private trains, fitted with salons, arrived at a local station, met by obsequious servants in bright red uniforms and caps, who then escorted the noble souls to majestic carriages decorated with gold leaf, which effortlessly carried them to their hotels.

Brand and the Prince had loaded the Duesenberg with cases

of Dom Perignon, pâte, and Viennese chocolates. Alcohol was not permitted in this sophisticated spa, and the cuisine could be pretty spartan, except for once a week when the famous chef, Mothnam, served his masterpiece of *Truite a la Meuniere*, laced with brandy mustard sauce, and his renowned *Bombe Brazilene* for dessert. This spectacular feast made the simple meals in between worthwhile.

Included in the Kruger party were Uncle Herman and his Wagnerian girlfriend, Frieda; Bill Harrington and the Prince; and Carl Anspach, the head of the National Bank of Danzig, with his austere-looking wife, Gretchen. It was going to be ten days of bliss.

They dined together, played cards late into the night, and during the day luxuriated in the sulfur baths, drank freely of the mineral water, had their bodies covered with loathsome mud, and then surrendered to massages vigorously given by supermen and Amazons. Many guests of the Park Hotel looked with disdain at this "different" group. "Money buys honey," as the wits noted and, after all, these "outsiders" had paid top dollar for their accommodations. It was unseemly to argue with wealth.

By the third day of their austere dining, Lucia had tired of mineral water, munching on carrots and celery, and having her body contorted into a pretzel each day by the never-ending staff of sadistic masseuses. But there was some private time between the schedule of organized health activities, and then she and Brand would walk the carpeted forest paths hand-in-hand like lovers. At night, in their resplendent suite bedecked in red and blue, the walls covered with gold satin, they rediscovered each other. It was fresh and stimulating, exciting being together. She now felt a great burden was lifted from her heart. Her crush on Bill was long over and Brand was never more loving. Life was good and fair.

Her father's words on the eve of her wedding day rang in her ears. "If you wait long enough, live long enough, things straighten out, and love always prevails if it is real love from the start."

"We are letting the years run from us," she said one morning as they took their obligatory walk. "I do know you love me. It's been a good marriage, all twelve years of it, but it has been so long since just the two of us have been together! Dinner parties, travels, you always away. Sometimes I feel we deliberately set up our lives to keep us apart. Even now. Why didn't we simply come here alone?" She took his hand and raised it to her lips, kissing it. "Brand, you are as handsome as the day I saw you for the first time from my window. Do you remember?"

"Of course."

"So proud and strong in your officer's uniform, parading with your cavalry. Such fire in your eyes as you looked up at the window. Father said, 'That is Brand Kruger, a distant cousin of yours.' There and then I knew I wanted to marry you.

'Let's invite him for tea,' I asked father, who was a little reluctant at first, but I knew, young as I was, Father feared I was going to be an old maid. Our city was full of nice Jewish men, but there was no one I fancied. I was determined to hold out for a love match, even if I was going to be the last well-bred girl in Warsaw."

They sat down on a large rock facing one of the many streams where the last traces of winter were being pushed along.

"How did your father find me?" Brand asked.

"Well, he called one of his old friends from Pilsudski's cavalry, and he was told that you were camped outside of Warsaw. When a messenger came with the invitation to tea at our house, all of them laughed because they thought it was from one of the prostitutes in town." Lucia laughed softly. "And there you were, tall and dashing at the door, a box of marzipan in your hands, smelling of lemon."

"I had been to the Jewish Market, Nalefke," Brand said, "and with the few groschen I possessed, I purchased marzipan from a sweet girl. I told her I had a date with a rich young lady in town, but that I had just a few groschen. She understood. She was so kind that she filled the box with more than she had to. Then she insisted I take several lemons. She knew all about cavalrymen who always smell of manure. She squeezed the lemons over my uniform, and told me to rub my face and hands with the juice, even to put some lemon peels in my pockets."

"It certainly did the trick," Lucia laughed. "You smelled like a blossoming fruit tree. We sat in the living room, not really at all comfortable with each other. Mother served tea and snacks on her favorite Rosenthal china, and . . ."

"I crossed my legs, and my damned boot knocked over the tea tray. What a wonderful way to make an impression!"

"My sweet Brand, I felt so sorry for you. My heart melted. It was that helpless look on your very crimson face that made me fall in love with you immediately. How could I resist? And those lemons," she teased.

"My men thought I had the best whore in town."

"Brand!" she exclaimed.

He looked sheepishly at her. "How could I tell them I was only chatting and drinking tea? Think of my image."

From the distance, Bill saw Lucia and Brand laughing and embracing like young lovers. He smiled and suddenly looked away. They'd all accepted the relationship between the Prince and him so casually as if here was nothing to be ashamed of. In his letters home, he had written about his noble friend, calling him an excellent guide and a generous mentor. He'd also hinted there was another friendship beginning to root between him and a young female art student. The white lie left him feeling sad, guilty, and very lonely as he tried to straddle two worlds, two cultures with very different rules

When Lucia and Brand came down from the little mountain,

they were met by Bill, the Prince, Anspach, Herman, and his Frieda.

"We decided," Herman said, "after a long drawn-out meeting of the board and by a majority vote, that we as a civilized group can no longer stand all this health food crap and carrot juice. My body is so purified that these *goyim* will canonize me."

"Get the champagne, the pâte, the duck, and chicken; we are going on a picnic far from the madding crowd."

Two young-looking men, wearing leather knickers and carefully cultivated mustaches, one carrying a hunting rifle, were standing close enough to overhear Uncle Herman. Both men were Germans who were staying at the hotel. They recognized the Prince, and exchanged looks when they heard the word *goyim*, but they said nothing.

With knapsacks filled, Herman informed the concierge they would not be having lunch at the inn and that they were going out into the mountains to a picnic.

They walked for nearly an hour, uphill through the pine forest, Uncle Herman puffing like a mighty steam engine. By lunchtime they found a plateau of grass, and with the very resourceful Prince and Lucia in charge, tablecloths, candelabras, Waterford crystal, and porcelain plates appeared as if from nowhere. It was magical.

By late afternoon the champagne was finished and Lucia was reciting poetry from Verlaine's *Fetes Galantes*. The banker's wife, a tall thin woman with wide black eyebrows and dark finger-waved hair, stood in the center of the circle of this happy crowd strewn over grass like a Monet painting, and she began to whistle, with a masterful talent, as she imitated the bluebird, then the red cardinal, and then went through several choruses of "The White Horse."

Anspach, ever the banker – even here in the pine forest – wore his white shirt, stiff collar, and tie. He edged over to Brand, who was blissfully stretched out on the bed of grass, his eyes closed. Lucia was swaying to and fro, never happier. Bill was enchanted by it all; thoughts of Ohio floated far from his mind.

"Brand, we have to talk," Anspach whispered.

"No business today," Brand said in a sleepy voice.

"This is not business. I am worried, I tell you, worried sick. The National Socialist Party will control Germany as soon as Hindenburg dies. Danzig will be Nazified soon."

"The world will never allow it, Anspach," Brand said. "What is going on in Berlin is simply not going to happen here."

"Brand, you are certainly not stupid, but you are dreaming. Your friend, Max Schiller, the grain company, and our friend, the Prince, want to form a conglomerate. If you sell your share to them you can still get a very handsome price. Brand, millions are waiting for you. Take it and go to America or Switzerland. You will never have to work again. Listen to me. I am your friend. Everybody is running. Einstein, Marlene Dietrich, Lotte Lenya, Kurt Weill, and Schnabel are already gone. Bruno Walter is planning to go, even Freud – if he can get out! So many of the intellectuals of Europe. The list is endless."

"They are all radicals, Reds," Brand said, now wide awake. "Nothing can make me sell this giant I built," he continued. "You are crazy. Paranoia, that's what it is. A world gone mad over a little man it would laugh at in a dance hall. And what if the Germans did own Danzig? How would that affect my life? The Bosch also once owned the Saar Valley, the Ruhr, Silesia – and they will get them all back in due time. Why shouldn't they? They belong to Germany."

"Brand, I am going to sell the bank," Anspach whispered, "and I am leaving in six months. I tell you this in great confidence."

"Before the election?" Brand asked incredulously.

"Come with me. We will go to America and build an empire.

It will be easy in America. They are so busy with their base-ball and frankfurters. The Depression has distracted them, and whatever business we want, we would buy cheaply. The time is right. My head knows it. My bones feel it."

"I am sorry you are leaving," Brand said. "You have a solid bank here. You belong here. Panic doesn't suit you."

"Wisdom, my friend, not panic. Life is more precious than money. And how much is freedom worth? It is over Brand. Are you so blind you can't see Hell is knocking at our door?"

The banker's words seemed to shake the leaves, but not Brand. A late afternoon breeze now sent a chill through the hap-py tipsy group sprawled out like Roman centurions after a fierce battle. Lucia took it as a signal to prepare for the trek back to the hotel. There was a sharpness in the air. Lucia even started shivering.

"Come children, gather ye rosebuds while you may. Time is flying. Let's go back."

They all rose from their comfortable positions, and not with-out difficulty. Each gathered something from the picnic. The Prince gently collected each of the flutes, as if they were delicate rosebuds, and placed each in a cotton container, then into his rucksack.

"Let's fold our tents and silently steal away," Lucia said in mock seriousness and hiccoughed loudly, causing everyone to giggle.

"Now we are getting literary," Bill mused.

"When Lucia starts quoting from memory, you know she has had too much," Brand laughed. "The whole world becomes her library."

Like a caravan on a safari, the rollicking group walked in a reasonably straight line, Brand and the banker leading the way down through the narrow paths of the pine forest. They came to the crossroad, staggering to a halt. The banker said, "It is to the left."

"No, it is to the right," the Prince said.

Brand had mentioned some landmarks when they first arrived at the open field and stretched out his arm to the right, a cavalry officer clearly in command of himself and his troops.

"When the Captain says to the right, we go right. Orders are orders," the banker stated.

Suddenly, a terrible scream tore through the forest. Everyone stopped short, immediately sober. No sooner had the echo faded than there followed wild, hysterical laughter, and a shower of rocks began bouncing around them. Lucia felt a sharp pain as one of the rocks hit her face. Brand ran over and saw that there was a small abrasion on her cheek and that it oozed slightly. Lucia wept quietly, "I knew we were having too much fun. How could it last?"

Then, a shot pierced the forest. Another cry, from the Prince this time. "I have been hit," he announced, almost calmly. He placed his hand on the growing red mushroom on his shoulder, and pulled his white silk ascot from his neck to cover the wound.

"Now I know what it is to be wounded," he sad, matter-of-factly. "A Prince must also know these things," he said, wincing at the hurt.

"Everyone flat on the ground! Crawl to the other side of the road," Brand ordered.

More shots, more hysterical laughter.

"We got the fairy. The *goyim* got the fairy!" resounded from the woods. "The fairy will fly no more!"

"Follow me, Bill," Brand said quickly, harshly. Crawling on their hands and knees – infantry style – they got to the other side of the woods. They saw two men there, one standing, the other crouching, a pointed rifle in his arms. When they came within a few yards, Bill ran towards the standing man and tackled him, hard. Brand jumped on the man crouching on the ground, twisting the weapon from his hand as he was about to again fire at the Prince. Brand raised the rifle high, smashing the steel butt plate of the mauser rifle on his head.

"Unfortunately, he is not quite dead," Brand said to Bill, trying to regain his breath and something of his composure. The other man had twisted away from Bill, running frantically back into the forest.

"I recognized them," Brand said. "Those bastards are staying at our hotel."

Chapter Eight

ℋIS PARENTS HAD BEEN gone only nine days, but it seemed like weeks, even months. His next-door girlfriend, Ala, was invited for dinner on this late May night. She was eleven years old and her puberty was starting early, like the buds on the roses in the gardens on the terrace. Fräulein Marlow instructed Cook to make large golbsens, meat balls stuffed with onions and parsley, accompanied by mashed potatoes with lots of cream, the way Jonas liked it; and to top it all, a chocolate pudding for dessert. The two children ate in silence, except for the occasional knowing glances they exchanged with one another as they did the food proud. They had been taught by their respective governesses to talk little at meals, and to listen rather than to participate in conversation, even if the result was a tomblike atmosphere. It was considered bad manners to speak with a mouth full of food. Only the poor and ill-mannered allowed a morsel of the meal to spill from their mouths.

"The Jews from the shtetl, farms, and Judenstrasse, the Jew street, use their hands and spit food out all over the table while they talk. But you are not one of those!" Jonas' governess had said on many occasions.

"Hold the knife in one hand, the fork in the other. Never, but never, use the knife as a spoon. You can cut your tongue. And don't openly pick your teeth. Cover your mouth with your hand and then do it, if you must. If you have to sneeze, turn your back to the guests at the table and cover your face with the napkin. Picking your nose is disgusting. Eat slowly, enjoy each bite, chew carefully. Don't gulp the food like Astor. Use your napkin often, and dab, not wipe, your mouth. Never use your sleeve."

Those were the rules of the house that she strictly enforced. They were for the civilized, the urbane, not for "shtetl slime," as Fräulein Marlow announced often.

"You can always tell what class a person is by watching how they eat. How you eat tells the world who you are. Understand?"

The two youngsters ate their meal as she idly turned the pages of a book.

If Jonas ate alone with Fräulein Marlow, it was another matter. She permitted him to eat in his pajamas while she tied her long cotton robe snugly around her body. At the table she never would wear her silky low-cut black robe, the one she dressed in whenever she expected Brand, the one from which her full breasts almost escaped as she walked and moved. Jonas sighed. That was the one he much preferred.

After the children finished the chocolate pudding, the governess left the table and said to Jonas, "Now, you be the perfect gentleman to Alexandria. Entertain her properly."

He whispered to Ala, "Let's go to our favorite hiding place."

The governess allowed them – even tactfully encouraged them – to run through the darkened house, up the elegant staircase, to his parents' sensual bedroom while she went to her sitting room. She knew their destination. They squeezed through the narrow opening where the large mirrored armoire met the alcove. The usual hand-embroidered blanket was on the floor, as well as Jonas' tin soldiers and little boxes. It was dark, but the lights from the hall slipped under the armoire, allowing them to see enough of each other.

Alexandria sat on the blanket, as she had done so many other times, her small legs tucked beneath her. "I don't want to play doctor tonight," she said.

"Just a little," Jonas urged. "I want just five minutes. You are my guest and you are supposed to do what I wish."

They went through a familiar routine, but one that was never really familiar; each time it was somehow new, fresh, and exciting, but in a different way. Alexandria lay back on the blanket, pulled her dress up and pulled her panties down to her ankles. Jonas started the examination by touching her stomach and then proceeded to examine the new silky hair beginning to cover the slit between her legs. Sometimes his enthusiasm brought a sharp rebuke.

"That hurts, Jonas!" she said. "You can look and feel, but don't stick your finger in me. It hurts. Do it gently."

"Do you have breasts yet? I know how they should look and feel," he said.

She pulled down her blouse in the shadows. "How do you know that?" she asked in a perturbed voice.

Jonas saw the tiny buds on her chest but did not answer her.

"They are beginning to grow," she said. "You can touch them, but if you hurt them they may not grow."

He touched them gently and Alexandria relaxed, closing her eyes.

"Jonas, promise to keep it a secret if I tell you something?"

"I swear I will," he said, "and I have something to tell you, too."

She sat up and nonchalantly pulled her panties to her waist.

"The examination is over," Jonas complained, "and you did not play doctor yet."

"I don't want to touch you tonight. I must tell you something because I love you."

"I love you too, Ala," Jonas said.

"We are leaving for America soon and not one person knows. I don't want to go," Ala added sadly. "I don't want to leave."

"I don't want you to go," an alarmed Jonas blurted. Then, "I want to go, too."

"Someday, when we're older, we can get married if you come to America," Alexandria brightened. "We are like being married anyway because only married people see each other like we do, and I will always love you, Jonas, even when I am in America. Will you miss me?"

"Yes. It will be sad without you, lonely and very sad. Why do your parents want to go?"

"I don't know, except I heard Father say something about the Nazis, that it won't be safe for the Jews."

Jonas was about to tell her that he belonged to the Hitler Youth Movement, that it was a lot of fun, and the Nazis were not bad at all, but just then he heard his governess call from downstairs.

"Jonas and Alexandria, please come downstairs. Her father is here," Fräulein Marlow called.

Slowly, they came down the winding stairs, Ala tucking her blouse into her skirt.

"Hello, Papa," she said.

Jonas clicked his heels at the bottom of the stairs and greeted him. "Good evening, Herr Greenspun." He extended his hand.

Grecia Greenspun, the tall aristocrat from White Russia, grinned widely and said, "Thank you for being such a good host to Alexandria."

Jonas clicked his heels once more and shook Ala's hand too, but he lowered his head to hide the sadness in his eyes.

"Thank you, Fräulein Marlow, for being so attentive. When are the Krugers returning from Marienbad?"

"Early next week."

"They are fortunate having such a distinguished young woman caring for Jonas." He was staring into her eyes, but his eyes wandered. He could not resist surveying her sensual body and peeking into her cleavage. She read his thoughts all too easily and calculatingly lowered her eyes in a girlish way that made her even more alluring. Let her tease the Jew, she thought.

"Thank you, sir. We love having Alexandria here. She is a perfect young lady. Well brought up. We hope to see you again. It is too quiet without the whole family being here."

He read her thoughts and said, "If that is the case, we certainly will return soon and help to liven up your beautiful home while the Krugers are away."

After they left, the governess noticed Jonas' downcast face.

"Don't look so sad, Jonas. Alexandria is a darling child. She can come back any time you wish." Jonas, burdened with his secret, shifted uneasily.

"I will never see her again," Jonas said with tears.

"Such nonsense, Jonas. You can invite her next week. Come now, my little man, get undressed and we will have a nice bath together and lots of bubbles, and I will make you feel nice and relaxed. Cheer up. You can sleep in my bed tonight if you like.

"We are alone here," Fräulein Marlow called over her shoulder as she went to fetch some towels. "Cook is off. It is just you and I, and we have to keep each other company. Tomorrow you can stay in bed as long as you wish. It is Saturday. The Rabbi won't be coming for your lessons, and we are not going to go to the Boy Scouts. But you can wear your uniform in the house, if you wish."

In the bathtub, Jonas pushed his small tugboat along the water, singing to himself. His governess arrived with a large sponge in her hand, disrobed, and climbed into the large golden bathtub filled with pink bubbles. He was not surprised. He knew what was going to happen next.

"Now stand up so I can wash you well."

She looked down at his pubis and frowned, "Jonas, you are getting small hairs. Your father, well, it is his job to explain this but he is very busy. So I have to tell you what will happen next. Something called puberty. Don't be frightened if one night your bed is wet. It is called semen, which comes from your peepee. When the sperm in your semen swims into a woman's vagina, the sperm and egg meet and then a baby is made."

As she washed him she explained that his voice would also deepen, probably around the time of his Bar Mitzvah.

"Good, Jonas? Does it feel nice?" she asked as she continued to wash him.

"Yes, it makes me feel strange." His body suddenly tightened, convulsed. She laughed.

"That is what grown-ups call orgasm. Even young boys can have one if they rub themselves the right way. It helps you to go to sleep."

At breakfast, he ate quietly, yawning, while Fräulein was shiny and crisp, her face sparkling.

"Look how beautiful it is; a wonderful spring day to go out. Today, Jonas, there will be a big parade in the square and you have been invited to march with the other boys in the club. One of our leaders has come from Berlin to speak to us. Is that not exciting?"

"Fräulein, I feel tired. I don't want to go."

"Then let's just go to Springer for some ices, and we can watch the whole show. We will ask Karl-Heinz to drive us there in the Duesenberg, and you won't have to walk."

"You are playing a dangerous game, Fräulein," Cook, back at her post again, said to her in the kitchen, clearly alarmed by the little Jew training to be a Nazi. Jonas had gone upstairs to dress so the women could speak freely. "If they find out what you are doing to that boy, they will throw you out on the street, or worse."

"And if you tell them I will see to it that your legs are broken, or worse," the governess added archly.

"It makes no difference to me, except that they have been very good to all of us. I don't give a damn about your crazy Hitler and his party. I have seen them come and go. The Germans, the English, the Reds, and now the Brownshirts, and that, too, will pass. I have cooked for them all, and these Jews are better than most. I think you are sick, Fräulein, sick with hatred."

"Shut up, you old maid! You are disgusting. What do you know about anything but cooking? Mind your business or it will go badly for you later. Understand?"

The square by the old Marin Church was filled with thousands of people and the buildings were draped with red, white, and black Nazi banners. The crowd came to hear Heinrich Himmler and his cronies speak. There were all sorts of people – children, bankers, lawyers, bakers, shop owners, workmen – all dressed in their Sunday clothing. The mood was festive and exhilarating. The very air was charged as if they had come to watch a wonderful event. There was an unmistakable recklessness; the masses were already infected by the nationalistic virus of hate.

"Germans, defend yourself against the Jewish Atrocities! New Beginnings for a New Germany!"

Such slogans were displayed everywhere on the square. Just a year ago the crowd was small and indifferent, even often shocked and disgusted, but now they packed the square in support of the new party, the party of hope. The party that made it all so simple and comprehensible: "The Jews – the unclean ones – have sapped the energy of the folk, devouring money, jobs, will. But no more! The vampire will be returned to the dark, with stakes in their hearts!" So screamed the orators from Berlin.

Springer's Café was crowded. It was, however, warm enough to sit comfortably outside around one of the charming wrought-iron tables in the square. Each table had a small Nazi flag standing on it. Everywhere there were Germans in the sparkling summer white uniforms of the SS. Some were sitting at the tables.

When Jonas finished his lemon ice, a tall blond-haired man marched over to the table.

"Ah, Fräulein, good to see you here today with your charge."

"This is Jonas Kruger," the governess said very proudly.

Jonas meekly rose from the table, clicked his heels and stretched out his hand.

"I have heard a lot about you, young man. I am proud of you, but why are you not marching in the parade with the others?"

"He feels a little under the weather, Herr Reichführer. Otherwise he would march, and gladly. Isn't that so, Jonas?" He wanted to answer the tall man but just now he felt nauseated and began to sweat as the wrought-iron table began to spin around him as if he was on the ferris wheel at Sopot. Suddenly, Jonas grew very pale, bent over sharply, and vomited unceremoniously all over the table. He wanted to run away from the cafe into the crowd never to be seen again.

"My little Jonas, too many ices," the governess said as she gently placed a napkin soaked in ice water on his face.

"The lad looks ill, Fräulein. Better take him home. Young man, you will get your chance another time," the German officer said. Jonas felt too ill to rise up from the table to make his customary formal good-byes of hand-shaking, bowing and clicking his heels.

They swiftly returned to the parked Duesenberg where the chauffeur stood waiting. The crowd by now had greatly increased in number and noise. It had become a seething mass.

Jonas climbed into the rear seat, perspiring profusely. He leaned against the leather seat, pale and frightened. The governess took hold of his hands, saying, "Your little tummy is upset. We will get you home soon, safe in your own house with Astor. You did not get enough sleep."

Fräulein Marlow had never seen the boy ill like this, and she began to feel somewhat uneasy, responsible, even guilty. Perhaps she had gone too far. She reviewed in her mind what they had eaten in the past few days. The boy suddenly lurched forward and vomited again, this time all over the shiny leather interior of the car. He then lay back against the seat holding his hands over his mouth, his efforts absolutely exhausting to him. "We better get back quickly," she told the Karl-Heinz, but the Duesenberg was unable to make such headway through the crowd.

"If you have to vomit again," she told Jonas, "take deep breaths and then hold your breath as long as you can." She placed her hand on his head, then kissed his wet cheek. With the perfumed scarf she wore around her neck, she wiped his face.

The crowd was in a frenzy as they heard the speakers on the platform. Jonas, holding his breath, stared blurry-eyed through the closed window as he watched the boys in their uniforms waving flags and shouting, "Sieg Heil! Sieg Heil!"

God is punishing me for last night, Jonas thought to himself.

The chauffeur shouted through his open window, "Let us through! I have a sick child in the car!"

At last, home was such a welcome haven. Astor led the way up the winding staircase to Jonas' bedroom. The governess did not have to tell him to get undressed. By the time she had removed her coat and entered the room, Jonas was lying under the duvet, Astor at his feet. His face was flushed and his eyes were half closed. She touched his forehead and said, "You feel warm, my little man."

In the medicine cabinet she found the thermometer next to

the valerian drops that Lucia used to make her sleep. She placed the thermometer under the boy's armpit while Astor carefully observed every move.

"One hundred and three degrees," she muttered to herself. "I have to sponge you down with alcohol," the governess said, "and I will call Doctor Citroen."

The doctor could not be reached and when she phoned the hotel in Marienbad, she was told that the Krugers were in the mountains on a picnic.

Jonas fell into a deep sleep while Astor stood by, vigilant at his bedside. The little boy twisted and turned, sweating more and more profusely as his fever soared. He dreamed he was marching in his brown uniform and Ala, standing on the curve of the long street, was applauding. Then a small bearded man – the Rabbi who came every Wednesday to give him Hebrew instruction – broke into a marching phalanx, shaking his finger meaningfully at him.

"*Shande, shande*, disgrace," the Rabbi yelled. "You, a Jewish boy! How dare you march with them?" The Rabbi grabbed Jonas by the neck and dragged him away from the riotously laughing crowd. The Rabbi's hands were hurting his neck! Help! he cried out to his governess. She was standing beside Bruno enjoying the parade, and she was naked to her waist. Her arms were outstretched, towards him, but not long enough to reach his own small, desperate fingers. Then, he was being pulled from one side by the Rabbi, from the other by Fräulein Marlow, now absolutely naked. Pulled. Torn apart!

When he suddenly awoke, he was drenched. The concerned governess was wiping his brow.

"My poor Jonas, you had such a bad dream," she said softly. "The doctor is on his way over to see you now. It will be all over soon."

"I don't want him to see me," Jonas said in a tiny voice. "He hurt me last time with all those shots for diphtheria."

"Jonas, he has to see you. You're very sick. He will help you," the governess said in a pleading tone. "Jonas, do this for me."

It was three in the morning when Doctor Citroen arrived. In spite of the hour, he wore a very dark suit and carried an ominous-looking black bag that no doubt contained long syringes for painful injections.

"How is my friend, Jonas?" the doctor asked cheerfully. As soon as he put one foot in the room Astor lurched at him with bared teeth. He growled and would have attacked the physician if the gentleman had not quickly moved behind the door back into the hallway.

"Tell Astor to let the doctor in!" the governess commanded. But nothing she said or threatened changed the boy's mind.

"All right," the doctor finally said in frustration, "sponge him down some more, Fräulein, and give him a tincture of belladonna and the phenobarbital. At least we will quiet him in bed."

By morning the fever had dropped, the doctor was long gone and Jonas felt hungry. After a breakfast of applesauce and a soft-boiled egg, Jonas was ready to begin his day. It was as if yesterday had never been.

"You have to stay in bed. The doctor said so. I reached your parents. They will be home by tomorrow, and then they can fight with you."

In the late morning, the Rabbi arrived to give Jonas his Hebrew lesson.

"You better not go in," the governess said. "Astor will attack you."

"Rubbish." The Rabbi entered the door. Astor excitedly jumped on him, licking his face with great enthusiasm.

"You do look sick, Jonas. I guess we will skip vocabulary and letters today, but I will read you a story by one of the great Jewish writers, a man called Sholom Aleichem."

Jonas fell asleep as the Rabbi finished the tale. When he awoke, it was late afternoon, and to amuse himself Jonas tore open the pillowcase and tossed the feathers into the air. Soon the room was so covered with feathers that it looked like a chicken-coop. He crawled out of bed and went into the library, Astor at his side, climbing the ladder leading to the forbidden books.

As he was about to pull out the volume with pictures of naked women in Africa, the governess stormed into the library.

"Get back into bed! You are really a bad boy. Don't you see enough of naked women?" she admonished.

As soon as Jonas was back in bed he began to vomit again, and once more his temperature began to rise. When Doctor Citroen arrived he again saw a very angry dog standing between him and a very sick boy lying in the bed.

"I have to get to him. Call the chauffeur and get a net. We have to get the dog out, even if we have to shoot it; otherwise, I am afraid for the boy's life."

"Jonas, please, let the doctor in the room. Tell Astor to leave. You are very sick. You don't want to die, do you?"

Karl-Heinz arrived carrying a long rifle and a net. As sick as Jonas felt, he ordered Astor, "Up, up on the bed!" He then placed his arms around the shepherd, whose body was tense in preparation to attack.

Jonas had to get to the bathroom as he became more ill. He crawled out of the bed and onto the floor, Astor very closely following behind him.

"Now we can get him! Shoot the dog!" the doctor ordered. But Jonas kept his arm around the dog, protecting him, until he arrived at the bathroom and vomited all over the floor. The chauffeur then took careful aim at the backside of the dog. Fräulein Marlow stood by, frozen in fear.

Suddenly, Lucia, Brand, and Uncle Herman came rushing into the room, just as Karl-Heinz was about to pull the trigger.

"My God, Jonas, my darling, what is going on here! Stop! Stop it now!" Lucia demanded.

She grabbed the boy off the floor and pulled him into her arms. Brand coaxed a reluctant Astor away and allowed the doctor to come into the bedroom to examine her son.

"Thank heavens, Frau Kruger, you came back," the governess said, tilting her chin toward the ceiling in gratitude.

"We were going to leave in the morning, but I insisted we leave immediately," Lucia said. She looked at Fräulein Marlow with a masked hatred in her eyes, as if the two women understood each other. Women-talking eyes, some called it.

Each day for the next month the doctor came, and so did Uncle Herman, who brought another new gift to make Jonas laugh. Once he even brought a goat into the room, wearing a dress. But the boy continued to vomit daily. He lost weight. He complained of head and body aches. His fever caused him to hallucinate and he uttered words such as "God punishing" and "Gerhardt."

"I thought at first he was coming down with measles or another childhood disease," the doctor said after more weeks had passed. "Now, I just don't know."

"We have to take him to Berlin," Uncle Herman said. "There is a famous doctor there, Sauerbrucher. He may make a proper diagnosis. I know him, and it may take time to arrange, but he owes me a favor."

"Berlin is a long way off," Lucia said. "He is too ill to travel."

Doctor Citroen feared now that Jonas was suffering from leukemia, because all of his glands were swollen, as was his spleen, and he agreed that if anyone could diagnose Jonas' illness, it would be Dr. Sauerbrucher, the distinguished physician at the Wilhelm Institute in Berlin. Precious time may have been lost.

Brand made all the arrangements for the long and arduous trip. With the help of Max Schiller, they boarded one of those luxurious trains whose carriages contained a bedroom and small living room. They even had a private waiter. The walls were upholstered in blue and cream velvet.

The morning train to Berlin was crowded with Jewish lawyers, doctors, judges, professors, and others, who had decided it was time to flee Danzig for Warsaw, the first stop.

Fräulein Marlow sat next to Jonas in one of the lush chairs by the window, feeling depressed and guilty.

Jonas liked the train and all the constant attention. He looked outside the window. In the distance, as the train departed from Danzig station, walking hurriedly with a pile of luggage, were Ala and her parents.

"Look, Mother," he pointed to the outside. "There's Ala and her mother and father."

He banged his fist against the window, to no avail. "They are leaving for America," he cried as Brand and Lucia looked on with despair in their eyes.

Jonas fell asleep as his temperature rose again. Several hours later they arrived at the Warsaw station, where most of the Danzig passengers de-boarded. When Jonas awoke he found a small present wrapped in tissue paper at his side.

"How is my brave boy feeling?" Lucia asked. She could not get over her feeling of remorse at having been in Marienbad while her son was so ill. She took the incident in the woods as a bad omen, a warning.

"I'm all right, except for my headaches, and my arms and legs hurt all the time, and I still have my tummy ache."

"Ala left you a present, darling," Lucia said softly.

He unwrapped the present and saw it was a paperweight similar to the one she had given him on his birthday, the one with the soldier and the princess inside. Now the soldier and princess had grown up to become a king and queen. He shook the glass and watched the snow falling in front of a castle.

"They went to America," Jonas said forlornly. "She told me it was a secret, but now it does not matter." For the rest of the train ride, Lucia and Brand sat quietly at his bedside, while the Fräulein busied herself reading.

When they arrived in Berlin it was dark, and the station was packed with people and SS men and soldiers. There was a peculiar air of gaiety among these somber looking men of war as they watched with interest the elegant family with their beautiful, self-possessed-looking governess descending from the train. In contrast to Jonas, weary eyed and feeling so ill, the Fräulein felt exhilarated in her natural environment.

Brand carried his son in his arms to a chauffeured blue Mercedes limousine.

They arrived at the exclusive Kisserhoff Hotel fifteen minutes later. Inside, there were hundreds of people in formal wear, while the SS, dressed in their black uniforms, stood at attention, rifles and bared bayonets at their sides.

The crowd was so dense that they could not approach the registration desk. From where Jonas stood, he saw only feet and backs. He looked up toward the thousands of lights. The ceiling was painted in flowing colors, with garlands of naked men and women and pink angels. He turned his young body like a carousel, following the outline of the naked women on the wall as Brand twisted with him. Jonas' mouth was wide open, his eyes widened in amazement. In the center of the fresco was a large face with a red beard. That must be God, he said to himself. He is watching me carefully.

Suddenly, the crowd parted like the jaws of a whale and formed a path on either side as a group of men and German shepherds marched into the hotel.

"What's going on?" Brand asked the man standing next to him.

"Did you not hear? Hitler is to become both president and

chancellor. Hindenburg is dead."

Then came a small man, wearing baggy pants and a raincoat, flanked by Rudolf Hess and a squirrely-looking man, the propaganda minister, Joseph Goebbels. The crowd applauded. Then they all broke into a frenzy. "Sieg Heil! Sieg Heil!" shook the great lobby.

Jonas wondered if he should not join in. He looked toward his governess, whose eyes were absolutely blazing with excitement.

The man with the mustache and raincoat suddenly stopped in front of where Jonas was standing, squeezing Lucia's hand.

"So late," he laughed, rubbing Jonas' hands in his. And then those hands ran through Jonas' hair.

"A good German boy should be home in bed now."

Fräulein curtsied and gave the German leader a radiant smile. Lucia and Brand stood frozen with fear. The child recognized the man with the mustache from all the posters he had seen at the youth meetings. Jonas felt warm and sleepy, wondering if he still was dreaming from the night before, especially when he saw so many Astors in one room.

Light bulbs flashed, and then there was more applause as Hitler and his entourage entered an elevator. Curious reporters came running up to Jonas asking, "What did he say to you?"

The concierge, Hans Schneider, personally escorted the Krugers to their suite of rooms, leaving the curious onlookers to wonder about the identities of the elegant man and woman with the beautiful governess and sick-looking child that the new leader of Germany had personally greeted so warmly.

Chapter Nine

PRINCE BRANDENBERG WAS the first to see the morning Danzig paper.

Kruger family in Berlin greeted by the new Chancellor of Germany. Jonas' picture was on the front page, the hand of Hitler on his head.

"My God," the Prince shouted to Bill, who was reading in the library. "Just what the Nazis wanted. Dammit. They will be lucky if they get out alive, especially when they tell that madman that he greeted a Jewish boy. I better give Rudi Hess a call. Perhaps I should go to Berlin. What do you think, Bill?"

"From what I have seen of these guys, you'd better watch your step. I would just call your friend," Bill replied.

At eight o'clock in the morning, the Mercedes limousine drove Jonas and his parents to the Wilhelm Hospital on the Kammerstrasse.

"You have to be a brave boy," Brand explained. "They will put you in a room, but parents are not allowed to be there except during visiting hours."

"Can Fräulein Marlow stay with me?" Jonas asked coyly.

"She is not a parent."

Lucia pulled her son toward her and kissed him. "You are so cute and so smart."

"You don't have to worry about little Jonas. He will draw circles around them," Brand said as the car smoothly changed lanes. "The apple has not fallen far from the tree. Don't be smart and start mimicking Hitler, because they will lock you up."

"Are you sure we are doing the right thing?" Lucia asked Brand. "They know he is a Jewish boy, and they just dismissed some Jewish doctors from the hospital."

"Lucia, dear, he is very sick, and Dr. Sauerbrucher is world famous. Do you think it will make a difference to him that he is going to treat a Jewish child? He will be paid very well, and our friends in Berlin have a lot of influence."

"These people here are not impressed with Jewish money," Lucia said, as bitterly as she had ever said anything. "They only want to get rid of us."

"That is enough," Brand said in Polish, as the car pulled up to the hospital pavilion. "Our driver is one of them. Enough, I say."

A pleasant-looking nurse met them in a spacious marble lobby. Swiftly, after Jonas barely had time to kiss his mother and father, he turned his small head with feverish eyes towards his governess who gave him a weak smile as he was escorted to a room located on the second floor. Lucia involuntarily clasped her hand to her open mouth, sobbing, "We may never see him again! My Jonas, my baby!"

The nurse walked so swiftly that Jonas had to run to keep up with her. He turned his head once more and saw Lucia crying hysterically and realized how serious everything was. But he was a soldier in the youth party and was determined not to cry or be afraid; to be above all brave, never mind his headaches, the vomiting and fever, or the pain in his legs and arms.

The nurse left Jonas in a small stark room, which contained a bed and white blanket with a swastika embroidered in the center. A picture of Hitler was hanging on one wall, a crucifix on the other wall. Next to the bed was a night table with a large silver tray covered by a white napkin. Jonas picked up the napkin and gasped when he saw four large syringes with long needles lying next to four test tubes and alcohol sponges. He covered the gruesome sight quickly and planned an immediate escape. He was too frightened to be lonely. He tried the door, which was locked, and pushed the only chair in the room next to the window, which was partially open. Outside there was a narrow ledge wide enough to stand on. The ground was not far down. He saw a large lawn in front of him with patients sitting on lounge chairs. Ivy grew down from the ledge. He had learned at the Maccabee Club gymnasium to climb down ropes, and that was what he planned to do. And then he would run from the hospital to the streets, even if everything hurt. In his pants pocket he had some groschens and an Austrian gold coin that Uncle Herman had given him as good luck charms before they left Danzig.

As he painfully inched himself through the narrow opening and was halfway out on the ledge, he felt a strong pair of hands grab his waist and pull him back into the room. The hands belonged to the largest woman he had ever seen in his life. She wore a triangular hat and carried a large cross around her neck that swung like a pendulum between two huge breasts. She was a nurse, but she was also a nun.

"For God's sake, what do you think you are doing?" she yelled at him with a thunderous voice. "Get undressed immediately." She closed the window and locked it, glaring at him furiously.

"For the sick child you are supposed to be, you behave like one of those ruffians in the streets." She threw a white gown at him and said, "Put this gown on, now, and get into bed."

Jonas felt too embarrassed and frightened to undress in front of her. He had done that often in front of his governess, but this was so different.

"Lie on your side," she spoke in a rough voice. "Pull your legs toward your body, and don't move." He felt a greasy thermometer snake into his rectum.

"Don't move or I will chain you to the bed."

He lay still as a rock, afraid to take a breath, because he pictured his arms and legs being chained to the bedside like a prisoner on Devil's Island. He squeezed the edge of the bed with his moist hands, pulling his lips tight together to keep from screaming. He was not going to cry in front of her. The nurse kept her large hand firmly on his back as the thermometer remained in place.

"Five minutes, that's all it takes; stay still. Otherwise, I will leave it in you for one hour. Make one move and you will be sorry you are still breathing, you little hoodlum."

Minutes later a cheerful blond, blue-eyed doctor bounced into the room, as if he were arriving for a birthday party.

"Well, now, what do we have here? Our visitor from the Free State of Danzig. The 'Danzig Kid' we'll call him. You look like a brave sort, because I am going to draw some blood from your arm and tomorrow the famous Dr. Sauerbrucher will come to examine you. Did you ever have blood drawn before?"

"No, sir."

There was no escaping now, Jonas thought, but he was not going to cry. He thought of Gerhardt at the moment, and wondered if he had been in the hospital with an ugly fat nurse that he hated. Gerhardt had moved away immediately after he'd recovered when his father took a job with a big bank in Hamburg. That episode still made Jonas shiver. Shivering now, he thought that if Astor were here, this happy doctor wouldn't be smiling.

Jonas felt a tightness around his arm as a red round rubber tube was placed around it. The nurse pulled out the thermometer from his rectum. The tall doctor kept asking him questions like, "Do you like Schlagball? What about soccer?"

He told the doctor he liked soccer best because he was small and could run faster than any of his friends. Jonas was afraid the doctor would ask him about Fräulein Marlow and their secrets or discover something wrong with his privates that would reveal all.

"Just a little stick," the doctor said. The nun was towering over him like a wrestler ready to put him into a tight hold. The doctor's face looked like white marble to him, like a statue he had seen at Schopenhauer Park. He tried to focus his thoughts on Fräulein Marlow, and how warm and safe he felt when lying against her soft milky skin. But he was too engrossed to follow that thought-line now. He watched instead with fascination as the long needle entered him. The doctor pulled back on the lever of the syringe, always smiling, showing his perfect white teeth. Jonas wondered if the doctor would be smiling if he had blood drawn from his own vein. The whole process intrigued his imaginative mind. The blood streamed into the syringe.

"We want to see if your blood is filled with little bugs." As he said that, Jonas pictured thousands of tiny bugs swimming in his blood, climbing into his nose, his ears, his mouth, into his head. The thought made him feel sick to his stomach. He would have to be careful that the bugs didn't travel to his mother when she kissed him, or to Fräulein Marlow. He looked over his naked body, checking to see if there were any already on his skin.

Jonas' arms began to hurt as he felt pins and needles in his fingers, but he was afraid to tell the doctor as he watched him transfer the blood from the syringe into the test tubes lying on the silver plate. When his arm began to turn blue he could not contain his agony any longer. He cried out, "My arm is hurting so much!"

"It's all right, Danzig Kid. We have other Jewish children

here, but none as brave as you."

Jonas did not stop crying and pointed to his arm. "But it hurts so much."

The doctor saw the arm was blue and now realized he had forgotten to remove the tourniquet. With one swift movement he released the rubber tube and Jonas held his limp arm at his side as the blood trickled from his puncture site. After the bleeding stopped, the nun said with an angry voice, "Now I will need to change his sheets before the professor comes. You should be more careful, Doctor." As she scolded the young doctor, he looked as scared as Jonas.

"Now give a urine sample," the nun demanded after the doctor left the room.

"I can't go," Jonas protested.

"You better, or I will force a tube into your little peepee."

Now he was certain he had to find a way to escape from this horrible place. Why had his mother and father put him here, Jonas asked himself.

"Come into the bathroom, you filthy little Jew devil!" she hissed. "Piss into this bottle or I will piss on you."

The more she talked the more he became frightened and was unable to fill the bottle. She escorted Jonas back to the bed and placed the bottle at his side.

"I will be back, and that bottle better be filled."

He fell back exhausted on the bed, his body burning.

The nun returned and saw the boy's face flushed and his body raging with fever. The young doctor returned. Jonas heard through his crepuscular state, "We better do a spinal tap."

Whatever that meant, it sounded terrifying. "He may have meningitis. Bring me the spinal needle," ordered the doctor.

They are going to put that long needle into my peepee, Jonas thought, because I did not fill the bottle. He reached for the bottle and placed his small organ into it, straining, but no urine came forth.

Through the corner of his eye he saw the nun coming toward him with a long needle and sponges on a tray. With her large rugged hands, she arched his back like a boomerang, as he felt a cold solution strike his spine. He was too weak to cry or to resist.

"Hand me the syringe, Nurse. Just a little stick, Danzig Kid, and it will all be over."

"You know, Doctor," the nun said, "had you not better check with Dr. Sauerbrucher to see if this is what he wants you to do?"

"Nurse, this is an emergency. Sauerbrucher is sleeping in his comfortable bed and won't like to be disturbed. I know what I am doing."

"Still, doctor, this boy was greeted personally by the Führer this evening," she said. "If anything goes wrong . . ."

"The Führer? Where?" He pointed the syringe towards the ceiling and thought for a few seconds. What if his hand did slip and caused a paralysis as he struck nerve roots? The nun was right. One hour or so would make no difference. Then he could ask the professor if he thought a spinal tap was needed.

The doctor replaced the syringe on the metal tray, sponged off the little boy's back, and covered his naked body with the starched white bed sheet.

"Very well then. Finish sponging him down, then give him aspirin and phenobarbital so he doesn't start convulsing." The physician tried in vain to become an authoritative person, but now the nun and Hitler were in charge.

After the doctor left, Jonas finally filled the glass jar and, with grateful eyes, handed it to the nun. He no longer hated her, and when she wiped his head with a wet cloth he liked her even better. She no longer screamed, but gently brushed her hands through his brown hair.

"Go to sleep, my little boy. You don't have to be afraid anymore."

Jonas wondered how someone one minute can be so mean and the next be so kind. Grown-ups are funny sorts of people.

Nuns.

Spit three times if you see two nuns walking together, he was taught. He feared them more than a pit of vipers. But this nun was nice after all.

In the morning when Jonas awoke he thought for a minute that he was in his own bed in Danzig. Had everything – seeing Hitler and the close call with the long syringe – been just a bad dream, a nightmare?

A young, fresh-looking nurse entered the room, arriving with a tray of applesauce and rice and some warm tea. "My name is Nurse Herta," she said cheerfully. "We have to give you a quick sponge bath, change your sheets, and make everything look fresh and clean for the professor."

"Are my mother and father coming soon?" Jonas asked in an anxious voice.

"In the afternoon, when we have visiting hours."

Herta placed a clean towel on the night table, along with a metal tongue depressor, a flashlight, a round headlight, an oph-thalmoscope, and ear scopes.

"You sit on the bed here, Jonas, and I will tell you a story while we wait for the professor."

Jonas felt his heart racing under his night shirt. Why would his mother and father put him through all this torture? And Uncle Herman and Fräulein had allowed it, too. When he got stronger he would definitely run away and never see his parents again, and then they really would be sorry, he thought.

The door of the room opened briskly and three doctors and two nurses entered, chattering. The tallest of the men was the famous Professor Sauerbrucher. He had a lean body with a kind, narrow face and gray hair.

"I'm Dr. Sauerbrucher," he gently said. He sat down on the side of the bed and took one of Jonas' sweaty hands into his own

"You have had a bad time, but don't worry, soon we'll make you better and you will go back home to your beautiful city. You would like that, wouldn't you?"

Jonas nodded.

"Do you have a dog?"

"Yes."

"And his name?"

"Astor."

"Astor, what an unusual name. I bet he misses you."

"Yes, I miss him too. He protects me."

"You don't look like the type of young man who needs protection." The doctor laughed as he picked up Jonas' chart. "Were you excited when you met the Führer?"

"Yes. He shook my hands."

"Your picture is on the front page of all the newspapers," the professor said.

He showed him the front page of the *Berlin Daily* where Jonas was standing with Lucia and Brand as Hitler bent down to greet him. It had been paper-clipped to Jonas' records.

"You are a famous young boy. So tell me, does Astor sleep in your bed?"

"No, only if I am sick; otherwise, he stays in the room. He is a German shepherd." Jonas liked this doctor.

"Ah, I, too have one. His name is Bruno."

Jonas began to giggle.

"What is funny, Jonas?" the doctor asked.

"Bruno is the name of my new chauffeur in Danzig, and he looks like a German shepherd." Karl-Heinz had been terminated because Lucia could not rid herself of the image of his carrying a rifle into her boy's bedroom to shoot their beloved Astor. "He is a friend of Fräulein Marlow, and he is also the leader of German Youth Scouts," Jonas added.

Dr. Sauerbrucher continued asking Jonas hundreds of questions, always interrupting him with a pleasantry as the other doctors stood by in silence and in admiration as they observed a real master at the work of doctoring.

While he was asking all the questions Doctor Sauerbrucher's long gentle fingers examined Jonas' neck and armpits, which made Jonas giggle, looking for swollen glands. The doctor pounded on his chest, then moved his hands to his belly, which caused Jonas to break out in spontaneous laughter. His laughter was so infectious that all the others in the room could not restrain themselves.

From Sauerbrucher's long white coat's side pocket, he produced a small piece of wood in the shape of a cylinder with a finely carved *caduceus*, the staff with two entwined snakes topped with wings that is the physician's insignia. He placed one end of the cylinder over Jonas' chest and bent his ear to the other. When he was finished, the professor placed his ear over Jonas' chest and told him to breathe in and out.

"Do you like this instrument?" he asked Jonas.

"Yes."

"Then you can hold onto it for a while and see if you can hear your dog's heart with it."

"We have to do some more tests, Jonas," he said in an encouraging voice, "but don't worry. There will be no more needles. We have enough blood." The doctor left the room trailed by a cloud of floating assistants.

The young pretty nurse wheeled him down the corridor to the x-ray suite where Dr. Sauerbrucher was waiting for him in a darkened room behind a screen and wearing a steel apron. For a moment Dr. Sauerbrucher looked like the butcher about to chop the side of a beef as Jonas once saw at the Jewish market in Danzig.

"Now take everything off, Jonas. Stand against the screen and I will move this screen up and down your body so I can see all your insides."

"What are you looking for?" Jonas asked.

"You are a curious one. Some day perhaps you will become a doctor. This is a fluoroscope and I can see your lungs move, your heart beat, and all your secrets. I bet you have lots of those. But I promise, whatever is written on your heart, I won't tell anyone. Your secrets will forever stay with me," he laughed. This struck Jonas with a knowing chord.

Jonas felt his heart race thinking of his Fräulein and his bathtub, as the doctor smiled gently, observing the rapid beat of the young boy's heart.

"Now Jonas, I see that your heart is very strong and healthy and that it is going to beat for a very long time for you. Next we will go get some x-rays of your intestines. But first you will have to swallow some white-like chalk. It is called barium and it tastes not too bad if you swallow quickly and make believe it is cold ice."

After Jonas was wheeled into another room, he had to swallow the white chalky material that did not taste anything like lemon ices.

He wanted to vomit but the nice doctor kept encouraging him to swallow quickly.

The nurse helped Jonas to step up to the steel table and told him to lie there and not move. "You are a wonderfully brave young man," the doctor told him.

Each day for the next seven days, Lucia and Brand and the governess came to visit Jonas. All the tests were finally completed, and his temperature did not rise any longer. Throughout his hospital stay Jonas heard words like leukemia, blood diseases, rheumatic fever, and cancer. At the end of the second week, the nurse-nun brought in all his clothes and said to him, "Now you can run away. We are releasing you. You can go home." She shook his hand and said, "You are a good, brave boy. May God keep you always well."

Jonas remembered something about her once having called him a Jewish devil, but that seemed long ago. He must have been mistaken.

He was escorted to the professor's office, where Lucia and Brand were waiting. On the wall were dozens of pictures of famous men and women who came to consult with Dr. Sauerbrucher.

He rose from his chair and proffered a long thin hand to Jonas and said, "You see all those pictures on the wall, young man? Well, I want you to promise to send one to me and in exchange I will give you a present. Here is the stethoscope that seemed to fascinate you so. Someday you might use it for your patients."

Jonas took the stethoscope into his hand, bowed and said, "Thank you, Doctor, for making me feel better."

Sauerbrucher for an instant was taken aback, and said, "Those are the nicest words I have heard in a long time." He turned to Brand and Lucia and said, "Your son is a real gentleman."

He continued, "All the tests show no leukemia or anything else serious. I suspect the young man is suffering from a form of undulant fever that will get better in time without any treatment, like most things in medicine."

Lucia and Brand were overwhelmed with happiness, shook hands with Dr. Sauerbrucher and hugged Jonas. The following morning they departed on the first train for Danzig.

Jonas bounded out of the limousine and ran into the house

where Astor jumped on him, bathing his face with his huge tongue. The large entrance hall was decorated with balloons and colorful welcome signs. They were greeted by the entire staff, including the cook, the chauffeur, and the chambermaid, with a loud round of applause.

Uncle Herman suddenly appeared from the library, dressed like a nurse, two balloons pushing out his chest, and he carried a huge cardboard thermometer in one hand and a long rubber stethoscope in the other. He hobbled over to Jonas and said in a high voice, "Doctor Sauerbrucher called and said to check your temperature." He gathered Jonas up in his arms like a sack of potatoes and pressed him against the balloons, breasts on parade, which popped loudly and delighted everyone except Astor.

The governess watched the clowning around and whispered to Bruno, "Disgusting! What they teach that boy."

Inside the library, the scene was not so jovial. The Rabbi and Metchnik were waiting grimly. They greeted Jonas warmly and then waited for the boy and the governess to leave.

"You two look like you lost your best friend," Brand said.

"It was a disgrace and humiliation for all eight thousand Jews in Danzig," the Rabbi said. "Here. Look at that."

The headlines: *Jewish Lad from Danzig Greeted by the New Chancellor of Germany*. The picture clearly showed Lucia and Brand smiling as Hitler shook hands with Jonas.

"You should have pulled Jonas away from that madman. You give the impression that good Jewish Danzigers welcome Hitler!"

"What was I supposed to have done?" Brand said, more than a little annoyed. "It all happened so quickly. We were thinking only of Jonas and getting him to the doctor. Any aggressive move on my part and the SS would have enjoyed bashing my head in and arresting us all. And that, I assure you, would not have appeared in the *Danziger Daily*."

"Listen Rabbi, Brand is a good Jew, like the rest of our family," Uncle Herman said. "I know these bastards. They might not have done anything on the spot, but one day they'd arrange a little accident – the Duesenberg gets blown up, or Astor is found dead, or even more to the point, my nephew disappears, possibly forever! If you really want to protest, get your Rabbi from New York to help you, and all those rich Jews and their beloved new President Roosevelt to protest. They are scared to death to say anything in America, and you expect one Jew in Europe, sur-rounded by the SS, to stand up to the new leader of Germany?"

"Brand is no ordinary man," the Rabbi said. "He is one of the very industrialists who sell them coal."

Brand sat silently in his large armchair listening as he was being scolded by the Rabbi. He looked at Metchnik, whose stern eyes were lowered.

"Rabbi, you are right," Brand said. He knew it was best to end the conversation as quickly as possible. It had advanced be-yond reason. The subject was too inflammatory.

Later that same day, Max Schiller called Brand and said, "You don't have to worry about future business with the new regime. The Reichstag is delighted with the priceless publicity you have given them."

"Life is fair." Brand remembered those words of Metchnik from long ago. He was recovering from the bullet wound he had received in his right arm on the field as the Russians attacked Warsaw. His men had abandoned him and Metchnik found him. He was lying in a four-poster bed in the guest bedroom of their estate. The walls were covered with blue velvet, and there were the largest curtains he had ever seen on the largest windows.

"You were saved for a reason," Metchnik told him as he sat at his bedside. "All your men were either killed or captured by the Russians. You showed courage and knew how to survive. The war is over. The Red Army has been stopped at the gates of War-saw, and you don't have to be a soldier anymore. But you must return to your regiment in Warsaw, and I will give you a letter testifying that you did not desert your men and were wounded. Otherwise, they will incarcerate you, put you on trial for deserting, and have you shot, especially since by now the survivors are blaming you for their blunders and they will tell that you are a Jew." Still, Brand knew it was his blunder.

It was a major error to lead his cavalry into an open field surrounded by trees during the day. He should have sent out a scout, but the men were so anxious to return to Warsaw that he did not use logic.

Now he was again faced with a threat to his life and his family. The right decision had to be made. This time another mistake could be the end of everything.

It was that quiet look on the old gentleman's face that made Brand stop for a moment to reflect on the words of the Rabbi. It was that same look he had seen on Metchnik's face as he sat by his bedside. Metchnik was a wise man, experienced in life. He was telling him to prepare for the worst.

Chapter Ten

𝒯HE PRINCE FELT TOO UNSETTLED to stay in Danzig for long, so once Jonas was safely home, he moved to Paris to think things through. His shotgun wound had healed nicely, and he had received a personal letter from Rudolph Hess soon after apologizing for the Marienbad ruffians. They had meant, Hess reassured him, merely to scare the party and not to harm anyone. But in a recent letter, Hess had also informed the Prince that it would be best to end the relationship with the American, as the new leader was drafting plans to make political prisoners of all the homosexuals, gypsies, and cocaine dealers.

"The new Germany will not tolerate deviants! Understood? For your safety, send the boy back to Ohio. I can only do so much for so long. Burn this letter. My dear friend, I care for you too much to have anything happen."

The following day he and Bill took a large parlor car on the Orient Express from Budapest to Paris.

"Paris is the most beautiful city in the world," the Prince said. "You will see none of the horror scenes of Berlin. Germany and Danzig are finished."

They arrived at the Gare St. Lazare in the early evening and stayed at Le Hotel on the Left Bank. "This is where Oscar Wilde stayed and where he died," the Prince explained. "I usually stay at the Ritz, but I thought this would be more romantic."

The suite was decorated in the Victorian style, massive furniture everywhere. There was a huge feather bed and red couches with blue down pillows. A bouquet of pristine peonies was on a small round table in the center of the room, along with a bottle of Moët and two very tall glasses.

"*L'avenir est a nous*," the Prince said. "The future is ours." They toasted, but Bill saw a melancholy in the Prince's eyes that he had never seen before.

They walked down the Rue de Seine and bought a baguette and ripe, delicious camembert from a cart bedecked with flowers, and then they sat on a bench in the Tuilleries, facing the pond, surrounded by thousands of red and yellow flowers. At night they went to the Casino Royale and heard the fabulous American expatriate Josephine Baker. Then they drank Pernod at the Café Aux Deux Magots. Everywhere there was art and romance and wonderful smells: flowers, good bread, cheese, wine. At night, they walked the narrow cobbled streets lined with brash but often beautiful prostitutes, who eagerly offered themselves, at a not unreasonable price, to the handsome men. Young lovers dotted the quais, while pretty girls sold flowers from the shadows.

"Everything is there for the free soul," the Prince observed with Bill as they drank coffee one morning in the Dome at Montparnasse. It was already early September and the city felt as fresh as baby's breath.

"Here is where many of your expatriates come, even more important than Josephine Baker. There in the corner, that fat woman with the masculine haircut? That's Gertrude Stein."

Bill looked. "Who's the man with her?"

The Prince roared. "Oh, my American ingénue, will you never learn? That man is named Alice." Bill rolled his eyes.

The Prince decided the moment had come. Pretending to

be casual, he said, "I prefer the Dome to the Café Romaniche. Perhaps you would like to stay here instead of returning with me to Danzig?"

Bill seized on his companion's meaning immediately. They had discussed their future in the way soap circles a drain. Bill knew his family was expecting him to return sometime that fall, the clock on his year of peripatetic indulgence having run out. Instead, he had succeeded in putting them off. A wealthy patron, he said, had "offered" to sponsor him in a course of advanced architectural study at the university in Danzig, and Bill had accepted. He had managed to buy himself another year. He took the Prince's slender fingers into his large palm.

"You show me Paris through your eyes and you think I could stay here without you?"

"Things are going to change soon," the Prince said, his eyes sad. "I wanted to see this all now."

"Then why don't we stay in Paris?" Bill said. "I could enroll in the Beaux Arts right here and we would get a cheap apartment on the Rue Jacob, near the school."

"Because, because, because, my lovely Bill, in spite of everything, I cannot run like a rat and abandon the sinking ship. Danzig is my home. I have responsibilities to my estate; there are still many people who depend on me. And yet I think it would be best if you return to America or stay in Paris. It is not safe for you in Danzig."

"I am not leaving. I am as safe as any American citizen."

The Prince did not want say that it was he, not Bill, who was in great danger. The letter from Hess had been prophetic. A prison camp, which people were calling a concentration camp, had been built in Mauthausen, and thousands of people were being taken off the streets of Berlin, from cafés, even from homes: homosexuals, transvestites, prostitutes, cocaine addicts, and most recently, some Jews and gypsies.

It was the beginning of the purification of the German race, the purging of the unclean elements that had stained and corrupted the Aryans.

A shade was beginning to drop over everything.

Chapter Eleven

SOPOT BY THE SEA, 1935, was as exquisite as ever, a jewel of a resort. This charming village was an international playground for the elite. White silky beaches stretched on for miles, lined by the famous boardwalk. They came to Sopot to swim, to sunbathe, to listen to the concerts, and to gamble at the casino, which was almost as famous as the one at Monte Carlo. This little village was nestled between Poland and Germany, and even the North Sea, which all but surrounded it, usually cruel and harsh, was as calm as a lake this June. Nevertheless, it was too early in the season for the gaiety of Sopot to have begun in earnest. Everywhere there was the smell of fresh paint and the sound of hammering. Sopot now belonged to the carpenters, the painters, the waiters shining the stemware, and the croupiers making ready for the arrival of the elite crowd.

Although it was still spring, Lucia decided to come to Sopot a few weeks early. With Jonas's illness last year, they had entirely missed the season. Now that he was better, the sea air and the warm sun could only have a salutary effect.

It had been a long, tough year for them all.

It took almost one full year for Jonas' temperature to subside and for him to begin to feel stronger again. The pains in his arms and legs left him tired and irritable. And so Jonas had remained home most of the time, away from his playmates and his outings with his governess, as Dr. Sauerbrucher ordered. Lucia knew this change would do her son good.

The Krugers owned a sprawling twelve-room villa, high atop the dunes, facing the ocean, only a few minutes from the largest boardwalk in Europe. Their house was surrounded by ten-foot hedges, immaculately manicured, and facing the sea was a lush garden and a rolling lawn dotted with colorful chairs and umbrellas. This was their home for the summer months every year, until the September chill announced unmistakably that it was time to leave. It was a forty-five-minute drive by car back to their home in Langfuhr.

When they first arrived, Lucia had warned Jonas, "We are going to have many guests this summer," thinking of her family in Warsaw. Her sisters and their children, as well as her parents, would spend a week in July with them. The Prince and Bill would follow in August, and Uncle Herman, and very likely one of his women, would come too. "So you will have to share your room with Fräulein Marlow, but it is, after all, the best room in the house." Indeed it was. From it one could see the beach, the sea, the boats, the boardwalk – everything!

Fräulein Marlow, standing next to Jonas, wearing linen trousers and an open-collar shirt with the sleeves rolled up past the elbow, said, "Well, Jonas, you will just have to put up with me. Don't worry, Frau Kruger. We will manage just fine. Jonas, you can have the bed by the bay window."

Jonas looked down at his sneakers, his face hot crimson, thinking that this summer, his twelfth, would turn out to be the best one of all. He loved it here. The house had once belonged to a sea captain, and his upstairs bedroom had large bay windows with a small widow's walk outside. The original captain's telescope was still in place, mounted on a brass stand, still pointing out to the sea.

For the first three days, Jonas stayed close to the house, taking a morning walk with his mother on the beach, Astor running happily around them. The governess helped Lucia put the house back in order, making it spotless for the many visitors to come.

In the evenings, Jonas played checkers with his mother and turned in early. He was usually in bed by 9:00 p.m. and asleep by the time Fräulein Marlow came to bed. Sometimes he feigned sleep and listened to the rustling of her clothing as she undressed. Through his half-closed eyes he saw her beautiful half-naked body as she climbed into her own bed. In the morning he waited for the governess to leave the bedroom, because he always awoke with a stiff erection, which embarrassed him; often, his sheets were soaking wet and sticky.

By the middle of the second week, Jonas was running on the beach with abandon. His governess watched him from the top bay window. In his white shorts and red shirt she could follow the boy for miles, and she watched as he and Astor explored the long white beach, always running by the edge of the water, kicking it, splashing it, delighted by its coolness. She marveled at how, even with a year-long convalescence at home, nature had asserted itself. Jonas' body was lean and lanky now. The sea air would tone it. Like his father, Jonas had a natural athleticism. The young boy was disappearing before her eyes. Jonas was growing up and perhaps away from her. She wondered now if she was losing him.

That afternoon Fräulein Marlow sat beside Jonas as he read on the porch. For Jonas, during his convalescence, reading became one of his greatest joys. Each new book introduced him to another magical world in which he lived vicariously. When he read *The Adventures of Tom Sawyer* for the first time, Jonas could identify with Tom's adventurous spirit. He volunteered to paint the picket fence around the Sopot house just as Tom did in the book. He imagined himself part of the round table in King Arthur's Court with Fräulein Marlow as his Guinevere. When he walked on the beach, he was Robinson Crusoe, isolated, alone, waiting to be rescued.

"Jonas, you read so quickly,, I can't get books fast enough for you," Lucia frequently exclaimed to him. He carried one with him at all times, and he used every free moment to read.

He loved reading Jack London's sea stories. He liked to read Conrad, too, even though he was more difficult. The family library in Langfuhr was a treasure trove, but thanks to Uncle Herman, who still brought the new releases with him when he visited, Jonas was introduced to new authors, too. He loved especially James Hilton's *Good-bye Mr. Chips*, which had just been translated into German.

"Jonas, you like to read so much," Uncle Herman had told him many months earlier as he presented his nephew with a handsomely wrapped package, "I want you to keep a diary, your own secret diary. Perhaps someday you will become a writer and you will have oh, so many things to write about."

It was a beautiful leather-bound diary with a little lock and key, and Jonas kept it under his pillow. Each night before he went to sleep he wrote, at first just a few words about his parents or his day, and then a whole page of everything he observed around him.

"I wish my father would spend more time with me, and mother loves me very much, but she likes to have a good time and is always laughing. I feel well now, but I think a lot of Dr. Sauerbrucher, the hospital, and the silly man with the mustache." He added, "I have a governess. Her name is Fräulein Marlow. She is like no one else. She tells me things and shows me things only grown-ups know, but never talk about." Jonas also became more contemplative and he had profound thoughts of life in general, his life.

Lucia also realized that summer that Jonas was hardly an ordinary boy. He had a marvelous memory and an inquisitive spirit. His zeal for reading was a side she adored.

She remembered Dr. Sauerbrucher telling her, "Your son is very bright. All he needs is to have some pool of knowledge open to him and he will suck it up like a fish out of water, gasping for air."

As the weeks passed, Jonas no longer waited for the governess to leave the room in the morning. He now awoke at sunrise, ran to the bathroom to relieve himself, laughing at the death of his erection, then was immediately out on the beach with Astor, a book under his arm. The governess, still sleepy-eyed, watched the young boy march to the bathroom, his pajama bottoms made taut by a ramrod.

On one of those bright beautiful mornings, he went to his favorite spot, not too far from the house, where the rocks jutted into the sea. There he sat on the edge, first watching the waves hit the shore, then reading by the light of the newly risen sun.

He felt alone and wished there were some boys his age to talk to or that his cousins from Warsaw would come visit soon and explore some of the caves on the far side of the beach with him. He made several resolutions as he sat on the huge smooth white rock facing the sea. He said out loud, talking to the waves as they struck the shore, he would become a doctor and help sick people as Dr. Sauerbrucher helped him and write books and stories that would also make people happy.

He thought of Ala, now living in America, and their promise to each other to marry some day.

In the distance he saw a small figure walking by himself. At first he thought his eyes were tricking him because the boy looked like his old friend, Gerhardt, whom he hadn't seen since that terrible accident so long ago. Then he thought that it must be a ghost, because Gerhardt had moved far away. The apparition of the boy passed by the jetty, and Jonas skillfully tip-toed over the rocks onto the beach like an escaping dainty sea-creature, and then started to run after the boy.

Jonas had never stopped thinking about Gerhardt, and believed that because of Gerhardt God had punished Jonas and made him sick. He was convinced, in fact, that he had driven Gerhardt into the streets and caused a car to hit him. He still dreamed of him at night.

"Gerhardt, Gerhardt!" he called against the wind, and ran as hard as he could.

The boy turned when he heard his name called. There was a long ragged scar across his face, and another that traveled zig-zag from his thigh to his toes, which looked like a road map.

"Jonas, I heard you were at the beach. How wonderful!"

"You are back! I thought I'd never see you again. Why didn't you tell me you were here? Gerhardt, this is wonderful!"

Gerhardt shrugged, kicking at the sand with his left foot. "I was in the hospital a long time, you know. Then we moved away." The strong Baltic Sea sun made Gerhardt wince and he raised his hand on his forehead to better look at Jonas.

The gulls encircled them as the waves burst against the rocks spraying them.

"Me, too. I was also in the hospital," Jonas said.

"I know. I saw your picture in the newspaper."

"Oh, that." Jonas paused. "Can we see each other tomorrow? I have a great bedroom with a real telescope where a captain once lived, and my father has a schooner, a big one. Oh, I am so happy you are back! I didn't mean to chase you into the street. I am sorry you were hit by a car. I was so miserable that for a long time I could not sleep from thinking of you." His words tumbled over each other, and he continued, "We can have a terrific time here in Sopot. Come and meet me in the morning, tomorrow, by these rocks, at seven, and we can spend the whole day together. You can sleep at my house. I heard there are some secret caves on the beach. I think I know where they are, and then we can go to the boat. Please come. I've missed you." His enthusiasm and genuine happiness over this reunion built with each word he spoke.

"All right, that would be fun. I will see you in the morning, Jonas. I am not angry at you. I don't remember much about what happened, anyway. The whole thing was probably stupid. Anyway, it's over. So there!"

Jonas wanted desperately to entice his old friend to see him again. He seemed the same inside, although the scars that raked his friend's body made Jonas quiver. He watched with sadness mixed with joy as Gerhardt walked down the beach with a limp. Excited, stumbling down the rocks, his feet pushing through the warm sand, Jonas ran into the house to tell Lucia the good news. She did not appear to share any of his enthusiasm. She was pre-occupied by some terrible rumors swirling about the elite sum-mer community, like the high winds on the beach.

Brand and Lucia became pariahs to the few remaining Jew-ish families, who deliberately avoided them. When Lucia went shopping or to lunch in town, she was no longer greeted with affection and kisses. Instead, her former women friends stiffened up and barely greeted her.

Was it her fault that Hitler had greeted them? They were just standing in the hotel lobby. They were victims of circum-stances beyond their control. And why couldn't they understand that they had done what any parent would do by bringing their sick child to Berlin for treatment? Who among them would have done anything differently? Now, even Jonas would be punished. Where were the playmates? The gods played a dirty trick on them.

These were the thoughts that raced through Lucia's head as Jonas stood smiling in front of her. In addition, many of her close friends had left for other countries. Some went to Poland, others to Argentina, Venezuela, even China, as they could not get visas to America. The Anspachs did get to New York, and with their money the Krugers could go to New York also. Brand had a cousin living in Baltimore, and he could send some money ahead.

They had a few friends left, but even at home in Danzig, none would allow their children to associate with Jonas.

And yet they simply could not commit themselves. It was not that they lacked the courage, though some might see it as such. They had obligations, and ties of love that bound them willingly as much as necessarily. Chiefly, Lucia's parents in Warsaw were old and retired, and they had no desire to change their lives so late in life.

"What am I going to do in America?" her father said whenever the subject arose when she visited. "Here I have a lot of money, a good life with servants. There, your mother would have to learn to cook. They don't have servants in America. They don't have servants in America unless you are very rich. And then to learn a new language, ach."

"I am too old for all that," he told Lucia.

Poland was safe for now, and they had a beautiful home there. Why tempt fate?

Lucia was about to have her morning bath when Jonas ran into the house. He stayed just long enough to tell her his news about finding Gerhardt and then was outside once more on the beach with Astor. She closed the bathroom door, undressed completely, and sat on the edge of the bathtub watching the water. Her morning routine was to fill the tub with hot water, then add to milk and gardenia gel and to listen to her small shortwave Blaupunkt radio that Brand had bought for her in Berlin. She was able to get Radio Warsaw and listen to Richard Tauber singing German love songs. Her body felt languid as the warm milk and water covered her. Above the bathtub was a Victorian round mirror that Brand had installed for her. At the age of thirty-four, she thought her body was as youthful as when she was twenty. Giving birth to Jonas had left her with barely a stretch mark. Her breasts were still taut and her belly flat. Her mother had told her to soak in milk to keep her skin soft and white and to always wear a hat because the sun will make a woman old fast.

Brand still made love to her skillfully, but of course the passion was different. She still carried the guilt of having yearned for Bill and for the clumsiness of her failed seduction. How pathetic she must have appeared. But she also realized that it must have been an act of God that Bill turned out to like boys better than girls. What a risk she had taken. All this time later, she wondered why she had been attracted to him anyway. Was it because he was so young? American? A trophy in her tight little community of bored wives? Or had she only been trying to catch Brand's attention? As some of her friends told her, Bill was a bed-warmer.

"Just what is a bed-warmer?" Lucia had asked her friend Lotte.

"It is someone you meet in the afternoon that makes all your insides flow and you are ready for the night. Men often have bed-warmers," she told Lucia. "They catch fire." She knew Brand had a few of those. No matter how many baths Brand took, or how much cologne he doused his body with, Lucia always knew when he had been with another woman. And although she never had caught him with the governess, Lucia knew. That one fact rankled her deeply.

"Why do you stand for it then?" Lotte asked her. "You are beautiful, sexy, and so young, you can get dozens of men. Leave the pig, divorce him, run back to Warsaw and take Jonas with you."

"Why, why? I ask myself a thousand times. And the answer is I love him and I know he loves me. And I know he will tire of her and always be mine."

She moved her lips in the bathtub as she thought of her last conversation with Lotte. Lucia had told her friend she thought, in fact, Brand was no longer seeing the governess. He had neither the appetite nor the energy. He was tired these days.

Fräulein Marlow knocked on the bathroom door, which startled her for a moment.

"I have some fresh towels for you; the chambermaid did not change them yet, Frau Kruger. Should I drop them in?"

"Please do, Fräulein. Come in please."

Fräulein Marlow came into the bathroom with two fresh towels under her arm. She gathered up the dirty ones as Lucia rose up from the bathtub, her body covered with droplets of water mixed with milk. Fräulein Marlow was taken aback for a moment by her employer's graceful, sculptured body, her youthful breasts and swollen hard pink nipples. This was the first time she had seen the mistress of the house naked. She handed Lucia a towel, and Lucia bent down to study her large painted toenail. As she rose up slowly she caught Fräulein's eyes staring at her. Fräulein blushed and felt a surge of warmth between her legs. Slowly, she backed out of the bathroom, stunned and confused.

"Thank you Fräulein, that was very thoughtful of you," Lucia softly called after her. She had performed her moves deliberately, to show Fräulein that her body was beautiful and desirable and that she wasn't just another naïve housewife. She had seen envy and admiration in Fräulein's eyes, and she was content.

The following morning, Jonas was up at the crack of dawn. He was almost breathless with anticipation. He rushed to the beach to wait for Gerhardt by the breakers. He had skipped breakfast, even risking the wrath of Cook, who had prepared warm rolls, jam, fruit, and hot cocoa.

He waited and waited, hopping back and forth just beyond the waves that chewed the sand. The sun was now high in the sky, blindingly high, but Gerhardt did not appear. Perhaps he was mistaken about where they were to meet. Back and forth Jonas ran on the beach, running from jetty to jetty, but Gerhardt never came. Disappointed and heartbroken, Jonas slowly returned to the house.

Why didn't Gerhardt come? I guess he must still be angry at me, he told Lucia. Lucia was having her breakfast on the porch, and was expecting his return.

"Gerhardt must have forgotten. Do you know where he lives?" Jonas asked his mother. "Maybe something happened to him," he said with a pitiful voice. She placed her arms around her crestfallen son not knowing what to answer.

"Jonas, he will show up somewhere. Come and have breakfast with me."

Lucia knew the reason why Gerhardt had not appeared. His family, like so many others, had no doubt also forbidden Gerhardt to play with Jonas, whom they had taken to calling "the Hitler boy." And while Lucia did not know that her son had attended the youth movement at the Toppengasse Hall, Danzig was a small town, and like all small towns, nothing remains a secret for very long. Everyone in the Langfuhr crowd also knew of Brand's business association with the German firm, Luirgi Company.

Brand arrived that same day and was running off to the tennis court when Lucia intercepted him. "Please, Brand, not today. Jonas is upset because of Gerhardt. I think today you could give him some of your precious time and forget about tennis." Her voice was almost strident.

"Sit down and listen please." She gave him a detailed account of the meeting with Gerhardt and when she finished, Brand said, "Those lousy bastards!" Lucia quickly retorted, "That is what they must say about us."

"You are right, as always. I will take Jonas with me today. This will be a good time to teach him to swim." Brand felt guilty for not teaching his son to swim during the many summers in Sopot. For a long time, Jonas had been terrified of the water following an incident at the pool back when he was little. Brand and Lucia had wisely decided to back off. And then time passed. As Brand came to Sopot only on the weekends, and much of that was reserved for tennis with the Chief of Police and for business meetings, the truth was that Jonas had simply not learned. But now Brand felt that perhaps there might not be many more summers spent in Sopot. The time had come to spend more time with Lucia and his son. "Call them at the tennis court," he said, "and tell them I can't make it."

Jonas was proud of his father and loved him very much, so any time they spent together was precious. He knew Brand was a very important and busy man, and a brave person who knew a lot about many things. But he was rarely home long enough to spend any time with Jonas. Once, while Jonas was convalescing after they had returned from Berlin, he showed his son a locked-up gun collection and promised the child he would teach him how to shoot when he became just a bit older. "I am going to teach you how to defend yourself. Every man must learn that." Brand told stories about when he was a cavalry captain as Jonas sat on the edge of the chair, enthralled as Brand described some of his adventures. "And you will learn how to ride a horse in the fall," he had promised Jonas.

So when his father now suggested that he would teach him to swim, Jonas quickly stopped sulking. The boy knew, too, it was well past time he learned. Brand brought out a long fishing pole with him and telephoned the captain of his schooner to meet them by the pier.

"I thought you said we were going swimming, Papa?" Jonas was surprised they were not heading for the club pool.

"We are, but we will need the fishing pole." Jonas looked at his father bewildered.

The dock located at the long pier was crowded with pleasure boaters and fishermen lounging around, displaying the morning catch. A mild morning breeze blew in from the North Sea, moving the spotty clouds above them, and bringing with it the slight chill in the air so characteristic of the northern port.

"All right, Jonas. I will put this strap around your body with the line attached and you will get into the water, off this dock. Don't look so afraid, just jump in the water." Brand placed a double fishing line around his son's frame. "Trust me, I won't let you drown." The captain of Brand's schooner stood by, near the shore, his arms folded against his chest as he watched Jonas jump in the water, the fishing line attached to him.

"It is freezing!" Jonas screeched. Brand stood on the pier, yelling down, "Kick and crawl on the water like a lobster. Keep your head up, don't swallow the water!"

Brand pulled harder on the line to keep Jonas above the water. The onlookers were amused that the boy showed no fear and they applauded, shouting, "Bravo, bravo, keep kicking, move your arms out and in," which gave Jonas even more courage. The captain stood over him as Jonas gracefully moved his body nearer to the pier. And when he felt confident that Jonas could negotiate the water successfully, Brand slyly detached the line as Jonas was swimming. He stayed easily afloat until he realized there was nothing holding him up. Afraid to do otherwise, he continued to do the crawl, and there was more applause. He started to swim out to sea, but then the captain wisely directed him back toward the shore and escorted him out of the water.

Brand knew the older the beginning swimmer, the more

afraid they were. He had seen adults larger, older, and stronger than his fourteen-year-old son, flail and thrash. Now he was so proud of the boy that Brand pulled a towel around Jonas' shivering body and hugged him. Jonas thought that was wonderful. His father rarely hugged him or kissed him anymore. Jonas could even smell his father's aftershave lotion, which he loved. He had never felt more secure.

"Wait 'til I tell your mother, and your governess. Will they be proud! But remember, you are never to go swimming alone. Not until you become a stronger swimmer. The ocean waters can fool even the most experienced swimmers. Either I or the captain must be with you. Understood?"

"I really did swim, didn't I?" Jonas laughed with joy. "Please, let me go in again by myself."

"Tomorrow, Jonas, we will go again," Brand nodded.

So often his father had made plans with him but something urgent always came about and it did not come to pass. Jonas was tempted to remind his father about all the times he had not kept his word. Uncle Herman always kept his word.

Perhaps this time it would be different.

Now he loved his father even more because he cared what could happen to him. The other men standing by congratulated Jonas: "Brand Kruger, when he does something he does it – with no pussy-footing around. That boy has courage." They returned to the house and Lucia also gave her son a warm hug and kissed him on his cheek. For now the disappointment of not meeting Gerhardt left his mind.

"My goodness, how quickly he grows," Lucia said, "But his skin is red as a lobster's."

"He swam like one," Brand added.

"We will have to get some soothing lotion on soon or he'll have a bad night."

After supper, Brand and Lucia went to the casino, and Jonas

went upstairs to his bedroom to use the telescope. The governess came into the room with a bottle of lotion.

"Jonas, you know what we have to do now?"

"Just a few minutes more, please. I want to find the North Star. Father said that if I find the Big Dipper and then the brightest of those stars, I will have found the North Star, the one sailors use for navigation when they are lost." He pointed to the sky. "See? Look, there it is!"

The governess peered through the telescope. "It does look like the North Star. Smart boy. Now, come," she added. "Let's go to work before you are up all night feeling like you are on fire."

Jonas took his shirt off and she gently rubbed the scented oil across his shoulders. It smarted just a little at first.

"Feel good?" she asked softly, enjoying this very much.

"Yes." He shivered not sure if it was the cooling balm or his governess' soft touch he was responding to.

"Now, let's get the rest of you," she said in a voice at once imperious and casual. "Take off those pants and shoes. You have had a bad day not seeing Gerhardt but you did learn how to swim, so it turned out to be a good day."

He pulled his pants down around his shoes and stood naked before her. There was a slight breeze in the room; it was as soothing and provocative as her gentle rubbing hands. The governess, dressed in a long skirt and summer blouse said, "I had better take this stuff off because this oil will ruin everything." She removed her outer garments and to Jonas' shock, she wore nothing underneath.

The oil slick on his torso grew slowly, tantalizing until a finger on the hand rubbing his belly barely touched his stiff member. Then another finger. Then the whole hand.

"Massages are the most relaxing thing just before going to sleep," she said in a controlled voice, as if lecturing. For a moment she remembered Lucia's look of triumph the other morn-

ing as she rose from her bath. Or was it disdain? No matter.
"People have enjoyed them for thousands of years, you know,"
the beautiful Fräulein continued, her voice now as soft as a whisper. One cool hand was in the small of his back, pushing him
forward. The other, in the shape of a fist, surrounded his penis,
and moved rhythmically up and back. Jonas' knees were buck-
ling. She understood the situation very well.

Chapter Twelve

$\mathcal{D}$OWN BY THE WATERFRONT, Brand's 100-foot schooner was being painted and refurbished under the supervision of Captain Kowalsky. Its luxurious cabins slept six and were outfitted with a full dining room, complete kitchen, and darkly gleaming bar. The schooner belonged to Brand's Baltic Kohlen Company and was primarily used for fishing and entertaining. Sometimes on weekends, she had been sailed to the Isle of Usedom, but this was now restricted. This was where Captain Walter Dornberger had been assigned to begin construction of a secret base for the building of rockets – Peenemunde. If Brand had known that his coal was being used to help build the V-8 rockets destined to destroy Europe, he would hardly have been so quick to deal with the Luirgi Company. Perhaps Brand was not greedy, as he was often accused, but merely naïve.

Each morning, Jonas walked with Lucia along the splendid white beach. He gave up looking for Gerhardt and his father did keep his promise to take him swimming the next day and every weekend after. Most weekends were spent on the schooner. Jonas did not feel so lonely or abandoned as he did in the beginning of the summer. And when his Warsaw cousins visited that July, filling his days with picnics, races, and digging for crabs, there was little time left to read.

The captain of the schooner was the tallest man Jonas had ever met. Were it not for his comforting smile and those twinkling blue eyes, he would have petrified the boy. He had large bushy red eyebrows and a full shock of red hair. When he smiled, as he did often, the captain displayed a line of crooked stained teeth; and his arms were tattooed with weird creatures and exotic serpents with endless tongues. Captain Kowalsky had been commander of Brand's schooner from the beginning. He had never married but claimed, without fanfare, to have fathered dozens of "little cannibals" throughout the Pacific, every one sporting red bushy eyebrows.

Jonas and his boy cousins, Samuel, David and even young Benjamin, were given paintbrushes and assigned to different little jobs, which they performed well. There was always a break, a rest period when they and the captain sat in the galley around the thick wood table drinking lemonade, and it was then that he told the boys wonderful adventure stories about his trips to Samoa and Fiji and Africa. Now the books by Joseph Conrad that Jonas had read came alive. The captain described the Galapagos Islands, where Darwin did so much of his work, and the natives of Bali, especially the gorgeous women. Jonas could smell and see the color of the islands, almost touch them. The captain's descriptions were so vivid that Jonas felt transported to each place he described. He, too, would someday go to sea, he told the captain, and might even write stories like Joseph Conrad did.

On one afternoon after Lucia's family had gone home, when the captain was not aboard and only a single member of the crew was, Jonas roamed freely, opening all the drawers and cabinets, looking for precious secrets. Jonas had long before decided that every place had a secret hideaway which waited only to be discovered. One door opened to a large pantry closet crowded with provisions and cylinders of water. Another door, located by the pilot's room, had a large black lock dangling from it, but the lock wasn't closed.

Jonas removed the lock and gently pushed open the door. Inside were dozens of rifles, guns, ammunition, flares, and knives. It was an arsenal. Jonas picked up one of the small handguns, and twirled it in his hand as he had seen Tom Mix do at the Arts Cinema in Danzig. If only he had a gun like this, no one would dare fool with him, not even the toughest of the tough guys. And, he fantasized, one day, when he became a German Youth leader, they would allow him to carry the gun in a holster. Fräulein Marlow would surely approve, but not his mother, father, or Uncle Herman, and certainly not the Rabbi. Jonas could sneak the gun out and it would never be missed.

All these thoughts danced through his mind as he teased the trigger and looked down the barrel. Suddenly, he heard the loud trampling of feet, and he jumped back, swiftly replacing the gun on the shelf just as Captain Kowalsky burst into the room.

"Jonas, my God! Those guns are all loaded! Don't ever, ever touch a gun, because it can go off and blow away your head!" The captain was so icily angry that he scared Jonas to tears.

"Come, up on the upper deck! Now!" he ordered. He took the small handgun Jonas had held. "I will show you what can happen." Kowalsky escorted the frightened boy up the narrow stairs to the deck, firmly pushing him in the small of the back.

"I will teach you how to use a gun if your father agrees; but for now, stand behind the wheelhouse, watch carefully, and learn."

The captain barely touched the trigger. The sudden report made Jonas flinch. Once again, the captain fired into the sea, emptying the five remaining chambers so quickly it sounded like a huge explosion.

"You see, Jonas, how little it takes to fire a revolver! You could have shot yourself in the head."

Suddenly, flying the flag of Danzig and the swastika, a German gunboat approached.

"We are coming aboard, Captain," came bellowing through the megaphone.

Jonas moved close to the captain, as two German naval officers in starched whites climbed the ladder and walked smartly toward the pair.

"Good afternoon, Captain Kowalsky. Why the shooting? A jealous husband, perhaps?"

"Very funny, Wolfgang," the captain said to one of the officers. "This is Brand Kruger's son, Jonas. I was merely demonstrating the dangers of a loaded revolver. I think he learned a lesson."

Both officers smiled. They had been teenage boys once and they immediately understood. "Fixing up the boat, Kowalsky?"

"Well, you know Kruger. He wants to go fish, cruise over to the islands, and have parties, special parties, I think. It is rumored that he is having guests from Berlin this summer, important ones," Kowalsky lowered his voice, "Perhaps even the most important guest of all."

"We have already heard. We will be providing extra surveillance. There are some radicals – freedom-fighters – they call themselves, on the prowl, looking to pirate some ships. So keep a watchful eye. This ship, after all, is a prize. Tell Herr Kruger not to sail out of reach, yes?"

"Come aboard tonight, Wolfgang. We'll have some beer and you can bring a friend. Better yet, since you're an adventurer, I will find someone nice who will know how to appreciate a distinguished naval officer."

Jonas stared at this Wolfgang, and at the polished black holster at his side. He was very grateful that the man was a friend of his captain.

"Why not, it's boring as hell out here. Who can resist an adventure on the high seas, even in the harbor? Tonight, for late supper, yes?"

Sopot, besides being famous for its resplendent casino and the longest boardwalk in Europe, was noted for its grand concerts and lavish operas. In the past, many of the greatest musicians had performed at the Sopot Music Festival. Now, only Wilhelm Furtwängler and his ilk, those sympathetic to Hitler, would conduct. Many of the others, like Artur Schnabel and Bruno Walter, had already left for the U.S. or England. Now only Wagnerian operas were permitted, those magnificent tributes to blood and race. On this beautiful August night, *The Flying Dutchman* was to be performed. Brand had eight excellent tickets for his family and guests. He decided that this would be a good opera for Jonas to see.

Everyone was dressed formally, beautifully, including the governess, who was breathtaking in a white gown, a Nordic princess. Her charge was dressed in a starched shirt, dark trousers, and a blue jacket. The governess had combed his long brown hair back and had generously applied pomade to make it glisten.

"Now you look like my gentleman." She kissed him on the brow.

Brand was elegant and confident, and he kissed Lucia on her slender neck. "You are the most beautiful woman in Sopot and tonight is going to be a very special night."

She wore a splendid sapphire necklace, and it sparkled when they descended the staircase of their summer home. Their guests turned to look at the brilliant couple. Among them were the Prince and Bill, who had arrived at the villa earlier in the day for a week's beachside holiday, and applauded the majestic entrance.

"What beautiful people," the Prince said. "We will all be the envy of the opera. They will say, 'There is the grandest family in all of Danzig.'"

Uncle Herman was still in his baggy pants and ruffled shirt. One sometimes wondered if he ever really undressed at all before going to bed.

"Herman, you are not dressed," Lucia scolded.

"I hate the opera. Lina and I will break the casino tonight," referring to his current paramour. This one was a redhead. "You people are too fancy for a poor peddler like me."

"Herman purposely buys his clothing from the war veteran's outlet, so he can look like a pauper," Lucia whispered wickedly to their other guests.

"Not really so. I like sausage and dark beer, and simple clothing, what the real people like."

"And loose women with long red stockings and hair under their arms," Lucia finished. Her brother chuckled and turned to Jonas.

"Is this really my nephew? He is getting too grown up to be my nephew. Ah, Fräulein, you are doing a wonderful job. You are teaching him well, preparing him for life. Soon the young women will fall at his feet, and I am certain he will know exactly what to do. Right, Jonas? You'll know what to do?"

Jonas snuck a look at Fräulein Marlow. Every boy has a secret, but usually he is able to share it with a friend. He wished he could tell someone about what he and his governess did when they were alone. This summer had quietly moved their cuddling and his tentative explorations to a new phase that felt frank and unabashed. Sometimes he had a feeling Uncle Herman knew because he was always giving him a knowing look. Jonas had read somewhere that masturbating causes mental illness if you do it too much, but he had never felt better.

"Right, Uncle," Jonas laughed, his face glowing red. The governess smiled slyly back at him. She caressed the cascade of her long blond hair and pulled her head back, a goddess posing for countless admirers.

On their way to the opera house, Brand explained the story of the Flying Dutchman to Jonas. "The captain of a mysterious ship is doomed to sail forever. He is in love with the young maiden on shore."

A full moon bedecked the open-air opera house set in a large park surrounded by oak trees and gardens. The sky and the sea were the natural background as the accursed ship rolled silently onto the stage. The elegantly dressed audience applauded the spectacle in sheer delight. Jonas, sitting next to his governess, was absolutely enchanted. Brand was at her other side, Lucia at his right. Bill and the Prince, remarkably handsome in beautifully tailored summer dinner jackets, sat in the center aisle. They, too, were enthralled by the evening and the stage sets.

By the second act, Jonas began to lose interest in the opera and moved uncomfortably in his folding chair. The governess tugged at his trousers and whispered to him. "Stop moving so much. Be good and I will let you touch me tonight."

Jonas broke from his reverie when the sailors on the ship began shouting, "Yo, Ho, Yo, Ho," and his body returned to normal. Now that he was older, his erection sometimes occurred without provocation. When the weather turned colder, he could wear his lederhosen, and then it would not be so obvious. And now that Fräulein had taught him how to touch himself to get relief, it made his life bearable. But would he go insane from all of that? It was on his mind constantly. "It will stunt your growth, grow hair on your palms, and make you die early," he'd heard from the boys at school. He was already taller than most of them. He looked at the palms of his right hand as the Flying Dutchman looked at the picture of his love.

Brand watched the governess out of the corner of his eye as he listened to the passionate music. He had not come to her bed since before Jonas' illness, and his appetite for her and her rough sexual passion had clearly waned. The danger and risk of having her had once been as intoxicating to him as closing a big deal. And she was still so chillingly beautiful.

He sighed. It is not easy to relinquish power and money, even now. Or a mistress, especially a mistress living in your own house who was also, as he was now certain, a Nazi. How could he manage it? What should he do now? How long could he continue in this fatuous way with them, who held more cards now than he, avoiding decisions that could have most unpleasant consequences?

Brand held Lucia's hand and closed his eyes. He tried to concentrate on the music, but his teeming brain would simply not allow it. He thought, in this peaceful surrounding, it is hard to imagine that right at this moment in Berlin a madman is convincing the German people to arm and conquer the world, and to rid the land of the Jews.

But the madman was making Brand even richer, he had to admit. He was shipping his coal through the new all-weather port to Germany. Now that he was on top of his trade, his wealth increased by leaps and bounds. Although the political picture was grim, Brand felt confident that business would go on as usual; it always did. Yet, there was always that uneasy feeling, a part of his brain that urged him to sell and run while there was still time. He opened his eyes for a moment and spotted the governess now stroking his son's hand, which left him with an odd sickly feeling in his stomach. He decided that she was only being nice and there was nothing more to it. Or was there? And had his own recklessness brought it on?

The Prince and Bill sat together, completely immersed in the beautiful music and gorgeous scenery. They had returned to Danzig at Bill's insistence, together, and had decided that in the fall they would leave Danzig together, and live in Paris while Bill studied at the Sorbonne.

The music at one moment became monumentally powerful and strong, and then came the tenderness, the sweetness of life, love, devotion, and sacrifice. Life is like Wagner, the Prince thought, as he looked at the only real love he had ever known. An unlikely lover, this American who was so unsophisticated and yet so caring; so naïve and decent and unaware that a world was about to change. He, too, had to make decisions. He did not have enough strength now to make the change he'd promised Bill. He did not want to luxuriate on the Left Bank of Paris, and let the rest of the world go to hell. He'd lied to Bill, sweet Bill, innocent Bill, who should have stayed in Columbus, married a nice university girl, and never have let his real self surface.

Bill had taken such risks for him, risks that overwhelmed the Prince and flooded him with joy, and with worry. Bill's family was not taking his ruse of further study funded by an architectural patron lying down. They had ordered him back, the political environment providing a convenient shield for their growing impatience. Bill's oldest brother had been dispatched, in fact, to bring Bill home – only to cancel his crossing upon hearing that Germany had become an increasingly inhospitable place, even to Midwestern Americans.

Instead, the Prince would take care of Bill. There would be no Paris. Rather, he would take Bill to Le Havre and give him a ticket on the *Liberty* back to New York. He imagined Bill sailing to his freedom in a beautiful stateroom, the Prince sacrificing his own true love in order to save him. It was an act, a plan, worthy of a grand opera itself.

"I will meet you in New York, my darling, I promise, and then we'll find an island where war or politics or other people will never touch us." That was the prepared speech. Bill had to leave this brutal, nefarious, horrible country. The German people were disappointments, brutes to allow this to happen. He squeezed Bill's hand one more time. His intuition was that something terrible was going to happen.

Jonas, in spite of the governess' titillating hand briefly on his, was becoming so bored from the endless-seeming performance that he decided to go to the men's room to at least take a break from it. As he turned abruptly towards the rear, he noticed a line of men, young men dressed in brown uniforms, carrying clubs. More and more of them were gathering there along the periphery of the park, like an army of hornets. Jonas recognized them.

"Look, Father, at all the people standing in the back." Brand took one look and, instinctively sensing imminent danger, pulled Jonas and Lucia from their seats in one swift motion, sweeping them away from the theater, shouting to the Prince and Bill to leave at once.

Before Lucia could even protest, they were heading for a large oak tree. The orchestra played even more loudly, resoundingly, as the Flying Dutchman came on stage with his men. This was the signal. The men in their brown uniforms swept down upon the crowd shouting and screaming, coarse and frenzied: "Heil Hitler! Germany is the future! Danzig must unite!" Brand recognized the man shouting into the megaphone. "The Jews are our misfortune. They must be destroyed." It was Carl Beyer, a man who had been one of Brand's employees ten years ago. Incompetent and argumentative, he had been let go. Now he had his day. He wore the uniform of an officer.

They used their clubs freely, striking the shocked and bewildered crowd, now streaming from their seats. The young thugs ran down the aisle to the front, even as Bill and the Prince were edging away.

Jonas and the governess and Lucia were standing behind the large tree when panic swept the spectators. One of the men rushed towards the Prince and struck him on the shoulder yelling, "No fairies in the Third Reich!"

Bill, suddenly enraged, picked up the folding chair he had been sitting on and swung it over his head as the men tried again to strike the Prince, who had stumbled across the aisle. Jonas watched in terror as events unfolded in front of him. Brand yelled at his son, "Lie down, lie down flat on the ground! Don't move!"

Furtwangler, the conductor, turned towards the screaming audience, shocked and crestfallen, and walked off the podium while the singers and musicians ran aimlessly every which way in this bedlam. The night scenery collapsed. The noises were unbearable. Jonas covered his eyes, but not before one of the hoodlums smashed a beer bottle over Bill's head and then clubbed his face hard. Blood spurted from the American's head, a terrible red fountain. Bill tumbled over the chairs, unconscious.

"Father, Bill is hurt! He is bleeding!" Jonas screamed frantically. The crowd tried to disperse, but instead they trampled each other, rampaging cattle in evening dress, crying and cursing. Brand rushed recklessly back into the audience trying to push people aside, away from the seething mass, but it was useless. The panic now created its own momentum. The Prince had fallen and was lying somewhere beneath the crowd. Brand shoved the people aside, desperately trying to reach Bill.

"There is an injured man on the ground! Let me through, for heaven's sake. Please, please!"

Brand pulled off his torn jacket and swung at the faceless bodies blocking his path. Jonas and Lucia watched, panic-stricken, as Brand struggled to get to the fallen American.

Sirens! Dozens of policemen came running into the crowd, and then the Brownshirts disappeared as swiftly as they had appeared only minutes earlier.

Brand stood over the body of Bill, screaming for an ambulance. He saw the Prince looking pleadingly down at Bill, holding his bleeding head in his hands, sobbing like a lost child. Jonas began to cry too, as he watched a grown man burst into tears. He had never seen a mature man cry. Jonas' world suddenly vanished before his eyes. He glanced angrily at the governess, seeing no longer a princess, but a witch dressed in a brown uniform. For the few weeks before he became ill, he had begun to have some doubts about his boy scouts, but they swiftly vanished after the governess overcame his resolve by reinforcing his father's pleasure at the fine work the scouts would be doing for the people of Danzig. "After all, your father is an important man helping Germany become strong. Soon, you will surprise him and tell him that you have been also doing your part and he will be as proud of you as I am."

Jonas heard his father whisper to Lucia, "They've killed Bill." He had never really gotten to know the young American, but Bill had always been nice to him, and now he was dead. And he realized he could have been one of the boys in the crowd.

There comes a time in a boy's life when his world of dreams and make believe simply vanishes. The tooth fairy, Santa Claus, and the bogey man, all somehow disappear. For Jonas the make-believe world was now gone. He saw his former friends beat and stampede an innocent young man to death.

The crowd opened a path for a stretcher; the Prince followed behind, a walking corpse immersed in the darkest of nightmares. That night, he, too, lost all his illusions and dreams. The serpent was upon him, gnawing at his soul.

A wind was blowing over the deserted beach; dark clouds filled the leaden sky. The beach was covered, as every morning, with hundreds of small and large beautiful amber stones swept in by the tide. Amber stones, the Baltic Sea trademark that few collected because they were as common as the seashells. When he was a child, Jonas had collected a handful and brought them proudly back for his governess, who knew they were worthless and placed them in a drawer to be secretly discarded later. Jonas nonetheless liked to hold and stroke their smooth surfaces, and to hold them up to the light and watch the sun shine through them. What mysteries they must enclose inside. Carrying his small satchel, Astor walking at his side, Jonas as recently as that very morning tested the water and had randomly bent down to look at an arrangement of stones. Gone now was any interest in taking home a prize. The shouts of the boys in town, "Kill the Jews!" still rang in his ears, and the blood spurting from Bill's lifeless body remained vividly, horribly, in his mind. It all made him shudder and tremble.

So in the immediate aftermath of the tragedy, Jonas kept to himself, refusing to eat or speak to anyone. He felt betrayed by his governess. In vain, she tried to persuade him that the night was an aberration.

"Those were just very bad people. They are not the same ones at the youth organization," she pleaded. "It was an accident, Jonas. The New Germany is not going to hurt anyone, I promise." But she was not able to convince him, perhaps because she now had her own reservations about the new Germany.

"It was not an accident," Jonas answered. "I saw one of the boys purposely hit Bill with a bottle. Bill was only trying to protect the Prince. The police did not even arrest the bully. If my father had not pulled us out we could have all been killed, like Bill. You, even."

Jonas found an isolated spot on the beach and made certain there was no one in sight. None of the new, non-Jewish friends he befriended that summer after it became evident his old playmates had dropped him had arrived yet. He sat down on the moist sand and removed a small shovel from his satchel, one he had often used as a little boy to build marvelous castles, complete with roads and bridges. The castle he wanted to live in with his Fräulein and Astor.

He rapidly shoveled a deep hole, Astor looking on curiously. Once satisfied that the hole suited his purpose, he opened the satchel, which contained a book, his magic stones, a crab shell, a small bracelet he had found on the beach which he had intended to give his governess, and his old Nazi armband and uniform. One by one he removed each item from the bag and stuffed them into the hole. He quickly refilled it, stamping down the sand and brushing his foot over the spot.

"Now, don't dig here, Astor, ever again! We don't want anyone to find this, or ever know that I was once one of those terrible boys."

Astor looked up, pushed his nose into the boy's body, as if he understood. Jonas ran off towards the water, relieved, free, his nasty secret buried forever.

"Hey, Jonas," he heard someone yelling. Three boys and one girl came running down toward the water.

"What were you burying?" one of them asked.

"I wasn't burying anything." Jonas' face became crimson. "I was looking for treasures."

"Did you hear that they had a riot at the concert hall last night and that one person was killed?"

"I know. I was there and saw it all," Jonas said as the young people gathered round.

"Are you telling stories?"

"No," he said softly.

"I can tell he is telling the truth," the girl in the crowd said. She was already fifteen and the oldest in the group.

"Won't you tell us everything, Jonas, please?"

"Let's go to the cave, and we can sit there while he tells us about it."

Fräulein Marlow was watching the scene from the top window of her bedroom. She was glad that at least Jonas had found some new friends and they were with him now so that he was no longer brooding alone. She watched as they crept toward the caves under the boardwalk. Last night's violence had unnerved even her. What was intended to be an act of harassment had turned into a brutal atrocity. Now the battle lines were clearly drawn, and she no longer felt secure and comfortable in this household.

Lucia and Brand accompanied the Prince back to Danzig, with the body of the dead American. Uncle Herman stayed behind with Jonas. They helped the Prince arrange the grotesque details necessary to ship the remains back to Ohio. The German news wires reported that the death of the American resulted from being struck by a hit-and-run driver. The Prince and Brand concurred that it was useless to say otherwise and cause even more pain to Bill's grieving parents. They would soon enough learn the truth.

Lucia marveled at how controlled and even emotionless the Prince seemed, while she, at the very mention of Bill's name, could not restrain her tears. She searched that handsome face she knew so well for a sign of any anguish, but found none; instead, there was a mask, cold and expressionless, a death mask.

Chapter Thirteen

THE NAZIFICATION OF DANZIG, underway for years, was now complete. Jewish children were no longer permitted to attend school during the day, and so Jewish parents formed their own school, under the direction of Emmanual Echt. This special school was on the Helligstrasse, the very street celebrated for the birth of the German philosopher, Arthur Schopenhauer, and it was not without savage irony that some of the parents of these "special" students recalled that the great man would have viewed the unbelievable madness as, in his words, "mere phantasmagoria of [his] brain."

All books by Jewish authors were removed from the public schools. The only music tolerated was by Wagner, Bach, and Mozart. Mendelssohn and Mahler were prohibited, having been born Jews. Any business owned by Jews was confiscated; Jewish bank officers were fired; Jewish stores were boycotted, posted with a yellow Star of David to identify them as places to be avoided. Brownshirts roamed the streets like hungry wolf packs, provoking, attacking, humiliating. Few Jews were left in Danzig, perhaps some five hundred. The other eight thousand had fled to any place that would take them. The doors of the United States were closed now. How easy it was even for the idolized

Roosevelt to shut his eyes and ears and hope that everything would somehow return to normal? Hitler proposed that the Jews all find a homeland in Madagascar. There was no way to get to the moon in 1938.

The Kruger family was one of the few permitted to remain unmolested in Danzig as Baltic Kohlen was simply too important to the Third Reich. The Krugers, and Hitler's mother's physicians, and hundreds of other Jews deemed essential, stayed on in Germany, their blood less important than the German need for them. These were "cleaner" Jews! Lunacy triumphant.

Three years after Bill Harrington's death, the Prince was now an officer in the SS, a ReichFührer. In this capacity he was holding a reception for Goebbels and Ribbentrop at the exclusive men's business club in Danzig. Although the club was totally restricted by this time, Brand was a notable exception and occasionally permitted to lunch there with the Prince, Max Schiller, and Paul Richter of the Danzig Police.

Metchnik refused to set foot in the club. Brand was invited to attend the reception, but the Prince warned Brand not to come. "Accept the invitation," he told his friend, "then send word that there was a crisis that needed your presence."

One day before the scheduled event, the Prince met with Jan Goldberg, the owner of Café des Artistes, where Bill had lunched with Lucia in the early days. Jan's eyes were still intense, his face more drawn than it used to be. "I know Hess is your old friend," Jan told him, "but you should have invited him also. We will never get this chance again. Anyway, after the dessert is served, three waiters will arrive with champagne. You are to slip into the bathroom and wait there until your butler comes to get you. He will escort you out, and away."

Hess had given the Prince an alternative: "Either you join

the Führer, or you give up all your titles and your holdings, and leave Germany forever, in one piece. More I cannot do for you, I'm sorry."

Being on the Reichstag staff, the Prince thought as a reasonable man, that in his own way he could do something to scotch the madness that was rising like a monster from hell. He even agreed to help Goldberg and his small group of patriots who were planning to assassinate the Nazi leadership and to establish a new government.

A long line of Mercedes and BMWs gathered before the Men's Club as SS soldiers dressed in their intimidating black uniforms emerged with Joseph Goebbels, Minister of Propaganda, a thin, tiny man with rat eyes, and with the tall stately Von Ribbentrop, the Foreign Minister. Goebbels and Ribbentrop were dressed in dazzling white uniforms. They entered the club in high spirits. The Prince greeted them with an affable smile.

As they were lunching and toasting the Führer, Goebbels whispered to the Prince, "I thought you invited the special Jew," he said.

"He telephoned and said that he had a crisis with one of the barges."

"Good, he doesn't belong here. What was the crisis anyway? Did some of the herrings rot?" He guffawed at his own joke. "You know, by the way, how pleased we are that you are so close to the Jew. I hear he lives very well, that thanks to his barges he leads a life of refined tastes. Soon, very soon, we will send him and his family away to a vacation in a far-off resort where he won't enjoy his luxuries." Goebbels gave the Prince a devilish grin, exposing his crooked teeth.

The dessert was served and the Prince excused himself from the table, as planned. He waited in the bathroom for the sound of gunfire, his heart pounding. Ten minutes later, the door suddenly opened and Goebbels walked in.

"You looked pale at the table, Prince. How are you?"

"I am fine," the Prince said, fighting to keep his tone even and wondering what had happened. "Just too much rich food for so early in the day, my dear friend. Come, we are all waiting to toast you."

The following morning the *Judenblatt*, the only Jewish daily newspaper the Nazis still tolerated, for reasons never really understood, announced in bold type that Jan Goldberg and five other men had been shot dead after a conspiracy was uncovered to kill the Prince and the special visitors from Berlin.

Jonas' life had changed drastically. His large playroom was converted into a classroom. There was a school desk and a large blackboard. At his parents' insistence, the old Rabbi continued to give him religious instruction and he attended the Jewish school from five to eight each evening. He had no choice. But Jonas was grateful to be able to continue some of his education which he supplemented with the large volumes of original editions in his family's library. He spent hours climbing on the movable ladder, removing from the shelves more and more books by the great writers of the past to read, especially at night. His governess spied on him as he sat by the long mahogany table with an opened book in front of him underneath the Tiffany lamp. When Jonas went to bed after he bid his parents goodnight, he locked the door of his bedroom. During the day he tried to take little notice of the Fräulein, who made every effort to provoke him, and he succeeded. In fact, he barely spoke to her, feeling ashamed and remorseful at having ever allowed himself to become emotionally and physically enticed by her.

Stefan's Park, across from his balcony, was converted into training grounds: barbed wire, trenches, tents, young men in brown marching, and target practice – the quotidian scene in

1938. Jonas recognized with some guilt and revulsion many of the young faces, and he was in constant fear that one of them would call him by name. How, after all, could he explain that to his parents? Every time Jonas left the house he expected some of the boys to engage him in conversation. He lived with this terrible secret, dreading imminent exposure and shame. He may have buried the relics of the Nazi regime in the sand, but he could not ever erase the sounds and images of his own participation.

Jonas was in the library waiting for the Rabbi to arrive. Astor sat waiting at the trolley stop. As soon as the Rabbi climbed down from the tram, Astor jumped on him, licking his beard, and then escorted the old gentleman back to the house, the young Brownshirts looking on, wary of the large dog. Brand had offered the Rabbi the use of the chauffeured limousine, which he refused. Lucia served the Rabbi tea in a tall glass with a slice of lemon floating on top with a lump of sugar, which slowly dissolved in the mouth. There were also open-faced sandwiches of deviled eggs and smoked salmon. Astor stood by watching, waiting for the crumbs to fall from the old man's white beard.

First they read from the Torah, and then the Rabbi lectured Jonas on topics about Jewish history and the role the Jews had played in Danzig.

"The Jews of Danzig originally came from Lithuania, early in the tenth century, and they established a most important community. It was they who built one of the synagogues still standing today, the Central Synagogue.

"The Prince was a descendant of the Black Knight, one of the Teutonic Knights. Although they were against the Jews, they allowed them to form guilds, and the Jews prospered, as did Danzig. But in 1600 they were expelled until 100 years later, when the Swedes invaded Danzig and the Jews were allowed to return, with the provision that they not worship publicly.

"Now, three hundred years later, it is the same story. Once again we are persecuted, but we will prevail now, as we always have. Your father thinks it will be better soon, and that is why he desires to stay. Perhaps, with God's help, your father will be right. Whenever we are free again, it will be because of our education, tradition, and family life; because we are the chosen people of the Great Book, the Torah, guardians of the moral and ethical values that helped shape the world."

After the Rabbi finished his lecture, Lucia gave him a handsome amount of money for his tutoring, Astor escorted him back to the trolley car and Jonas had to leave for school.

Jonas hated going to school at night. All his friends were gone, except for Gerhardt, whose family still refused to let him associate with Jonas. Having no friends, he spent most of his time reading and being alone. He read *The Odyssey* by Homer and felt as Odysseus did at being drawn in by the Sirens. Fräulein Marlow felt Jonas' resentment when he looked at her with angry eyes.

It was early November, 1938. Jonas took his satchel with his books, put on his leather jacket, and waited outside with Astor for the chauffeur who would take him to school. He reflected deeply on what the Rabbi had said and, with his next birthday just weeks away, wished with all his heart that his father would also leave Danzig. While he waited, he watched the Brownshirts strolling with their parents across the street. They carried shopping bags stuffed with newspapers and rags, and when they saw Jonas they started to laugh, sticking out their tongues, shouting, "Eenie minee mouse, a Jew is nothing but a filthy louse."

Three teenage boys suddenly deserted their parents, ran across the street to Jonas, and started spitting into his face. One of them carried pepper in his handkerchief and threw it at Jonas' eyes. He was blinded momentarily, his eyes tearing and smarting. The boys and their parents found the scene amusing. Jonas took off his leather knapsack and began to swing it like a sling at their heads just as he once had at Gerhardt. But now here was a real enemy. He suddenly thought of David and Goliath and somehow gathered the courage and strength with which to overcome his abject terror. The boys, in turn, surrounded him like animals, rabid dogs waiting for the kill.

"Kill the Jew!" He heard those familiar words and in a rage, thrust his fist into a face, making it bleed. They threw him to the ground. Astor attacked the three teens, savagely. The parents now stopped laughing and came running to gather up their sons, but not before Astor took a measure of revenge, inflicting large and bleeding gashes on several boys' arms and legs.

"Get them, Astor! Kill them! Kill the Nazis!"

The teenage boys and their parents ran; it was their turn to feel terror. If Jonas had not yelled for Astor to return, he would have pursued the vermin to the ends of the earth.

Although at that moment Jonas felt little pain from the thrashing, there was a deeper pain born of bitterness and rage. "Good boy, Astor! You taught them a lesson!"

He walked slowly back to the house, Astor following behind. If his father and the captain had not given him some basic instruction in self-defense following that terrible incident in Sopot, he would surely have been seriously hurt, to say the least.

"If ever you are attacked by the hoodlums," they had said, "find a wall to lean against so they can't attack you from behind. Kick them in the balls, and go for the eyes." There was no wall, but he had done well.

At the indoor Stadt tennis courts, Brand was in the middle of the second set with the chief of police, Paul Richter, when he learned that Jonas had been in a fight on the street.

Paul had been a friend for many years. Each Christmas and

Easter, Brand sent over presents for his family and special bonuses for his extra diligence in keeping the barges and the Baltic Kohlen offices from being vandalized. The police inspector was an elegant Prussian, descended from a long line of police. His grandfather had saved one of the Hapsburgs from being assassinated in Sopot in 1902.

Much to Paul's dismay, his entire police force was gradually taken over by the Nazis, and he was forced to join the party or lose his job.

"Get a bodyguard for Jonas," he told Brand as they hustled swiftly from the tennis palladium. "Quickly get to the families and make them an offer; otherwise, we will be forced to kill Astor. They will demand it."

Brand, that very next afternoon, went to the homes of the three boys, paid for all the medical bills and gave each parent a few thousand guldens as well as one year's supply of coal for their furnaces; with winter coming, a gesture not without real value. Each boy also received a thousand guldens. Brand knew his friend was right; that if he did not swiftly compensate these savages, Astor would indeed be put to death by the police.

In one of the homes Brand saw dozens of shopping bags stuffed with newspapers, exactly as Jonas had described it to him, and as he drove he saw dozens of youths on the street with their parents, many of them young children, each carrying bags the same way, as if they were going to a party. He stopped at the Prince's home, next door.

"What is going on?" he asked. "The whole town is gone crazy. All the children are collecting newspapers and stuffing them into bags."

"Perhaps it is a new craze," the Prince shrugged it off. "Young people, what can I say? And so, my friend, tonight I will come to your home and I will bring the daily paper – and some Polish ham and herring in a brown bag."

It was the first formal dinner party that Lucia had given since Bill died. No one, frankly had had the appetite for it. But tonight they were celebrating. It was Lucia and Brand's eighteenth wedding anniversary. In the Jewish tradition, eighteen was an important number. It stood for luck. Brand had insisted they mark the occasion.

Still, it was a sedate evening. The world begged for a sedate evening, although Lucia insisted that everyone be in formal wear. It was their usual set. Uncle Herman was accompanied by a voluptuous new girlfriend, a secretary who worked at Gestapo headquarters. The Prince came alone, as he always did now. Still he was dressed to perfection and Lucia seated him to her left, just like old times. Tonight she wore a white gown with a splendid diamond necklace around her fine neck, an anniversary present from Brand. They drank champagne from beautiful Baccarat stemware. The governess, sitting next to Jonas, drank too. Jonas was quiet, even solemn. His face was swollen, covered with black and blue marks; his arms and body ached like a boxer's days after a fight.

The Prince raised his glass and toasted to Jonas. "The first to resist and fight back, but not the last. He is our Joe Louis defeating Max Schmelling."

Everyone applauded. Lucia sprang up from her seat and planted a loving tender kiss on her son's bruised and blushing cheeks. The Prince was on his fifth glass of champagne, and only later regretted making his sympathies so obvious to the governess and the secretary.

From behind her champagne flute, Fräulein Marlow sighed and thought about how many times she had sat at the Krugers' table as she did tonight. She was not without nostalgia for those absent like the young, unlucky American, the mignon, and for those now grown, seemingly beyond her reach and allure. The governess failed to seduce Jonas into the Hitler Youth, but she did beguile and seduce him. Passion is hardly selective. In spite of Jonas' resentment, the governess had lured him, trapped him, imprisoned him. She had taken him from childhood to adolescence and into the exciting and exotic world of carnal love to meet her own needs: a fury at Brand for no longer desiring her and at his wife, who had won.

So why then was she still there? Surely the boy, soon turning seventeen, no longer needed a governess. Yet they refused to let her go. And what about her? She told herself that she was still there to help the Führer, to be his eyes and ears in this Jewish house. In reality, she had found more joy in initiating her sweet boy – pure and good and without shame, who had trusted and loved her -- than she did with her bullfaced Bruno, also still here, his swastika armband tucked inside his chauffeur's uniform. Yes, they both had jobs to do, and so they stayed.

"Tonight," Bruno had told her earlier, "the reign of terror for the Jews of the world will begin. Their days are numbered." She sipped her champagne and watched Jonas. What a tall handsome devil he is going to be one day, she thought. Who was addicted to whom?

A few blocks away from the Kruger home stood an ancient synagogue. It was a small house of worship where the old Rabbi, who taught Jonas, was in his study with some of his advanced students, studying the complexities of the Talmud.

Deeply immersed in their studies, they did not hear anything amiss until the unlocked door was suddenly burst open by a group of young teenagers in those familiar brown uniforms. They grabbed the old Rabbi by his beard, pulling him like a goat up to the altar of the sanctuary. The two Talmudic students were also bearded, and they wore the traditional black silk garb and long ringlets suspended from the sides of their heads. The teenagers, screeching like hyenas, pulled them by the ringlets, as other young boys crammed into the synagogue, carrying their stuffed brown bags. They threw the old man to the ground, tore the holy Torah from the ark, and ripped off their golden crowns. The bearded students screamed in horror and frustration as the blond-haired hoodlums tied their hands to the altar railing before urinating on the Holy Scriptures. The Rabbi lifted his head to the sky, begging for God to intervene in this moment of terror just as one of the wolves kicked him hard in the head, knocking him to the ground where he lay unconscious. The newspapers in the bags were lit, and in minutes the synagogue was on fire, the Rabbi and the students powerless to save themselves from the inferno.

All over Danzig and Germany, the same grotesque scene was taking place. Jewish stores and businesses were shattered, glass strewn everywhere. Thousands were attacked. Hundreds died. Hitler called this night *Kristallnacht*, the night of shattered glass. It was a night of shattered hopes and lives, the true beginning of the beginning.

Brand and the other guests smelled smoke even through the closed windows of the cool November night. When they ran out into the street, their nostrils were assaulted by the sickly sweet smell of seared flesh and they saw that the sky was aglow; it was as if the entire city of Danzig were burning. They followed the path of the glow, as did dozens of others from this elegant neighborhood. The glow led to the synagogue. Astor ran ahead as Jonas yelled, "The Rabbi is inside!" The shepherd dashed into the burning old building that was now like a sacrificial tribal bonfire stacked with human flesh. Astor vanished through the flames. Heart-rending minutes later, his fur singed, Astor emerged, dragging the charred remains of the dead Rabbi into the street.

The stunned spectators stood in absolute silence, paralyzed by these monstrous events. Policemen and Brownshirts directed traffic and dozens of teenagers, now empty-handed, were escorted to their homes by their parents. The party was over. At least for now.

The Rabbis of Europe met in Evian, France, several weeks later, appealing to the world, especially to the United States, to demand an end to the torment and murder of Jews. But the pleas were unheard.

Powerful Jewish groups in America remained relatively silent, either not convinced that the unbelievable should be believed, or afraid lest they themselves become victims, even in America. Others simply feigned ignorance as they walked their quiet, peaceful streets. Germany, after all, was so far from New York City. How can one be sure of what was really happening? Thus there would be no economic sanctions, no severing of diplomatic relations, no easing of immigration quotas.

That March, Brand was sitting before the fire in his library, reading the report of the Jewish congress following months of futile discussion, when the Prince arrived.

"This is my favorite room, Brand," the Prince said. "The old Victorian mantle, the beautiful embroidered tapestries, the velvet armchairs, the leather-covered books, the greatest words ever written, right in this marvelous room. The only things of real and lasting value in life are right here. To think these monsters burned all those great books. Someday, perhaps, there will be some justice, retribution, for every woman, man and child who has swallowed this poison."

"It is not to be believed," Brand said. "In the history of the world there never has been such concerted government-sponsored violence against so many innocent people. *Wildgewordene Spiessburger!* Little men gone wild!" Brand spat indignantly as he quoted a familiar German epithet. "This is butchery!"

Just days before, Brand was in Berlin with the Prince at a meeting of industrialists at the Adlon Hotel. They sat with Speer and Krupp, Farben, and other men of industry, and they planned who was going to change the face of the world. When they departed, they arrived on Kammerstrasse. A huge bonfire, not unlike the *Kristallnacht*, made the world orange. German youth, dressed in their ominous tan uniforms, with glowing faces, were throwing in mountains of books, nearly all of them by Jewish authors, among them some of the greatest works ever written. The men were shouting obscenities as they hurled the books into the fire.

Brand had been mesmerized by the incomprehensible scene. "This is what Dante's Inferno must be like," he said as he covered his face with his embroidered handkerchief to shield himself from the heat and ashes encircling their heads like little red devils. "Surely, these hooligans cannot know what they are doing, destroying the very soul of civilization," he finished.

"Not so loud, otherwise you will land on that pile," the Prince had urged at the time. "They would welcome your corpse on top of the books by Stefan Zweig and the Old Testament."

Now the Prince approached his friend as he surveyed this beautiful library. "The time has come for you to leave," he told Brand. He did not mince words. "Don't you see that now? They will put you and your entire family in a concentration camp for political prisoners, and they will kill everyone. I can protect you for only so long. As you know, I am myself not in a secure position. I will try to sell all your interests and holdings and smuggle the money to Switzerland, because they won't let you take out one mark."

"I have some cash, although nothing big to speak of," Brand ruminated. "It is all tied up in barges, boats, buildings, billiard tables, the company. And the football stadium I recently bought. They have imposed an 80% tax on all Jewish store owners, which includes me, of course. I started to make arrangements awhile back," Brand continued, his voice dropping to a whisper. "The walls have ears, Fräulein ears."

He raised his finger to his lips and reached behind a glass bookcase, where a safe was hidden. Brand showed the Prince the passports, visas and five first-class tickets on the *Queen Mary*, open tickets, for which he had paid thousands of dollars a few years before.

"And here is $100,000 cash, in American dollars," Brand said.

"A small fraction of your fortune," the Prince whispered. "For you, Lucia, Jonas, and Herman, of course. But for whom is the fifth ticket?"

"Do you think our family could leave without our best friend? You, dear man. Uncle Herman and I concluded that the very day Hitler was elected."

The Prince, deeply touched, brushed his hand over temples that lately had started to gray, then said softly, "I guess I will have to start learning English."

The governess was standing directly outside the room, trying to make out the low conversation through the thick oak doors. Finally, frustrated in her efforts, she knocked on the door.

"I am sorry to interrupt you, sir, but I've come to speak for the staff – Cook, the gardener and the chauffeurs, and myself.

"Herr Kruger, we do not agree with everything Hitler is doing. We remain loyal to you and your family, but if you feel you'd rather not have any Germans in your home, we will understand and, of course, leave."

"Fräulein, you are part of our family, and we would not dream of your leaving us. We have had wonderful years together, and we have hopes that things will soon get better, for all of us."

She curtsied innocently, although bending her body slightly

to reveal the swell of her breasts above the low-cut blouse.

She looked particularly lovely this afternoon, her long blond hair catching the firelight, like silk in sunshine. Her eyes were sharp, intelligent, dangerously convincing. She smiled to herself as she felt her magical charm had not failed her.

"You are a lucky man, Brand," the Prince said after she departed. "To have such loyalty these days is most uncommon. And then, also, Paul Richter can be counted on as a friend."

"Money buys honey," Brand said, "except the governess. She remains her own person, loyal to that madman, but not to us. I have never trusted the Nazi bitch."

Brand, fearing he had been stupidly indiscreet, suddenly threw open the library door. Now satisfied that Fräulein Marlow was gone, he continued.

"She works for the Gestapo, as does Bruno." He had resolved to keep enemies close and friends not too far. That was why he had not let her go. The day could come when she might prove useful.

Brand removed a brown folder from behind one of the original Guttenberg bibles he owned.

"My will, for safekeeping, just in case, and here are the 100,000 dollars, no counterfeits. And the visas, passports, vaccination certifications, and affidavits; otherwise, they won't let us enter the land of the free and the home of the brave. And, here are the open-ended tickets on the *Queen Mary*. She sails every two weeks."

"Metchnik left for South America, Grecia and Lotte left for New York, and we," the Prince laughed, "when do we go? I have not only to learn English, but to get myself some cowboy clothing too. Can you imagine? Prince Tom Mix!"

"I need just a little more time," Brand said, his face tightening, his jaw frozen. "Besides, it may still blow over. The madman may change his mind and realize that without the Jews he will never make it. No power in the world has survived for long without Jewish brains and know-how."

"That is nonsense," the Prince said. "You better not wait until the fall. Rudolf Hess told me that Hitler is going to march in a few months. He wants Europe. He has Austria, the Sudenten; now he will take Danzig, Poland, England, and the rest of Europe. America will not enter the war. The Bund does good propaganda there. Besides, the isolationists are thriving. How safe they feel, surrounded by two mighty oceans."

"Don't be so sure my friend. There are many Jews in America who have more power than you think. I cannot believe they will stand by and allow that little prick to ruin the world."

Lucia spent most of her time now in the house, except to go to the Friedenau market where she could still get fresh fruit, cranberries, dill, and cucumbers; and from there it was only a short walk to the old Hangergasse where the few remaining Jewish vendors sold meat and bread. Every day she read the *Judenblatt*. It listed, uncensored, the names of Jewish families who had left Danzig, the businesses which were closed, and those who were sent to concentration camps. The newspaper even reported any violence that occurred. The news was then sent to America for the American Jews and the world to read.

At the end of June 1939, the family left for Sopot, which was still blooming with tourists. The casino was opened, but all of their old friends were gone. The old fashionable Jewish establishments of the long pier were boarded up, although the concert hall flourished, packed each night with visitors listening to music written only by "acceptable" German composers, skillfully conducted as ever by Wilhelm Furtwängler.

Sopot was also crowded with Nazis parading in white uniforms, and with the less elite in Brownshirts. Uncle Herman made Lucia's life bearable. They went to the casino whenever he came to visit, accompanied by his new girlfriend. He allowed her to play blackjack as long as she wished, and if she lost, Herman placed fresh rolls of gulden in front of her. Brand hired 24-hour guards to patrol the house, and Astor never left their side. Lucia felt abandoned, like a lost child, and became depressed and angry because they still had not left the country. And, of course, it was far too dangerous to see her family in Warsaw. She hadn't seen them in months, another heartache. On the positive side, the governess had been forced to remain in Danzig. Lucia could no longer stand the sight of her.

"Better to keep the snake in sight," Brand had pleaded. But on this issue, Lucia prevailed.

Never having done any housework, she took quickly that summer to cleaning and polishing the furniture, making the beds in the morning, and even cooking breakfast. The work was good for her anxiety. The cook, an elderly spinster from Poland, taught her how to make roasts and chocolate pudding for Jonas and white borscht and nalesniki, the fruit crepes Brand loved, for when he came each weekend. Anything to keep Lucia from the constant fretting and waiting. She had a small suitcase packed with underclothing, a makeup kit, and a book of poems by Pushkin, in case she was suddenly taken to the concentration camp.

She wandered through the quiet house like a woman obsessed, constantly securing the bolts on the windows, checking the locks on the closed doors, and rearranging old books. There was little to occupy her. During the day Lucia sat on the velvet cushion by the bay window of her bedroom, where she could see the beach and watch and hear the mighty sea rolling. At night, it was the soothing sound of the waves lapping the shores that finally lulled her to sleep. Her life, she mused, felt like the waves, reaching the shore, just touching it, but never arriving. Waiting, waiting for that truculent storm that she could smell in her nostrils and her soul, no less well than any sailor on the high seas.

Every morning, discreetly, a young English teacher came to the house to give Lucia and Jonas lessons in reading and conversation. Brand had arranged for these lessons and they were her great symbol of hope, evidence, at last, that soon they would be leaving. The young man was tall, thin, and earnest, and he wore a well-groomed mustache. They sat in the garden on the large porch swing, learning sentences like, "What time is it now?" and "I feel O.K."

Jonas liked the sound of "O.K." so much that he soon incorporated it into his everyday speech. After the lessons were over, Jonas was driven to the schooner where he and the Captain made daily trips, sometimes going to Tiel Gurato, a peaceful village by the sea where time seemed to have stood still, except for an occasional reminder of the Third Reich, whose gunboats patrolled the area. The Captain knew most of the sailors on them by their first name and was always careful to slip them a bottle of brandy when they were invited to come aboard.

Lucia now looked forward to the daily visits of the English teacher and the smell of his English cigarettes and English cologne. At first she wore simple house dresses when he arrived. One morning after a few weeks, she wore a blue bathing suit covered by a white silk kimono, and had carefully arranged the soft dark waves around her lovely face. The slow steady motion of the porch swing and the timid stare of the young teacher made her feel alive again. Brand had not touched her in months.

After Jonas left for the schooner, they sat and drank coffee, ate warm rolls and butter, and discussed Chekhov's *Cherry Orchard*.

"It was Flaubert who said that an unfulfilled woman has it written on her face. You, Frau Kruger, read like an open book," the tutor ventured.

At first she felt offended by the young man's audacity and

wanted him to leave, never to return. She looked in the mirror, searching for the tell-tale lines on her face that the teacher evidently found so readily. She remained silent, too weak to protest the obvious truth. She did find one small wrinkle near the corner of her eye.

It was after midnight and Lucia felt restless following a dream in which she and her English teacher were lying on a pile of books, undressed, caressing each other.

A beautiful full moon shone into her bedroom this late July night, and in her languid state she looked out towards the beach, which was covered by a soft haze. She spotted the English teacher wearing white pants and an open shirt, strolling slowly by the edge of the water, his eyes focused, frozen on her window. In her nightgown, she quietly opened the front door, motioning the guard to allow the teacher in. Astor was at her side in seconds, but once he recognized the young man, he withdrew. "You are walking so late," she said, her throat dry, her heart pounding.

"I like walking in the moonlight and reciting poetry. Tonight it is so sultry I could not sleep. The moon has magical mysterious effects, does it not? It does more than make the tide come in."

She invited him inside the house. Brand was still in town, not due back before the weekend. Her nightgown was pink, diaphanous with moonlight from the window behind her. Her softness revealed, she felt warm, desirable, feminine. She thought she could hear the pounding of the young man's heart through his half-opened shirt. They sat in the living room, drinking Armagnac. The air was heavy, humid.

He said, "I have walked here every night, hoping to see you. I have sensed how afraid and lonely you are. And so I have been reluctant to tell you that I must return to England. It is just too dangerous to stay here. I will be leaving in a few days."

Lucia's face changed, as if a cloud covered the full moon. He touched her thigh through the silk gown and she sighed softly, resignedly, and placed her arms around him, a pink flush on her cheeks. She felt his torso stiffen, as if the thrill of anticipation was coursing through his entire body.

"No," she whispered, dropping her arms, "please leave. I just can't. I am sorry."

The next day she sat by her window peering out into the Baltic Sea. Lucia had always loved it for its biting honesty, for its predictable tides and dark depths. Last night had been the end of something that never started. She didn't know if she felt worse because she had misled the young teacher or because he was leaving her behind.

On Friday morning two weeks later Brand was at the Baltic Kohlen office, finishing his paperwork. The Nazi officials came, as they did each morning, to look at the financial records. When they had gone, he phoned Max Schiller, transmitting an urgent message the officials had left with him, one of such importance that it had Albert Speer's signature and stamp. The barges would henceforth be armed with firearms and accompanied by gunboats. They would transport their precious cargo of coal and lumber directly to Bremerhaven and to Peenemunde, the rocket base being completed at a feverish pace. In other words, his personal services were no longer required.

The general manager of the company, Fritz Werfel, came into Brand's office. His head bowed, he spoke humbly, haltingly, perhaps even apologetically.

"We members of the staff want to thank you for being such a kind and considerate employer. We know that these are hard times for you and we want you to have this little present from all of us."

Bowing again, he presented Brand with a large sculptured piece of coal bearing the simple inscription, "Baltic Kohlen."

Brand was so moved by the gesture and by the significance of
the moment that he rose from his large leather swivel chair and
embraced him.

"We have survived other crises," Brand said, "and all this will
seem to have been just another test if we all stick together."

"You and your family will always have our loyalty."

When Brand left his office, he stopped and gazed at the magnificent building. It was centuries old, four stories high, with tall
narrow windows, and surrounded by its own cobblestone square.
A statue of a brave Danziger, holding a mighty spear, stood at
the entrance, in memory of the twelfth-century defense against
an invasion by the Teutonic Knights. He had the oddest feeling
that he would never, ever see this building again, this marvel of
architecture and finance where twenty years earlier his Baltic
Kohlen Company was born. With his broad business interests
and many investments, there seemed little reason to feel so uneasy at this particular moment, but Brand couldn't shake the
feeling that something terrible was in store for him. Yet, despite
the premonition, he felt fatalistic – nothing he could do would
change the inexorable events that were unfolding.

He took a last long look at the golden plaque on the building
façade – "Baltic Kohlen" – and then, heavy-hearted and weary,
he climbed into the gleaming Duesenberg parked in front. He
drove through the Danzig old town, with its beautiful ancient
streets, and then through the city's many neighborhoods, seeing
everywhere old and reliable friends: the statue of Schopenhauer,
the museum of old ships, the revered university, his newly acquired football stadium, the marvelous Hanseatic buildings with
their magnificent stone balconies sculptured with wild animals.
He was seeing all of them as if it were for the first time and for
the last time. He drove deliberately to the Danzig shipyards and
stopped to gaze at his line of barges packed with coal. Baltic
Kohlen, the pride and flagship of his fleet, sat low in the water,

although its name, appearing in large gold letters on the bow, remained visible. Men dressed in black, his men, were silently securing the bulkheads and getting ready to depart. The tugboats were blowing smoke from their stacks and making sounds like belching animals as they prepared to leave the port. Brand gave out a silent sigh and drove on.

It was early afternoon when he arrived at his house in Langfuhr. He planned to change his clothing, then go to Sopot for the weekend. Large dark clouds, reflecting his mood, covered the lackluster August sky. He climbed the stairs to the master bedroom, exhausted. The door to the bedroom was slightly ajar and he heard movement inside.

Fräulein Marlow, partially clothed, was pulling the sheets over the bed. She turned, and there was a look of surprise on her fresh and beautiful face when she saw Brand enter the room. Her long blond hair was loose, partially covering her magnificent breasts. She straightened up, stood defiantly in front of him, and then removed the rest of her clothing. Not a word was exchanged. She sensed his outrage, intermingled with his heightening passion. He brutally pushed her back on the bed, attacking her with his hands, slapping her face, all of which aroused her. She clutched her attacker, pressing him to her, into her, almost through her.

Her ecstasy poured from the very depths of her being. Over and over again he thrust into her like a frenzied gladiator. She pushed up to meet each thrust, tearing the skin on his back. It was very brief. Spent, angry, weary, he had to strike her face smartly to free himself from her grasp.

"I know everything," he told her. "What you did with my son. It is all in his diary, you pitiful monster. Damn your soul!"

Brand had had no intentions of reading Jonas' diary, the one Uncle Herman gave him several years back. But there it was, peeking out from the pocket of Jonas' old rain jacket, probably forgotten. Just days before, Brand had gone into the storage closet where they stowed their bad-weather gear and had found it. It was not locked. At first, he had read the confused descriptions of sex play – a boy's fumblings and worshipful desire to please, like a sacrament – with amusement, thinking it merely Jonas' fancy and imagination, a written daydream. That is, until he suddenly remembered the way the governess caressed his son's hand during the concert that summer. Then Brand realized it was not fiction.

He left her on the bed, in shock, crying from the pain and from being so humiliated and shamed. In his rage, Brand had nearly strangled the woman. She now almost wished he had. Through the open door, she listened to his movements, waiting, waiting for him to return. She had never seen such hate and anger in a man's eyes.

After he showered and dressed, he went to the library. This door, too, had been left ajar. He whistled "Lilli Marlene." He opened the safe, removed 1,000 guldens, wrote the combination of the safe on a piece of paper and stuck it in the pocket of his newest tuxedo shirt, in the armoire, along with a note: "Dearest Lucia, this is the combination, just in case. I am ever yours, Brand."

Dressed in his white duck trousers and a white shirt, he placed his boatsman cap smartly on his head and climbed into the Duesenberg, as the governess, still naked, watched him from behind the curtains of her bedroom, tears streaking down her swollen cheeks.

The sky now looked almost black and smelled of rain. It suddenly grew even darker and the wind picked up. Brand pulled the convertible roof closed just as the rain came down in sheets, like a waterfall rushing down a mountain. The torrent was mixed with hail and the winds now blowing in from the North Sea were of gale force. On and on he drove, the visibility very poor as he continued to make his way slowly along the periphery of Danzig Harbor. The waves grew huge and white, the winds now dangerous. He observed the mighty sycamore trees bending like saplings. He suddenly panicked – Jonas might be on the boat, perhaps even at sea!

He eventually stopped at a small service station and phoned the house. There was no answer. "All the lines are out," the garage attendant told him, "and the roads may already be flooded. You must drive with great caution. Perhaps you had best wait it out here."

Brand pictured Jonas being swept out to sea. The gods are angry with me, he thought, and they are right. Lucia was so right. He thought of the years the boy had been in Fräulein's care, alone. It grieved him to think of the poisons that woman drew into little Jonas' mind and body. The devil resided in her. Why hadn't he seen it? He had stopped just short of choking the life out of her. Had he done so, he would have descended into the same hell that was all around them. He would have been no better than they. Still, he thought himself a coward. He hadn't run when he could, and he hadn't struck back with the relevance this madness deserved. His guilt, about not seeing what was happening all around him, about not leading his family to safety, overwhelmed him. This Brand, this man who had risen from nothing to something, was no great man after all.

Sweating in the car as he inched along the flooded road, he continued to confront the nakedness of this truth. Was it now too late, he wondered? Would Lucia and Jonas forgive him? Could he ever forgive himself? Then he saw in the distance a man standing in the middle of the road, waving his arms over his head. A checkpoint. The road was deserted, and the man was wearing a black SS uniform. Brand decided to ignore him and to drive on, but he could not accelerate the car through the foot of water. The SS soldier did not move, and Brand slammed down on the brakes, skidding to the side of the road. He reached into the glove compartment for the loaded Luger and placed it in his belt, behind his back.

The man approached the Duesenberg. His blond hair looked like wet straw over his sunken drunken eyes. It was such a young face, Brand observed, thinking that he once might have been a university student, perhaps even in Danzig. A zigzag scar ran from the man's eyelid to the angle of his small angry mouth.

"Get out of the car! I order you in the name of the Third Reich. Show me your papers!"

Brand sat firm, looking directly into the soldier's eyes, his hand behind his back, fingers on the trigger. The soldier's trousers and body, soaked by the rain, must have felt as if they were drenched in blood. Was it not the same feeling he experienced on the battlefield so very long ago when the Bolsheviks swept down on him with their bloodied sabers? The SS soldier had that same bloodied look. Perhaps all men look that way when they are out to murder. Brand sat in silence, waiting, and then the door of the car was flung open and Brand was pulled out, the soldier pounding his head, screaming, "Filthy Jew!" and kicking him in the ribs, kicking and kicking, Brand thought from a place deep inside himself, in a ritual of punishment and redemption. Kicking him to his senses. Then, standing above him, the soldier drew the sidearm he was carrying and pointed the gun at Brand's head. Brand quickly drew the Luger from his belt, and shot at the blond face. With one bullet he silenced them both, this boy, and the woman who had scratched his dear boy's innocence. This bullet silenced them – their hate, and possibly also some of the crushing guilt he carried for this desperate mess.

The soldier's eyes were staring, disbelieving. He fell on Brand. His blood mixed with water, a widening circle of red grew around the dead soldier, and a thin red stream now flowed swiftly down a crack in the road. Brand pushed the corpse off his body. He was wet and sticky, smeared with sweat and blood.

There was no one else in view. The road was deserted. He rinsed his hands in the water at his feet, splashed his face, and struggled to climb back into the car, holding his ribs with one red hand. Each time he took a breath he felt the stabbing pain of broken ribs. The leather seat was soon covered with his own blood, dripping from his torn face. It was dark, but surely the people living in all these peaceful-looking houses would have seen everything. No one these days would dare venture out into the street themselves, but they were surely witness to what happened – a drunken soldier out to kill an innocent man who did what had to be done to defend himself. What reasonable man or woman, after all – if indeed any were left – could dispute that? There was no other narrative for him because if Brand now ran away, the guilt would shift to him, especially as the murdered man was SS The uniform told the story. They would hunt him down and kill him – and Lucia and Jonas, too. Now they would have a perfect excuse to do what they no doubt intended to soon do anyway, when neither the Prince nor Hess nor Kruger's own fortune could help him.

Limping, holding his side, Brand came to a small provincial house where an aged widow lived. He rang the bell, knocked on the door, the rain splashing over his anguished face. As he was about to leave to find another house, the door opened just a crack, and a small furry brown cat eyed him suspiciously.

"I am hurt," he said softly through the narrow opening. "May I please use your telephone?"

A tiny old woman wrapped in a black shawl slowly opened the door.

"Someone tried to kill me," he told her. "I have to use your phone to call the police."

"Come in," she said. "Let me bring you a towel and some hot soup. I am sorry to have made you wait. These days, you know, there are Jews escaping, looking for hiding places. You look like a gentleman."

He left a puddle of water beneath his feet and apologized.

"If you allow me, I would like to compensate you for your troubles." He did not wait for her answer, but slipped 100 guldens from his wallet and left it on a small round table covered with an embroidered tablecloth.

In the mirror of the bathroom, he saw how his face was bruised and swollen where the SS man had kicked him. His cut lip was oozing blood, and his side was aching. The woman must have seen everything from her window, and if she would be honest she could help to save his life. The phone worked now, and he called the police station, asking for the chief, Paul Richter, his tennis partner. "He is not here. Who is calling?" asked the desk clerk.

"Brand Kruger. I want to report an accident. A man ran in front of my car and tried to kill me when I came out to help him. He is dead. I shot him." He told them the location of the house and the site of the accident.

The old woman sat in the living room, her hands folded in her lap, her back straight, a steaming cup of hot soup on the table opposite her. Brand came out of the bedroom, composed but weak, in scorching pain and utterly exhausted.

"I must make one or two more calls. Please take this extra 500 guldens, Madam, for being so patient and kind, and I would like to reward you some more. These must be hard times for you."

The Prince answered the phone. He was about to leave for the weekend, too, for the charming Baltic village of Kronenbourg where he had taken a cottage. The Prince listened with horror and motioned to the valet to give him a change of clothes.

"Don't run, Brand! Stay put, and leave the rest to me."

"No, listen," Brand said. "Lucia has been wanting to go on

a little vacation. Please take her and Jonas – tonight! I promised them. Tell them I will see them on Sunday."

"You mean to Switzerland, now?" the Prince whispered.

"Yes, now is a good time." Weakened and now perspiring profusely, Brand sat on the couch waiting, trying not to faint. Even if he decided to suddenly break and run, he lacked the strength to do so. At least this diversion would give Lucia and Jonas time to cross the border to Poland. He waited, trying to gather his wits and his strength.

The storm was raging, and the phone lines were evidently down in Sopot. He could not warn her, but he knew the Prince could be relied on to do what was necessary. He would take them by chauffeured limousine to Warsaw, then by train to Geneva, to safety. Brand tried to light a wet cigarette, and groaned quietly to himself. This was not the way it was supposed to go.

Lucia stared at her watch, the gold Piaget that Brand gave her for her thirtieth birthday. She was in the bedroom, examining her jewelry, touching it playfully, wistfully, a naughty child sur-rounded by the soft duvets lying on the bed. It becomes quite cool in August in Sopot, but it was still too early to start up the coal stove. Jonas was in a deep sleep in his bed. The storm was subsiding, but the swells of the water had reached the house, cov-ering the beach and flooding the street. Tiring of playing with her jewelry, she sat by candlelight, the electricity having failed earlier. The private guard had left when the hurricane started, and there was just Astor lying on the floor at her feet. Brand had left her a small revolver, fully loaded, in the night table.

"I don't want to learn how to shoot a gun," she remembered saying when Brand first gave it to her. They were aboard their schooner when Brand taught her how to fire it.

"Squeeze the trigger like a nipple, slowly, lovingly." She

laughed to herself, now, at Brand, so clever, so charming. Her mind cleared of memory, and she listened to the splatter of the water against the eaves. It was too dark to see what was happening outside. There was no car to take her and Jonas to dry ground, and even if there were, she did not know how to drive.

"In America," Brand had said, "everyone drives a car, and along with our English lessons you should also take driving lessons."

"In America," Lucia said, "I will learn to drive a car."

Then she cried to herself when she thought of the English lessons and that boy she would never see again. She cried because she had almost betrayed her husband and was suddenly grateful that she would not ever have to see the teacher. She thought about poor dead Bill, too, for the first time in a long while, and thought about the strange things loneliness does to people. Leaning back on the sofa, she closed her eyes, listening to the sounds of the storm.

None of them had really come back after Bill died. She and the Prince had personally packed up Bill's belongings to return to his family. They had composed a dignified letter to his parents that followed the cable they had immediately sent. The letter described how the young architecture student had blossomed under the European sky, how well-mannered and brave he was, and what a privilege it was for them to befriend and look after him. The beauty and power of that truth was a consolation of sorts. No mention was made of the young female art student Bill had concocted for his parents' satisfaction. When they were done, the Prince, wearing the ring he had given Bill in the first blush of their friendship, had cried as Lucia held him, his trembling body surprisingly supple and boy-like.

Now the old house was trembling too, making cracking sounds, like a ship straining against a heavy sea.

Lucia thought back to the day they had bought the house so

many years ago. Jonas was still a baby and there was no Fräulein yet. They returned from the closing, the boarded-up place was now theirs. It was an ugly, raw winter day. They had built a fire and vowed to love each other forever as Brand had slowly removed her clothes and made love to her on the floor next to the glowing hearth. Afterwards, they smoked cigarettes, drank wine, ate cheese and pâte, and planned how they would paint and decorate the house. During the summer, a nursemaid tending to Jonas, they swam naked at night in the ocean, and then ate supper on their veranda. Brand always ordered a formal four-course meal from the casino dining room, and the best champagne – all of this served by a waiter dressed in a tuxedo. Brand liked dining in formal wear. Ah, those were such spectacular days.

Why did it all have to change? Lucia cried quietly, and fell asleep on the couch.

The wind finally subsided, the storm ended. She was awakened by the sound of a car. Thank God, Brand was back. He must have been stuck on the road and could not telephone. What time was it?

Astor was up at the door, growling. "Shame on you. It is Papa," she said, happiness animating her voice. She was transformed, glowing with relief. She ran outside in her bare feet, through the puddles, to the long circular driveway. But there was no Duesenberg; instead, there was a long black Mercedes driven by three men in SS uniforms. Her hand went to her breast as she gasped with fear. Astor barked furiously as the men drew their guns.

"Stop, Astor, sit!" she screamed in panic, terrified that they were going to shoot the dog.

"Frau Kruger, you are under arrest. Please go into the house and dress swiftly, and bring your son."

"Arrested? For what reason?"

"Please, no questions now; everything in time."

"Where is my husband? What happened?"

The spokesman of the three men was a small, fierce-looking man who wore a lecherous expression on his face as if it were a badge of honor. He eyed Lucia in her transparent black silk nightgown. She had worn it for Brand. Now it was to be her shroud.

Her body trembled with fright as she rushed into Jonas' bedroom. He sat up in bed, rubbing his eyes.

"Is Father home?" he asked with a sleepy voice.

"Quick, Jonas darling, get dressed. We have to go with these men." The three men were standing by the door as Astor began to growl again.

"Stop, Astor, please." Jonas placed his arms around the dog's head and held him against his face. "I will dress quickly," he said. "Please don't hurt my dog. Where are we going?"

"Just get dressed, and don't ask questions, before I put my boot into your Jewish head."

"Easy, Rolf," the other one said. "They are all friends of Berlin."

Lucia went into the bedroom and started to remove her nightgown. "Please close the door," she implored.

The men did not move; they waited like three hungry dogs. She moved into the closet and pulled her nightgown over her head when the ugly man called Rolf flung the door open, gaping at the unclothed woman.

"Rolf," the other said, "We have to bring her back."

Astor rushed into the bedroom jumping on Rolf, who drew his revolver. Lucia pulled the dog away, her naked body shaking. She cried, "Please stop, Astor. They will kill you!"

The SS man hesitated and placed his revolver back in the holster. Lucia slipped on a simple dress and reached for her underclothes. "You won't need those, Frau Kruger, where you are going. Now hurry up."

"Can I not at least take my make-up kit?" She reached for the night table where the loaded gun was inches away from her hand. She had heard what Nazis did to women, and at this moment her life was not particularly worth anything. She was dazed, in shock. Her only desire was to kill that ugly face staring at her. Her brain was numb, drugged with hatred, as if the Nazi's poison had already entered her soul. The SS man grabbed her by the arm and pushed her through her bedroom door and outside into the black sedan. Jonas was sitting in the front seat, waiting, too petrified to say a word. Lucia was directed into the back seat of the car between two of the uniformed men. She sat motionless, as if she were already dead. She no longer gave a thought to any human being – not her son, not her husband. Her fear insulated her from the rest of the world. She felt nothing, not even the rough hands under her dress, groping, kneading her body. She did not resist, which made the two SS thugs breathe harder and continue with even more enthusiasm.

"She likes it, the Jewish slut. Here, take this," one of them said.

The man in the front seat yelled in disgust. "I order you to stop, you filthy pigs!" He was the ranking officer.

They stopped, ever obedient, even with their flies undone.

Chapter Fourteen

THE PRINCE RUSHED INTO the house, and when he saw the nightgown on the floor, he gasped in despair. Astor barked from behind the bathroom door. Once freed, he ran through the house looking for Jonas and Lucia.

"Poor Astor, I'm sorry. I came too late." The dog peered through the darkness at the entrance of the house.

Rudolf Hess was at home with his wife and child, still awake at four in the morning. He was known in the inner circles of his friends to be a peculiar sort of person, paranoid and cruel, and yet, sometimes even kind. As a young man, Hess had come to prominence by penning an award-winning essay entitled, "How Must the Man Be Constructed Who Will Lead Germany Back to her Old Heights." In it he had opined that bloodshed and the shedding of old friendships might be required to reach that noble goal. Oddly, his long affection for the Prince had stopped the Nazi lieutenant from adding Brandenberg to his lengthy list of ill-fated associates.

The Prince called him on his private number, as Hess sat in his chair smoking a cigarette, working on plans and logistics.

"I thought you would be awake," the Prince said, knowing the man was a notorious night owl.

"Did they get you?" Hess asked, "Because I warned you to watch your step. I can't protect you much longer because they will come after me."

"No, it is not for me, Rudi. My friends – you know them, the Krugers – were arrested in Sopot. I have never asked you for a favor; you owe me a few. We must help them, and I will not ask you for anything more."

"I will see what I can do but this one time only, understand?"

"I do."

"All right, but I need to know. What did he do?"

"He killed an SS man, but he had to defend himself. The man was drunk, was beating him, threatening him with a gun."

"You don't make life easy, do you? Don't do anything stupid. Leave it to me."

The black Mercedes, carrying Lucia and Jonas to Nazi headquarters in Danzig, drove down the long street, past the Marienkirche. The dark streets were deserted and shiny from the rain. They stopped on the Toppengasse, across the street from the Central Synagogue. Hitler had ordered that this synagogue, now occupied by the Gestapo, be preserved as a sadistic monument to the former Jewish population of the city. Jonas climbed the familiar entrance stairs of the old building, his mother grasping his hand. They came to the large entrance hall and were escorted upstairs, in silence. The room was small, with just a bench, some chairs, and a dreary lamp on a small wooden table. On the wall was a large school clock with a picture of Hitler.

Jonas sat next to his mother, watching the movement of the pendulum. He got up and tried the handle of the door, which turned with ease. Standing outside was a soldier with a rifle. The soldier slammed the door when he saw Jonas inching it open.

Every week for three years, the Fräulein had brought him to

this very place, which might now become his tomb. Never before had he realized how he had betrayed his father and mother. A prisoner of the same persons who almost converted him to something he was not! He had never told his parents, but now he would have to! Perhaps one of his guards would recognize him. He decided he must also plan an escape to save his mother. Surely if he could just get to them, his father or Uncle Herman would come to the rescue, perhaps Fräulein Marlow. She told him over and over again how much she loved him. Surely even if she was one of them, she would not let the family die.

Lucia sat motionless, then she looked at Jonas and started to weep.

"Don't worry, Mother, Father will save us." He placed his arms around his tormented mother. This was the first time Jonas had ever seen his mother cry so bitterly and look so disheveled and old – like one of the women at the fish market, wearing black rubber aprons, yelling, "Mackerels and flounders, fresh today."

His mother was always neatly coiffed, a joy to the eye. He looked at the black lines under her eyes, and the hair in strands, as if it had never known a comb. Her face was streaked with tears, lined with tension, her gentle features now squeezed like an accordion. There were no windows in this death room. No possibility of escaping from the prison. What would the Katzenjammer Kids and Captain Kowalsky do now, he asked himself. They would have a plan, so he must have one too.

The door suddenly opened and an SS man marched into the room and pulled Jonas by his shirt collar.

"You come with me," he said roughly.

"No, take me," Lucia pleaded. "I will do anything you want. Leave my son." She fell on her knees embracing the black boots, pleading, unashamed. "I can give you anything you want. We have lots of money, and I can make you very happy."

He pushed her away with his foot and dragged the terrified

boy into another room where two Gestapo officers were sitting, their black boots resting on the table, their arms folded, grinning widely.

"Now, you little Jew, what is your name?"

"Jonas, sir," he answered with a strong voice, and clicked his heels like a young prince, just as his governess taught him so long ago.

"How old are you?"

"Fifteen next month," he lied.

"You look older than that." Jonas stood erect and proud. Stung by their laughter, he exploded at them, almost crying in his anger.

"Why are you keeping us here? I was one of the Brownshirts; just ask the group leader, Becker. Every week I came to this building. Let me go free and I will show you. Ask Fräulein Marlow, and she will tell you what a good German I am. I have my uniform at home, and my medals. You are making a big mistake. My father is a good friend of the Führer, and the Prince. You'd better let us go before they find out and they put you in jail. Let me run home and I will come back with my uniform." If they let him go, he thought, he'd get his father's gun and free his mother.

"Did you know, Jew bastard, that your father killed a German officer and that he will die, and that you will die with him, as will your mother? How do you feel now?"

"Sick. I want to urinate."

"Go and do that right here, in your pants, you little pig," and they all laughed like hyenas.

"Get undressed, everything off, pig. We want to be sure you are not hiding anything from us."

"Go easy on him; the Führer may hear of it," one of the Gestapo man warned.

"If the Führer heard that his father had killed one of his SS, he would cut the boy's balls off and feed them to his dogs."

Lucia was, meanwhile, lying on the bare wooden floor, screaming, begging God to take her, striking the floor with her head. "Kill me, kill me, not my Jonas!"

A huge woman came into the room, her blond hair cut short, her nose flat, the nostrils flaring like a hippopotamus'. She looked like a male wrestler.

"Undress quickly, on the floor, and spread your legs." She smacked her lips when she saw the naked body beneath Lucia's dress in front of her.

"Lie down, quickly!" Lucia held her breath, as she smelled sweat from that disgusting woman bending over her, touching her breasts and groaning like a bear in heat. Lucia screamed in pain as the filthy woman pushed her hand into Lucia's vagina and then into her rectum.

When the guard finished the search, she left Lucia lying on the floor, weeping from the pain and humiliation.

This is my punishment from God because I was a bad mother. I deserve this suffering. But Jonas should not be punished for my sins. He is a good boy. What does he know of life, she thought, her despair palpable and complete. She had never in her life felt so utterly powerless.

Then Brand was escorted into the little room – their tomb – by two SS men, his face bruised. At first he did not see Lucia as his eyes were fixed on the closing door. He shouted, "You have no right to treat me like this! I demand to see Chief Richter. You don't know who I am!" He turned his body away from the door and gasped in surprise when he saw his wife lying in the corner on the floor, half-naked. He picked her up in his arms and quickly covered her body with her dress. "My God, what did they do to you?" he yelled. He wanted to scream and beat them senseless, but he knew that if he fell apart now all would be lost forever.

"I am all right. They only searched me, but they took Jonas away." And with that he started to become hysterical again. Brand swiftly rose from the floor and banged on the door.

"I demand to see Paul Richter, and to call Berlin at once. You must let me talk to Max Schiller and Speer. Where is my son?" He continued in this manner, naming all his friends and connections in Berlin.

The door swung opened and Jonas was brought in. Both parents swept him up and covered him with their arms, protecting him with their bodies. He tried to push his parents away as he was ashamed of his pants soaked with urine. "They made me pee in my pants," he cried pitifully.

"They will never take you again, Jonas," Brand said with tears in his eyes. He explained to Lucia the events of the past twelve hours and reassured her that they would soon be rescued. They sat huddled together in the corner of the room like gypsies, Lucia quietly crying, Jonas shivering, and Brand encircling them both in his arms. There was no possibility of escaping. All his threats and shouting were of no avail. They stripped him of everything including the Swiss Army knife he always carried with him. His body ached badly from the battering he had sustained, and he felt utterly drained. For the first time in his life he realized that he had no escape route, no plan.

At eight in the morning Paul Richter came to Gestapo headquarters. The Prince had already been waiting there for hours.

"They've got the Krugers."

"I know, I heard," the police chief said remorsefully.

"I have a telegram from Hess, ordering their release, and these idiots would not honor it until you arrived."

"I am sorry, Major," the officer of the day said to Richter, "but we had to follow orders."

"Brand will have to stand trial," Paul said to the Prince.

"That was the agreement."

Uncle Herman came into headquarters, greeting the secretary and officer in charge like old friends.

The door to the little room opened and a guard stepped out, ordering the Kruger family to follow him quickly. "The Chief wants to see you," he said. Once inside Paul's office, Brand cried, "Thank God, Paul, you are here!"

"Don't say anything," Paul said. "You have to stand trial for the shooting, but they have agreed to let you and your family go home with the police guard, under three thousand guldens bail, until the trial."

Uncle Herman paid out the money, slipping an extra fifty to the guard.

"We are doing this for you, Herr Kruger," Chief Richter said loudly, "because you have been a good friend of the Third Reich, and because Berlin regrets the accident which occurred, but we have to go through the courts to clear you. Read the telegram from Rudolf Hess. We want the world to see that in the new Germany, justice prevails."

A sedan drove the Krugers back to Langfuhr, the guard and Uncle Herman in the front seat. The Prince was joking with the guard as Brand and Lucia sat silently, observing a master at work. "A surprise for you, my little Jonas. Astor is waiting for you. I had my valet run up to Sopot and fetch him." Once in the house, Lucia ran upstairs, showered quickly and changed her clothing. Jonas was hugging his dog, and the Prince took the guard into the kitchen for some beer and cigarettes where he found Fräulein Marlow seated at the table.

"Ah, Fräulein," the Prince said, "I want you to meet Sergeant Kessler. He will be staying with us here for a while, and we want to make the officer comfortable. He will be eating with us. Tonight he will sleep here."

The pudgy SS guard understood immediately what the

Prince had in mind. He licked his dry lips.

The Prince went on: "Now, Fräulein, Frau Kruger has asked if you would please be good enough to buy some food at the market, since we were not expected. Go and see my friend, Fritz Heller. He will give you sauerbraten, and fresh bread, a goose liver, salami, and whatever else our friend would like." He whispered to the guard, "They are filthy rich."

"Schnitzel and beer. I like a good schnitzel," answered the guard.

"Here is five hundred guldens, Fräulein, and please keep the change for all your troubles."

The governess sighed but did what she was told. She disliked the Prince intensely. He had always made her feel like an insignificant servant. He, too, was an Aryan living among Jews. But he had never once recognized their common bond. The minute she left, Brandenberg left the SS man with a bottle of brandy and a pack of American cigarettes.

"We have about thirty minutes before she returns," he whispered to Brand.

Brand removed the money, visas, and tickets from behind the Gutenberg bible and handed the Prince fifty thousand American dollars. Lucia quickly sewed ten one-thousand-dollar bills into Jonas' pants, into her dress, and into Brand's clothing.

Jonas watched her work with amazement, as Brand whispered to him. "Not a word! Don't even play with or touch your pants. Our lives depend on it, Jonas. No monkey business, yes?"

"Your mother will take you to Sopot right now by train, and I will come separately by car with the Prince, and so will Uncle Herman." Brand had just sent Bruno on an "errand" to collect suits he pretended he had ordered from his tailor downtown.

"What about the SS man, Father?" Jonas asked.

"It will be taken care of."

"Are you going to kill him, too?" he asked.

"Keep quiet, Jonas. We will talk later."

In a few minutes, they heard the Prince and the guard laughing uproariously. Then the door closed behind them. As soon as they heard the Prince's engine roaring, Brand kissed Lucia and Jonas.

"Now run. I will see you at the pier in about one hour. Look happy." He kissed his son. "Take care of your mother, Jonas. I am depending on you. We have to leave now. If we stay, they will kill us." There were tears in Brand's eyes.

"Can't I take Astor with us? He can protect us. He is no trouble at all. I can take care of him," Jonas pleaded.

"Hurry, Jonas. Get into the car."

"Please, Father. I can't leave Astor." He was sobbing.

"No, Jonas. Astor has to stay, like everything else in this house. It has to look like we are returning in a few days." Lucia began to cry, too.

"Look happy, for heaven's sake. You can cry later."

"How can you be so cold?" Lucia asked. "Everything you worked for – everything!"

"Stop it, Lucia! This is all worthless now. Take your jewelry. But only our lives matter. Please. We must control ourselves."

Jonas scurried in panic to find something of his own to take with him. He ran into the library and grabbed the piece of coal on Brand's desk and then to his bedroom for his diary, a photograph, and the small paperweight Ala had given him on his ninth birthday. Brand left a note for Fräulein Marlow: "We will be back a little later. We are at Gestapo headquarters for a hearing. Please feed Astor, as we did not get the chance."

Then he sent a letter to Gestapo headquarters that the governess and Bruno had helped them to escape, and that fifty thousand guldens were hidden in the governess' black shoes in her bedroom.

Astor lay down on his blanket in the hallway, and Jonas, with tears in his eyes said, "Be a good boy, Astor. I am sorry I have to leave you, but I will be back. In the meantime I am taking your picture with me." He hoped that Cook, returning any day from her summer holiday, would keep the dog. Jonas kissed Astor, who seemed to understand and began to whine and roll on the blanket. As they climbed into the Prince's car, Jonas, crying hysterically, looked back at the house, toward his room and balcony and the large chestnut tree in front.

He was waiting for Astor to come to the door or the window. Just one more look at his beloved dog. The street was deserted on this late summer day. Already a certain decay had set in. The lawns of these resplendent homes were unattended, the sidewalks unswept, and the balconies, the beautiful balconies of Danzig, were drab and funereal in appearance. This time of the year they were once bedecked with flowers; now they looked like grand tombstones: ornate, bathed in the shadow of the death that was soon to come.

"Take a good look, Jonas, a hard last look; we can never come back again," Brand said. His voice choked up uncharacteristically. "This is the end of a life, a civilization that will never be again."

"Father, please don't talk like that. We will come back one day."

The Guterbanhof railroad station ran trains to Sopot every hour on the hour on weekends during the summer. Vacationers with their beach paraphernalia, the Danzigers, were boarding the train joyfully, oblivious to what they left behind – a once-peaceful city that they had handed over to the Nazis, a takeover that they had even applauded. They had rid themselves of the Jews. These everyday folks – bakers, butchers, shoemakers, school teachers – proudly wore their swastika armbands and carried small flags, symbols of the new order, the new world. Brand kissed his son and wife and said, loud enough for everyone, "See you in a few days. Have a nice weekend."

Once in their first-class compartment, Jonas took a seat by the window, peering at all the people, at teenage boys his age boarding the train for the seashore. Once in a while, there was a dog being pulled by a child.

Jonas would never become a Nazi, as he almost had. He should have told his father after he went to that first Bund meeting, told him all about Fräulein Marlow. But he had loved her. She had been so good to him. Now he loathed her for being one of them. Why did she lie to him so? With the book in his lap he tried reading, but his nervous brain would not let him. His diary, started only this year, was now almost full, just a few pages left. Into it he had poured out his heart these last sad months. Now as he wrote the last entry, tears came to his eyes.

"On the afternoon of August 13, 1939, we left our beautiful home in Danzig, and everything that belonged to us. Father allowed me to take only a few mementos, including this diary. All my things, and my Astor, were left for the Germans. Soon, they will be in our house, living, sleeping in my bed, and using all our belongings. We may never reach America, as Father plans; and if not, then we will all be killed by the Germans, because we are Jews. Someday I hope I will understand why it is so bad to be a Jew in Germany. The worst thing that can happen to anyone is to be deceived for so long, like I was by my governess. The Rabbi said to believe in God and everything will work out. Yet, he was killed, and Bill was killed, and they did not hurt anyone.

"Father and Mother look so old. I am glad the Prince and Uncle Herman are coming with us . . ."

The compartment door was suddenly opened by two young SS men who entered, smiling. Jonas' heart began to pound so hard through his summer shirt that he feared the men could see it. He closed the diary and slipped it into his rucksack.

"Papers, please," the younger of the two asked in a soft, pleasant voice. He studied the papers for a long time and then looked at Jonas.

"Frau Kruger, are you going for a holiday?"

"Yes, we have a summer house in Sopot."

"No luggage, then?"

"We keep our summer things there. It is very convenient."

The two left, still smiling, carrying Lucia and Jonas' papers with them. Jonas and his mother sat and waited; the train was held up. If the SS men called Gestapo headquarters, Lucia thought, then she would never see Brand again. Jonas saw his mother holding her hands tightly. He had promised his father to take care of her. If they escaped now, left the train, they could hide in the caves on the north beach of Sopot. He touched his pants and felt the bulge of money sewn into the seams, which made him feel secure.

Jonas rose from his seat and pulled down the window. The station was empty because all the people were on the train except for a few SS men standing in a circle smoking cigarettes. He chinned himself up to the opening. One more push and his body would be out of the window. "Jonas," Lucia whispered tightly. "Get down! You can't escape; we will be saved. So, please, you must come down!" It started to rain as the train made a sudden thrust forward and Jonas lost his hold on the window and fell to the floor. Lucia rose from her seat to help him back up. She was about to say, "That served you right," when the two SS men appeared again, smiling. They entered the compartment. Jonas rose from the floor, and sat down next to his mother.

"We checked your taxes, and everything is in order. Sorry to have you wait, but you know our rules," one of them said, referring to the 80% tax all Jewish businesses had to pay every six months. Failure to pay meant being jailed immediately or sent to a concentration camp. "Frau Kruger, enjoy the beach!" The SS man's eyes glowed with warmth and he cordially extended his hand to Jonas, who took it reluctantly, and clicked his heels. "One minute they want to kill and torture you and the next they act as if they are your friend," Jonas whispered to Lucia as the train was on its way. The SS had not called Gestapo headquarters, but the tax office. Thank God Brand was careful to pay last week's taxes, Lucia thought.

The train arrived in Sopot, passing Casino Park with its yew trees. Jonas remembered going with his Warsaw cousins and Uncle Herman to the beautiful park to ride the donkeys. A lifetime ago, he thought. After a few more minutes, the train slowly pulled into the station. Hundreds of tourists ran onto the platform looking for relatives or friends or to board the train as it journeyed on. Lucia and Jonas left their compartment and walked to the exit of the train not knowing what to expect next. As they emerged onto the platform, they did not see anyone waiting for them. Then, Jonas spotted a horse and buggy, a *droschke*, at the old station. Their gardener was sitting in the driver's seat wearing a wide hat. Jonas ran over and was the first to climb in as the gardener winked to him.

The *droschke* passed the Wisering Grottoes graced by swans and hundreds of goldfish. The grottoes were surrounded by fruit trees and cast iron green benches and statues of naked nymphs. They arrived at Casino Park where children were riding the colorful donkeys, each donkey wearing a garland of wild flowers around his neck.

The long pier was crowded with vacationers in swimming outfits. Weathered fishermen were sitting on the dock, dangling their long feet over the side. As the *droschke* slowed in front of the schooner, Jonas jumped off while it was still moving and ran up the gangplank to greet Captain Kowalsky, who was standing with Uncle Herman. Steam was rising from the smokestack, and the Captain held the mooring lines impatiently in his hands. Lucia paid the driver and was stricken with panic when she did not see Brand. He was to leave Langfuhr with the Prince immediately after them, driving up to avoid being publicly seen, with his swollen and bruised face certain to arouse suspicion. Lucia's eyes filled with tears.

"Hurry, we have to leave now!" the Captain ordered. "There are many boats today. We won't be spotted."

"But where is Brand?" Lucia asked in a timorous voice, afraid to hear the answer.

The Captain pointed to the galley. Standing over the navigational map was her husband, his battered face partially covered by a brimmed hat, and the Prince, too, his hands on his hips. He looked up when he heard her sob. The Prince had worn his officer's uniform to smooth the way through checkpoints, and Brand had ridden past these on the back seat floor, a dark blanket obscuring him.

"Lucia, thank God you made it! We are leaving in five minutes!"

Uncle Herman climbed down into the galley, with Jonas right behind him. There was nothing jovial about his round face today; there was, instead, a tinge of terror in his tight smile.

"Listen to me, all. There is little time, so don't argue with me. I can't come with you now. You have to go without me."

Lucia gasped and Jonas' face crumbled.

"Don't say anything. I have to finish some things, then I will leave for Warsaw."

"Don't be a fool, Herman. I have a ticket and visa for you. There is no more to be done here."

"We have our parents and sisters, our family," Herman said, "and I can help them get out. I will come to America in a few months." He kissed Lucia and Jonas.

"I have to do what I have to do," Herman continued. "Try to understand, Jonas. Someday, you will. Lucia, I will see you in New York. O.K.? O.K. Oh, I almost forgot." He gave Jonas a tiny Prussian soldier carrying the Danzig flag.

"This was once a free country. Always keep this soldier, Jonas. It will give you courage."

"I will, Uncle. Please take good care of yourself, and take good care of Astor."

Uncle Herman knew his nephew was grief-stricken about his dog. "Jonas, once we are reunited in America I will buy you a new dog. One who will live a long life in freedom."

The Prince had to look away, as he felt his eyes moisten and a terrible dryness in his throat. The scene was unbearable. As soon as Uncle Herman had descended the gangplank, the anchor was raised and the schooner began steaming toward Southampton. The Captain raised the swastika. They were all sitting on the deck, holding fishing poles, and drinking champagne, listening to "The Ride of the Valkyrie" as they passed the other boats. Soon, as they sailed past the peninsula, they saw the German gunboats on patrol.

The Prince wore a striking white hat he had once purchased in Havana, and dark sunglasses. Jonas sat next to him in a deck chair, and Lucia was lying on a chaise lounge, in a bathing suit, looking surprisingly relaxed and predictably seductive. Brand stayed below so as not to expose his swollen and bruised face; also, he was studying the navigation map.

Five hundred long miles to freedom and an ocean of sharks on the kill, he said to himself.

Fräulein Marlow returned with the groceries and found Astor lying silently on his rug. She found the note by her bedstand and rushed to the telephone. Bruno, returning home to find the family missing, had rushed to Gestapo headquarters. The guard was gone, too, paid off and told to return to Gestapo headquarters until another one could replace him.

"They are gone!" she reported. "Their note says they were taken to headquarters. Have you seen them?"

"No one here gave orders for them to be brought back," Bruno barked at her. "Are you sure they are gone? When did they leave?"

"Not more than an hour ago. I went to get some groceries after you left for the tailor. And now they are gone."

"Well, they are not at Gestapo headquarters. Was the guard with them?"

"Of course. I left him talking to their Uncle Herman in the kitchen."

"You idiot! You are either incredibly naïve or simply stupid, Marlene. They sent us both out so they could escape. We will get them anyway. Did they say anything at all? Think. Your very life may depend on it."

She hesitated, and then said, "Yes," her face strained and drawn. "I overheard them whispering something about taking an excursion boat down the Vistula to Krakow."

She was lying, and she was glad. Suddenly, Bruno made her feel sick to her stomach. Had he been using her all this time? Or was it the way Brand had shamed her for what she had done to Jonas? She would never forget his eyes, so filled with hatred and disgust. With his hands around her neck he could have pushed the very life out of her, she realized, but he hadn't. Why was that? Anyone else in his situation certainly would have. Kruger had been decent to her, to the end. Or was she heartsick by the way Jonas, the boy she loved in her own secret way, ignored her and now had the same hatred for her in his eyes as his father? So much so that it became painful to even look at him?

At that moment, she knew that they had an escape plan. She was certain the Krugers were on their boat, heading for freedom. It was such a simple trick of the Prince to send her out for groceries. So clever of the elegant Brand to fool Bruno into thinking he'd ordered new suits for the fall.

The governess returned the receiver she was still holding to its cradle. She stood up and pressed the folds from her black shirt and re-tied her long blonde hair. If she had not witnessed the brutal killing of the young American and the horror of the Kristallnacht, she might have gone along with the new Germany. But she now saw that these men of the Third Reich were scurrilous, ruthless characters who enjoyed killing innocent people without one morsel of regret. And Bruno was the worst of them. This family had taken her in with trust and honor, always treating her as if she were one of them, and she, in her bitterness, sought only revenge because she felt like life had dealt her an ugly hand.

As all these thoughts raced through her head, she grew ever more remorseful. How stupid she had been. The Krugers would have taken her along with them if she had not betrayed their trust. To America! Now she was alone, marooned here among the thugs and thieves. Her life, once genteel and lace-edged, was as gray and empty as her future had ever been. Maybe even more so, now. She lay down on the rug next to Astor, who heaved a deep sigh. She placed her arms around him and cried bitterly, still smelling Jonas on the dog's body.

After a while, she raised her head and went into the guest bathroom and washed her face. She drew several long breaths. The police would be here soon to look in the house for evidence and to question her. She went to find the small Beretta that Bruno had given her and then returned to the kitchen and gently kissed Astor on the head.

"There is nothing left for us now, Astor. They are all gone. There is no place for us anymore; we have no home."

She would never know about the letter then being read at the Gestapo headquarters, and how Brand had exacted his revenge. She didn't know that the Gestapo would soon be on their way over to arrest her for conspiring in the Kruger's escape, or about the fifty thousand guldens Brand had hidden in her clothing. They would find it and it would be case closed. Rather, she only knew that she'd been left behind to rot in her own shame and isolation.

And so she raised her blond head, pursed her lips. She pointed the gun at Astor's head and pulled the trigger. Her body was covered with his blood. Then she pointed the gun to her breast, and fired once more.

Through the field glasses, Brand spotted a German gunboat racing towards them.

"Quickly, everybody down below. Prince, you stay on board, keep fishing, and look happy, a little tipsy." He gave the Captain a machine gun, which he placed under the cushion of the pilot's house.

"Let them come aboard," Brand said. "There are only three of them."

He raised the trap door, which led into the engine room. The Prince was left on deck with a large fishing pole, sitting on the "barber chair," as Brand called the seat used for catching tuna. His Havana hat was comically perched on his head at an angle.

Captain Kowalsky was in the pilot's room smoking his pipe and drinking coffee from a mug. He slowed the schooner as the gunboat approached. There were two men on the deck with rifles and one man in the machine-gun nest.

The captain recognized his friend, Wolfgang, who was speaking through a megaphone. His fingers touched the machine gun under the cushion.

"Good afternoon, Kowalsky. Aren't you out a little far for a recreational sail?"

"Hello, Captain. We are going for the tuna."

"Do you have any passengers?"

"Yes, of course. Prince Brandenberg. I mean ReichFührer Brandenberg. I promised to take him fishing."

"Did you know they arrested the Krugers?" the gunboat captain yelled.

"So I heard. Why not come aboard for a little refreshment? They won't be bothering us anymore. I am sure the ReichFührer wouldn't mind."

The Prince waved his arm like a ballerina, welcoming the German gunboat officers aboard.

"We would be honored," the Prince added.

"Your boss has escaped from the Gestapo," Wolfgang said to the Captain as the gunboat prepared to tie up with the schooner, "and we will have to search your ship. I am sorry, but I have my orders.

"Please do," the Prince said, "and I will commend you for your efforts. But, frankly, you'd best look for them on the train to Warsaw, which they are probably boarding now, if they did escape; or, more likely, they may have made their way to Switzerland by car. That Jewish pig told me one night when he had too much to drink that he had sent money to the banks there, just in case. Come on board and you can use our radio to call Danzig. I will wager they are at this very minute at the train station."

Brand stuck out his head from the cellar, holding tight to a loaded rifle, and then he lowered the trap door. Lucia and Jonas were hiding behind the coal bin, covered with a dirty canvas. This was not real, Jonas thought. He could not picture his father ready to kill the man who would open the cellar door. Yet his rifle was cocked, ready, waiting. Jonas stared at the sweat running down his father's shirt. Lucia lay trembling beneath the canvas; Jonas was beyond fear, as though he were merely watching a scary adventure movie on Saturday with Uncle Herman instead of living one, and then when the movie was over they would simply go home, where Fräulein would serve him his dinner. And then he would take a warm bath and go to sleep in his governess' arms.

"I will come aboard just to make sure," the young officer said. The Prince handed him a glass of champagne as he stepped onto the deck.

"My, you are a tall one." He appraised the naval officer just enough to elicit distaste and hasten a quick search and retreat. "How do you manage to sleep on those small bunks with your long handsome legs?"

"I am sorry to have to do this. Just take me through the boat so I can send my report." He took the glass of champagne and said, "*Prosit!* To the Führer and the Third Reich."

"Heil Hitler!" the Prince bellowed.

All three men felt ridiculous saluting like that, but each was afraid not to follow suit.

They went to the radio room where the officer called his commander. The Prince stayed at his side, and Brand heard them moving about directly above his head. The monotonous humming of the engine drowned out the terrified breathing of Lucia under the canvas cover. Brand sat crouched at the top of the stairs, waiting, waiting. If the officer opened the trap door Brand would take him hostage and have the officer order the other men to come aboard to have "lunch."

As they entered the master cabin, the officer spotted Lucia's nightgown on the bed, next to her makeup kit. The Prince quickly grabbed it, spun around, raised his chin and said, "We all have our weaknesses. Yes, this belongs to me. Do you want to join us? Our beds here are much longer than most, as you can see," the Prince said as prettily as he could.

The officer looked at the Captain in disgust.

"You don't have to report this, do you?" Captain Kowalsky added.

"I never thought you . . . I better get along. Thank you for the champagne." He saluted the Prince and could not leave the boat fast enough.

"*THAT WAS QUICK THINKING*, but I will never be able to show my face in the port of Danzig again," the Captain said, not entirely amused.

"You won't have to!" Brand said as he emerged from below.

They watched the German boat disappear in the distance until it was just a speck. Half an hour later, when they were certain the gunboat was not returning, they all stood on the deck raising champagne glasses. Jonas stood watch on the bow. "We are safe now," Brand said. "Except for the British patrol boats," the Captain countered. Brand swiftly lowered the swastika flag that was hurling in the wind and raised the Danzig flag.

"Welcome the British," he said as he tossed the Nazi flag into the sea. They all applauded as each of them watched the flag slowly sink into the ocean. Jonas remembered how he buried his flag into the sand on the beach of Sopot. Someday he was going to tell them all the truth about what happened with him and then . . . . Watching as Brand reached for Lucia and softly touched her cheek with his fingertips, he thought, Well, not everything.

"Now for something to eat," Lucia declared. "Anyone hungry?" A little later she appeared from the galley with a tray of smoked salmon sandwiches, and everyone ate, even Brand, who was standing like a soldier with his binoculars searching the horizon for boats. He told Jonas, that just when everything appears safe, that is the time to become most vigilant. For Jonas, standing next to him on the bow munching his sandwich, the boy saw another picture of his father that day. The man crouching down with a rifle ready to kill the Germans, and now a man who still had the wisdom to be alert, conversing with the Captain, giving him instructions if they were stopped again. Jonas decided he'd do his part and went to the stern of the schooner as he once did on the balcony of his room, although instead of looking for soldiers he searched the horizon for boats. The sea was calm as a lake. Sea gulls encircled them, following their small vessel. If he'd looked harder, Jonas would have spotted a submarine that was lurking behind them. "It has to be a British one," Brand whispered to the captain, "otherwise we would have been torpedoed already. Don't tell the others."

For the rest of the trip Lucia read and Brand played chess with the Prince when he was not on watch. Jonas worried whether Astor was fed and if Uncle Herman was safe. He knew how smart his uncle was. Would he keep his promise to come to America and maybe even find a way to bring Astor?

Four days later as they entered the North Sea, not far from the English coast, Jonas' efforts were not wasted as he spotted a large ship speeding toward them. "There is a boat coming towards us," he shouted as he ran to the pilot's room.

"They can't be Germans, we are too far west," the Captain said with assurance.

One hour later, they were stopped at the Skagerrak Peninsula by a Danish ship. They were boarded and then escorted several miles through the North Sea. The British warship *St. Thomas* met them at the mouth of the Shetland Islands, and they arrived at Southampton the day before the *Queen Mary* was scheduled to depart for New York.

Captain Kowalsky decided to enlist in the British navy, and Brand presented him with the papers to the schooner, to do with as he wished. A gracious gift for a good and gracious man.

On August 25, 1939, twelve days after leaving Danzig, they boarded the *Queen Mary* as it prepared to steam toward New York. The first-class deck looked down on the tourist-class section – one of the criticisms heard about this new and very luxurious Cunard liner. Jonas roamed the many lounges of the first-class section, marveling at the expanse of green carpets and the gold inlays on the walls. Each morning as soon as he awoke, he went to the stern of the ship and watched the cabin boys in their smart blue uniforms with the line of white buttons in front being inspected by the headwaiter. They held out their hands to have their nails checked, and their shoes shone brilliantly, like glass.

There were kennels aboard ship, too, and after morning inspection, Jonas watched with an aching heart as the cabin boys took the dogs for their first stroll of the day. He often thought of Astor, wondering if Fräulein Marlow or Cook was feeding him and giving him the marzipan his pet enjoyed so much before bed.

Part of Jonas' morning routine was to go to the swimming pool on the B-deck and then have breakfast with his parents at eight o'clock. In the evening he again dined with them, but this was always special fun because the Prince also joined in. They were the only first-class passengers who were not dressed in formal wear at dinner. Sometimes they were invited to dine at the Captain's table, which faced a large mural depicting a rustic wooded scene of a lake and swans with birds alight.

After dinner, Lucia and Brand went dancing and drank champagne until the early hours of the morning. Jonas liked to play ping-pong and checkers with the Prince.

In the spacious theater he saw a grand American movie, "Robin Hood," which starred a terrifically dashing Errol Flynn.

Jonas understood two words, "O.K.," and "good-bye." There were no subtitles, but it hardly mattered. It was wonderful.

Most of the passengers were Americans, returning from Europe, but there were many others – Jewish doctors, lawyers, professors, musicians, and businessmen – who were fortunate enough to have visas and the money for the trip, along with just enough left over to survive for a short period of time in the new land.

Brand's face still showed traces of the beating he'd received at the Nazi checkpoint. He explained to the few friends they made during the crossing that he had been involved in an automobile accident prior to his departure. For the most part, the family kept to themselves, knowing neither enough English nor feeling quite comfortable speaking German with some of the other passengers.

Brand paced back and forth on the deck, becoming bored and impatient with the long voyage. They were traveling 25 to 30 knots per hour, and with the weather holding out – it was absolutely splendid – they would arrive in New York on the seventh day, as scheduled. The long hours made him feel remorseful, anxious. Were it not for the cheerfulness and optimism of Lucia, he would have fallen into a deep depression.

"You saved our lives," she told him each day. "If you had not planned so carefully we would all be dead. Remembering even those taxes," she said admiringly. "Brand, you are remarkable."

"And you are too generous. I almost destroyed all of us because I was crazy enough for a very long time to think that we could stay and survive. Wishful thinking, stupid and dangerous! It was simply good fortune that the German bastard tried to kill me and we were forced to escape. God in heaven, the irony of it all! I only hope your crazy brother is on his way out soon as well. Dear man, he should be leaving with your family by the first week of September.

"We lost so much," Brand continued. "If I had only listened to Anspach and left five years ago, we would have no worries, none at all."

"Don't worry. We have plenty of money sewn in our clothing," Lucia said. "And my smart husband will be a millionaire again in America. It won't take long!"

Brand knew differently. There were desperate times ahead. America was still in a depression, and Roosevelt's economic program was not really working; certainly it was not the hailed miracle everyone hoped for. But they were, after all, alive and together. The money was really trivial. Still, it was hard to believe they would never return to their beautiful home and everything they loved. Brand had some contacts with the coal people in the United States, but he was without any substantial support; and, he knew just a few words of English. It would be a tough road for them, starting over.

"I heard," he told Lucia, "that in New York they have special names for people like us, names like 'Greenhorns,' and that they don't really like foreigners. I never in my life felt as insecure as I do now. How in the hell are we going to live?"

The fourth night out at sea, the last night of August, began with a warm breeze and spectacular stars. There was a soft glow from the huge moon, which lighted up the deck. The Prince, Jonas, and Brand met on the port side of the A-deck at midnight for a special ceremony. It was the Prince's birthday, and with a special bottle of champagne, partly secured with the dollars that had been sewn into their traveling clothes, they toasted him and then they toasted America. Arms around each other, they hugged and kissed, even danced. They were off to new lives in America. The name thrilled them even as much as what awaited understandably unnerved them.

"And now, dear Prince," Lucia asked, "what will we call you in America?"

"I will change my name to Roosevelt or Rockefeller. In America, everyone changes names," the Prince said, and they all laughed.

"But what will you do in America?" Brand asked in a voice reflecting the evening's champagne consumption.

"America loves a prince. I will be the Prince of New York, and will be toasted by the rich. The Morgans and Vanderbilts will seek me out!"

Brand knew the Prince was now as poor as he was – unless he had the good sense to send money ahead of him. He wondered if he would search out the family of his dear friend Bill, much-missed and never a day forgotten, and pay his respects.

"I could never live in Danzig again," Brandenberg said. "I am no longer the Prince of Danzig. Danzig is dead." By now, his speech was also becoming heavy, syrupy.

Jonas had never even seen his father or the Prince drunk. They swayed back and forth, singing German songs, recalling good times in much happier days.

The next morning, day five of the voyage, was September 1, 1939. The air was chilly. Brand and Jonas were playing shuffle-board on the A-deck, waiters in uniforms were serving hot bouillon. Lucia was lying on the chaise lounge, buried under many blankets. The Prince was again in a drunken stupor.

Lucia bought some clothing for them all at the fashionable shops aboard ship. With her own sparse collection of clothing, she felt uncharacteristically unstylish alongside the elegantly dressed ladies. But never had her jewelry sparkled so brilliantly.

There was a strange silence – a lull – on this voyage, despite some shenanigans, because so many of the travelers were still traumatized from what had happened to upend their lives. Every one of them had a story to tell. There was grief, and there was thoughtful and prayerful gratitude, too, that they had been among the lucky ones.

Perhaps most of all there was a sense of wonderment and love. In their hearts they loved this haven called America before they had even stepped on the soil of that blessed land.

The loudspeaker suddenly bellowed. Everyone expected that, as usual, there would be an announcement about the gala events planned for the evening.

"Attention, attention, this is the Captain. I have an urgent message for us all."

Consternation gripped the passengers. This was not what was expected. Also, there were rumors of U-boats in the area, and stories of ships being torpedoed. Brand instinctively looked for the nearest lifeboats and jackets, and was already preparing himself for the next calamity.

"It is with a sad heart that I must inform you that as of five this morning, the German training ship, *Schleswig-Holstein*, is in Danzig harbor bombarding and demolishing the city, and that General von Runstedt and his divisions have marched into Poland. England and France, who have guaranteed the independence of both Danzig and Poland, have declared war on Germany. We are not in any foreseeable danger, but we are heading full steam for New York. The wind is at our stern, and we should be able to make and maintain better than thirty knots. I will keep you informed when I have more information. Thank you. God save the King! And God bless us all!"

The passengers on the deck were silent, stunned, and then came the outpouring of tears, laments, and sobbing. Lucia was beside herself with worry, thinking of her family in Warsaw. Had Uncle Herman been able to get to them? Jonas' thoughts raced to Astor and his governess. Astor surely would be smart enough to hide. For each on board, there were personal thoughts and fears. Another war!

The Prince, almost always loquacious, now stared out at the sea, a peculiar look on his handsome face. From this point on he remained mostly in his cabin, skipping all his meals. Only at night in the glow of the misty moonlight could he be seen on deck, walking slowly, like a ghost. The mood aboard had turned to one of despair. The orchestra no longer played. Brand tried to engage his old friend in conversation, but the Prince only looked at him dumbly, as if in a delirium from his drinking, which now became constant. His fetish for immaculate appearance ended with shocking abruptness. Unshaved, unkempt – a man in a trance cast by the Devil himself – Prince Brandenberg repeated only one sentence: "I should have stayed behind."

On September 3, 1939, before dawn, the *Queen Mary* slowed its engines. It was met by Moran tugboats, which majestically escorted the *Queen* into New York harbor. The air was cool, thick with fog; and there was a stench of dead fish, oil, tar, and smoke. The water was calm.

The decks were crowded with staring passengers, trying to see through the fog as the first light of day lit the horizon. Brand was standing next to Lucia, and Jonas climbed on the small captain's deck, a forbidden deck, and waited. From there he could see the gray dark horizon, the shore, and look down on the people below. The ocean liner's captain was stunned by the impudence of the young man from Danzig, no more than a boy, really, but he was impressed, too.

"Let him be," he said to his chief engineer. "He needs the moment. He will never have it again."

Brand, failing to see their friend, said to Lucia, "I better wake the Prince. He shouldn't miss this. He is probably still drunk, or hung over."

The cabin was in total disarray. Bottles of champagne were strewn on the floor, soiled clothing covered the room, and an empty ceramic bottle was on the bed, opened, a few crystals of cocaine still clinging to its sides along with a tiny silver spoon. The bathroom was empty; the cologne bottle uncorked and drained.

The Prince's cabin was located on the starboard side. Near the railing Brand spotted a familiar silk robe, neatly folded, a pair of blue velvet slippers, and a scarf with the embroidered Brandenberg crest.

A shaken Brand stretched his body over the railing and gazed emptily at the still sea so far below. And for the first time since he himself was a boy, Brand Kruger's body convulsed with tears.

"*Prosit*, Prince. Rest in peace. Europe is gone forever. You've taken her with you."

The deadly stillness was broken by the jubilant playing of "Liebestraum" by the orchestra as the ship slipped slowly passed the Statue of Liberty. The Lady was thrilling. The foreign passengers stood gazing at it wide-eyed; some cried, others applauded, but not one head turned away from the sight of this magnificent symbol of freedom.

Then, as the sun rose on the horizon, an apparition.

Suddenly Jonas saw the magic city of tall buildings rising up from the sea like some great silvery ocean monster.

From his privileged perch he watched the Queen being nosed into the dock as burly men scurried about, tugging at the massive lines that secured her.

"All refugees and passengers not holding American passports will now depart from the A-deck for customs inspection. Please have your passports ready," came the announcement.

"So now we are refugees." Brand looked up to the heavens and said a silent prayer.

Jonas found Brand and Lucia in the long line that led down the gangplank. His face was sparkling with excitement.

A red-cheeked Irish customs inspector met them at the bottom of the gangplank: "Welcome to the United States of America. Let's see your passports, and get your luggage please."

He pointed to the huge pile of luggage on the pier, where the porters in their blue uniforms were waiting for their tips.

Brand said, "No luggage. Only what we are wearing, and this satchel."

"Where is the Prince?" Lucia asked, worried.

"The Prince is not coming. He was delayed. We will meet him another time," Brand said softly.

There was so much noise and distraction coming from the pier that Jonas did not hear his father's words. He smiled because he understood something that the porters were yelling:

"O.K., O.K., O.K."

The End

AUTHOR'S NOTE

*A*s I sit in my medical office holding the sculpted piece of coal the employees of Baltic Kohlen gave my father, I think that truth, indeed, is stranger than fiction.

I wrote *Twilight in Danzig* as a novel because most of the principals had died and much of the documentary evidence is lost – and because I was so young at the time. (I was born in 1930, six years later than my fictionalized self, Jonas.) But all the main characters in the story are real, with two exceptions and one important omission. The young American, Bill Harrington, and Jonas' friend Gerhardt are my creations. And I left out my older brother Leo, a successful attorney in New York, because of our difference in age.

Since this is a novel, I have taken poetic license, but most of the events in the story are founded on fact, and the dates of historical events are accurate. My parents were fabulously wealthy and owned priceless art, including paintings by Edvard Munch, the whereabouts of which are currently unknown. Fräulein Marlow did secretly enlist me in the Hitler Youth, but some other details of her life, including an affair with Brand Kruger, are invented. My father did survive an attack from the Red Army after World War 1 and did know Albert Speer and Rudolf Hess. He did shoot a Gestapo agent and our family did escape by boat through the Baltic Sea. I did suffer what is called brucellosis (a kind of undulant fever) and was taken by a private train car to

Berlin for treatment by the impressive doctor. And I may indeed have the dubious distinction of being the only Jew Hitler touched after 1934.

I still have in my possession a photo of myself as a boy with my beloved Astor, (see cover and picture inside).

Sadly, my Uncle Herman and most of my mother's family perished in the death camps during the War.

As how I fared in the New World, well, that's another story...

Siegfried Kra, M.D.
Yale University, 2018

Siegfried with his parents, Mr. Henry & Mrs. Lucy Kra.

The governess, Fräulein Marlene

Siegfried and Astor

The governess, Marlene, and little Siegfried between two friends on the beach.

A piece of coal, Siegfried took with them when they fled Danzig, and still has today.

Sign of the Sopot resort town.

Father (Henry) and Mother (Lucy) on the beach with friends.

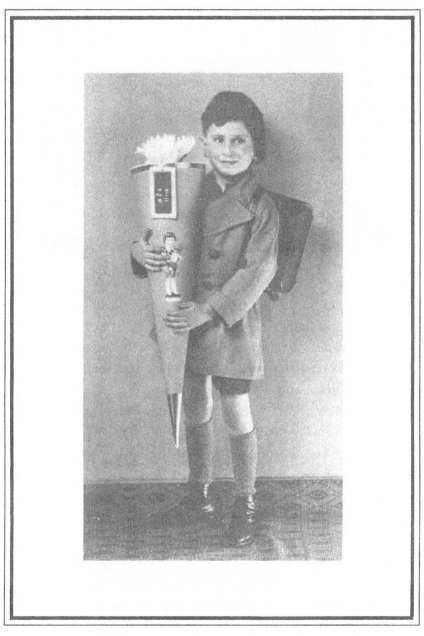

The large tube in the picture was given to children on first day of
school, in rich families, filled with sweets, marzipans, etc.

$\mathscr{S}$iegfried Kra was born into a wealthy family in Danzig in 1930. After escaping from the Gestapo, they emigrated to New York, where Siegfried learned how to speak English without an accent. He attended CCNY, then went to medical school in France and Switzerland before completing his training in cardiology at Yale. In a half century of practice, he treated tens of thousands of patients, some of whom inspired his fictional story collections. Dr. Kra has published over a dozen books, including *What Every Woman Must Know About Heart Disease* from Warner Books, and *The Three-Legged Stallion* from W.W. Norton. His passions include opera, growing orchids, and tennis, which he still plays weekly at age eighty-eight. He also still teaches as an Associate Professor of Medicine at Yale University School of Medicine and at Quininipac University Netter School of Medicine.

THE FIRST EDITION OF *TWILIGHT IN DANZIG*
was non-fiction and titled *Twilight in Danzig:*
A Privileged Jewish Childhood During the Third Reich
Canal House, 2015

OTHER WORKS *by* SIEGFRIED KRA

The Collected Stories from a Doctor's Notebook
CreateSpace Independent Publishing, 2014

How to Keep Your Husband Alive: An Empowerment Tool
for Women Who Care About Their Man's Health
Lebhar-Friedman, 2001

Physical Diagnosis: A Concise Textbook
Elsevier Science Ltd, 1987

What Every Woman Must Know About Heart Disease: A No-nonsense
Approach to Diagnosing, Treating, and Preventing the #1 Killer of Women
Grand Central Publishing, 1997

Coronary Bypass Surgery: Who Needs It
W W Norton & Co Inc, 1987

Aging Myths: Reversible Causes of Mind and Memory Loss
McGraw-Hill, 1986

The Good Heart Diet Cook Book
Ellen Stern, Jonathan Michaels & Siegfried J. Kra
Ticknor and Fields, 1982

Examine Your Doctor:
A patient's guide to avoiding medical mishaps
Houghton Mifflin Co International Inc., 1984

Is Surgery Necessary?
Macmillan, 1981

The Three-Legged Stallion: And Other Tales
W. W. Norton and Company, Inc., 1980

Basic Correlative Echocardiography Technique and Interpretation
Medical Examination Publishing Company; 2nd edition, 1977

CPSIA information can be obtained
at www.ICGtesting.com
Printed in the USA
FSHW02n2333230518
48424FS